Hunters and Gatherers

Hunters and Gatherers

Francine Prose

Picador
Farrar, Straus and Giroux
New York

www.picadorusa.com

Picador® is a U.S. registered trademark and is used by Farrar, Straus and Giroux under license from Pan Books Limited.

For information on Picador Reading Group Guides, as well as ordering, please contact the Trade Marketing department at St. Martin's Press.
Phone: 1-800-221-7945 extension 763
Fax: 212-677-7456
E-mail: trademarketing@stmartins.com

Library of Congress Cataloging-in-Publication Data

Prose, Francine.
    Hunters and gatherers / Francine Prose.
       p. cm.
    ISBN 0-312-42283-0
    1. Women—United States—Religious life—Fiction. 2. Goddess religion—United States—Fiction I. Title.

[PS3566.R68H86 1997]   96-35461
813'.54—dc20   CIP

First published in the United States by Farrar, Straus and Giroux

First Picador Edition: September 2003

10 9 8 7 6 5 4 3 2 1

To Georges and Anne Borchardt

and Denise Shannon

Hunters and Gatherers

Women paired off and gazed warmly into each other's eyes until they fell into melting embraces; then, regretfully, they separated, and each floated off down the beach to another woman, another gaze, another soulful embrace. Everyone was hugging everyone else, but no one was hugging Martha, who was sensibly determined not to take this personally as she moved through the crowd of women gathering by the edge of the sea.

The women all seemed to know one another and to have come here for a purpose, unlike Martha, who had just wandered down from a short distance up the beach because she was bored and lonely and suddenly sick of pretending that she was enjoying this rare chance to do nothing and be alone. In fact, it wasn't a rare chance at all, and Martha had only herself to pretend to, though lately she'd had a persistent sense of being watched and judged and found wanting, even when no one was looking and she was the only one in the room.

Today, on the beach, this feeling had been cruelly intense. In the glaring sun, she'd shivered under the scrutiny of that unseen eye that missed nothing and despised everything (her pale, twiglike body sticking out of its skimpy swimsuit; her newly-hatched-duckling Mercurochrome-orange hair, a regrettable recent mistake; her huge black eyes, all pupil, like those of some sort of lemur or sloth), so that simply lying on her towel had paralyzed her with stage fright, despite her having managed to find a deserted stretch of sand away from the groups of suntanned gay men, and parents anxiously chasing their toddlers.

When she'd noticed the crowd of women assembling on the shore, she'd been wondering, as she often did, how a reasonably intelligent person could have made a series of choices that seemed less like clear decisions then like a series of stumbles down the path of least resistance, a path that had dead-ended in a cul-de-sac so grim, most people would need a lifetime to get as lost and stuck as this.

But why should Martha feel gloomy just because she was thirty years old and spending Labor Day weekend alone with her friend's elderly parents on Fire Island? Because everything had come to seem symbolic of everything else: her lack of invitations for the holiday weekend was only the tip of that iceberg she jokingly called her life. And thirty was a critical age: only this year had it struck her that things could go on this way forever, that this actually *was* her life and not some stage she would soon outgrow.

Six months ago, her heart had been broken by a man named Dennis after a romance that lasted a year and died a lingering death. Now she could still think about how badly Dennis had treated her and about the many faults in herself that had given him no choice, but the absence of the physical Dennis gave her more perspective, or at least more time in which to consider how much else had gone wrong: for example, her current job as a fact checker at a fashion magazine, a job not merely boring, underpaid, and demeaning but also pointedly symbolic of what she most despised in herself: her starchy literal-mindedness, her unintuitive narrowness.

These were but two of the numerous character flaws that had been helpfully pointed out by the men with whom she'd been involved in a string of romantic disasters culminating in Dennis. How magically her lovers had accomplished the barely perceptible transformation from impassioned suitors into kindly amateur psychiatrists coolly discussing her problems and suggesting quick ways to fix them. **(5)**

In the weeks before Dennis left, he'd been generously forthcoming about her serious but remediable physical and spiritual defects. An actor with a day job as an appliance repairman, Dennis could quote from *Othello* while fixing small engines and motors, a range of expertise that qualified him, or so they both agreed, to offer Martha the loftiest and the most down-to-earth advice. All winter he'd suggested she spend more time this summer at the beach, acquiring some color and muscle tone and working on her body. He'd reminded her that she liked to swim, and she'd asked without irony, "Do I?" because for one vertiginous moment she honestly couldn't recall.

Now at last she was taking his advice, though too late for it to matter, spending Labor Day on Fire Island with her friend Gretta's parents. Gretta was a bouncy, pretty young woman, so solid and pleased with herself that beside her Martha felt wraithlike, transparent, and funereal. Currently, Gretta was madly in love with a Venezuelan named Xavier and, as she'd told Martha on several separate occasions, was spending the weekend in bed with him with the phone shut off.

In a burst of the reckless charity that new love so often inspires, Gretta had arranged Martha's weekend visit as an efficient combination favor for her parents and Martha. But from the minute the frail old couple met Martha at the ferry, it was clear that they would be disappointed in their fond impossible hope that a weekend with Gretta's friend might somehow approximate a weekend with Gretta herself. Each minute with Martha only doubled their longing for their daughter and reminded Martha of how the pain of recent lost love is never so sharp as when one goes out on a bad date with someone new. Just last week Gretta had fixed Martha up with a former insider-trader who over dinner told Martha that at nearly every social gathering he usually found himself to be the smartest person in the room.

Gretta's parents spoke English but clung to their lilting Hungarian accents and to the modest Fire Island Pines condo where for years they'd summered among gay men, like vaguely addled colonials posted amid a tribe with endearing rituals like tea dances and Sunday brunch. They introduced Martha to several of their neighbors: friendly, likable fellows, some of whom had mastered the clever trick of chatting intimately even as they looked past you like restless party guests scanning the room for someone more attractive.

But the women gathering on the beach weren't like that at all! Intent on each other, they snapped together like pairs of Scottie-dog magnets. Martha saw more women coming over the top of the dunes, pausing to inhale the salty air and kick off their shoes and sandals; a few gave fierce little war whoops as they skated and slid down the sand. Some wore vests and jeans and rawhide bands tied over feathery haircuts; others had long flowing hair, robes, and paisley skirts. Jewelry jumped and clinked on their breasts—scarabs, tusks, and fangs. Scattered patches of glitter winked in the late afternoon sun. A number were in costume—Greek maidens, fairy princesses. Some had shepherd's crooks or magic wands and stick-on angel wings.

At first Martha thought the smiling and hugging was governed purely by proximity, that each woman was randomly greeting whomever she could grab first. But eventually she noticed some women getting more hugs than others, who shambled around, eyes averted, unseeing and unseen. The visible and the invisible—it felt like a junior high dance, and Martha couldn't help noticing that the same rules of selection applied. The graceful, the pretty, the confident danced; the others stood around watching. And Martha found herself doing just what she'd done in junior high: seeking out the lone wallflower, writhing with discomfort, someone who would be grateful for any company, even hers.

Standing off to one side was a squarish young woman with glasses, and blond hair gathered in pigtails, severely curtaining her wide, furrowed forehead. She was hungrily smoking a cigarette, which she then stubbed out in the sand. As Martha approached she must have assumed that Martha wanted a smoke and held the pack in front of her like a cross to ward off a vampire.

For one mad second Martha almost flung her arms around her, though normally she was uneasy hugging and kissing hello. She much preferred shaking hands and only hoped her handshake seemed intriguingly formal and European, and not, as Dennis said, like a hostile kiss-off masquerading as a greeting. She was at once envious of, and horrified by, the ease with which perfect strangers fell into each other's arms; that was why she was so impressed by these cuddling, nuzzling women. At the last minute, good sense or inhibition prevailed and Martha extended her hand, which she then withdrew from the cigarette pack the stocky blond woman was pressing into it.

"They're American Spirit brand," the woman said. "Supposedly nontoxic. Made exclusively from organic Native American tobacco."

"No, thank you," said Martha and, when the woman's

worried face crumpled, added quickly, "Hi, I'm Martha," so she wouldn't feel rejected but, on the contrary, would be pleased that Martha had come to say hello and not just bum a smoke. But why should Martha be overwhelmed by a sudden acute awareness of what—or what she imagined—this total stranger was feeling? How lucky men were, with their confidence that everyone felt just as they did. How blessed they were to be spared this raw, useless empathy, which Martha had come to identify as a pathological female complaint.

"I'm Randi," said the woman. "But my Goddess name is Hegwitha. That's what everyone calls me."

"Fabulous name," lied Martha, though Hegwitha did seem a more appropriate name for this person than Randi.

"Thank the Goddess," said Hegwitha and then waited, a little bullyingly, for some sign of complicity or even comprehension.

Martha forced a rigid grimace, and Hegwitha relaxed enough to notice: in her swimsuit and baggy white T-shirt, Martha was underdressed. Hegwitha's brusque, forthright scrutiny was quite different from the way men regarded you: with acquisitiveness or disdain, as if you were something costly or fragile they might pick up, decide to buy—or simply drop and let shatter. Hegwitha was all business; Martha felt she was being frisked. She wrapped her arms around herself. Hegwitha's lip curled slightly.

"I'm not . . ." Martha said. "I was down the beach and I saw . . . I'm not sure exactly what this *is* . . ." This was risky, allowing Hegwitha to see Martha as a contaminating outsider who might nudge Hegwitha even farther toward the edge of the group. But Hegwitha didn't seem bothered. In fact, she visibly brightened as she warmed to the role of Martha's instructor and guide.

"We're here to worship the Goddess," she said, and again waited for Martha to give some sign of comprehension.

Martha's throat constricted, a reflex conditioned by all the occasions on which a man had referred to some obscure fact he thought she should have known. At first men liked playing professor and student, and the truth was that Martha had learned more from men she'd wanted to please than from the years she'd spent in school, watching clocks on classroom walls. But the appeal of instruction wore off; men quickly grew impatient and attached no value at all to what you might know and they didn't. At the end Dennis took a sadistic pleasure in mentioning some unknown actor or brilliant unproduced play and waiting, drumming his fingers, for Martha to say, "What?" Once, he'd asked why talking to her felt like translating into another language. How was she supposed to reply? "*What* other language?" she'd said.

Now Hegwitha gave a shrug of ironic resignation—not directed at Martha but at the whole unenlightened world. "Many women," she said, "are reclaiming their spirituality by honoring the Goddess, the original female deity whom the matriarchal cultures have reverenced since the Stone Age."

"Oh, wait a minute!" Martha said. "We did a piece on that!" In fact, the article got only as far as Martha's desk and stayed there long enough for her to contemplate the alarming prospect of phoning the women quoted in the story to check their statements about women's blood mysteries and about using black magic to hex batterers and rapists. At the last minute she'd been saved when the *Mode* editors killed the piece for being too weird and creepy.

"Who's *we*?" asked Hegwitha suspiciously.

"*Mode*," Martha said. "The fashion magazine."

"I wouldn't have seen an article there," Hegwitha said.

"I don't suppose you would have," agreed Martha.

"The Goddess was honored everywhere," Hegwitha lectured on, unperturbed. "The Middle East, Africa, Central America, Europe—archaeological evidence proves it. The Aztec pyramids were built by priestesses who worshipped the healing powers of the earth—"

"Wait!" said Martha. "Those were *sacrificial* pyra-mids! They ripped out their victims' hearts and pitched them over—"

Too late, Martha caught herself. That was the fact checker in her, chilly and superior, insisting the details be correct.

"Where did you get *that* information?" Hegwitha asked. "Your fashion magazine? Well, sure. The media would love to destroy us. The truth is, human sacrifice began only after the male sky-god religion stamped out Goddess worship and taught us to mutilate and rape the earth. For centuries male religion suppressed the Goddess tradition, burning our healers as witches. But now women are channeling their energy to get back past the church and city religion, back to earth religion and the reawakening Goddess."

"Oh," said Martha limply.

"What I wonder," mused Hegwitha, "is how far they'll let us take this before they start burning witches again. But I suppose it's important to let all that negativity go—and focus on the positive. Tonight is a Druid holy night, a late-summer revel and gathering-in of female force. All over the world women are honoring the harvest and Persephone's return from Hades to rejoin her mother. In Sicily there's a lake that was Persephone's passageway to the underworld. And guess what Italian men have done? Built an auto track around it!"

"Look! The harvest witches!" Hegwitha pointed to four women in white; each carried a long wooden post. Tied to each post was a scarecrow, a human-sized corn-husk doll.

"Check out the dolls' dresses," Hegwitha advised. "They're really special, they come from us all. Each woman can contribute a scrap from her personal life-experience attic. I cut a piece of an old lab coat from the hospital where I work."

"You work in a lab?" said Martha, but Hegwitha was not to be distracted by the facile seductions of job talk.

"The crucifix and the maypole," Hegwitha said, "were sacred symbols of the Goddess until male religion made them instruments of torture and death—"

Suddenly, she grabbed Martha's arm. "Look! There's Isis Moonwagon!"

But Martha had already sensed some new current of alertness rippling along the beach, so that even the women who'd drifted away from the group and stood facing the sea now felt the crackle and abruptly ended their dialogues with the ocean. Hugs and conversations trailed off as everyone craned for a better look.

"The one in red," Hegwitha said.

Martha saw a tall angular woman with a halo of blond curls, her crisp, girlish prettiness blurred only slightly by fatigue and middle age. Her suntanned face had the crinkled buttery softness of an expensive doeskin glove and seemed to float above a spectacular robe made from patches of red Chinese silk, a costume not unlike the dresses on the cornhusk dolls, though the attic *it* suggested was that of some dowager empress. Tied behind her head in a bow with many loops and streamers, red ribbon banded her forehead as if her cranium were a gift. Smiling beatifically, she was speaking to a circle of women but had to pause every few seconds when someone came up for a hug. Though each hug lasted forever, the other women waited calmly, beaming.

Martha moved a few steps closer. This seemed to annoy Hegwitha, who lit another smoke. She thrust out her cigarette lighter so that Martha couldn't help but observe: on both sides were holograms of a Hindu deity.

"I live in an Indian neighborhood!" Martha volunteered. "Lexington and Twenty-eighth." On holidays her landlord's children brought Martha trays of neon-colored sweets topped with shreds of silver foil, agony on her fillings.

"It's Kali, the destroyer Goddess," said Hegwitha. "Perfect for a lighter. I know the Goddess religion is supposed to be nonhierarchical. Power's not supposed to matter, we're all priestesses together. But what do you do about someone like Isis who's so incredibly special? Not only is she a really centered priestess-shaman healer, she was a heavy-duty academic philosopher before there was Women's Studies and the only females on campus were secretaries and dieticians. She knows everybody. She knew Mother Teresa before she was even famous. Of course, when we meet in covens in someone's house we're all equal together, but I guess in a group this size that could get pretty out of control."

At that moment, Isis lifted one hand and tentatively wiggled her fingers, as if waving at someone who might not be the person she thought. Within seconds, the women had all joined hands and formed a circle.

Hegwitha's hand grasped Martha's, its hot, damp pressure firm enough to keep Martha from bolting. When escape no longer seemed possible, Martha felt a lurch of queasy terror that the group would do something embarrassing that she would be forced to do, too.

"It's all right," Hegwitha was saying. "This ceremony is really loose. It's just about feeling the spirit in every living thing. You don't even have to believe in the Goddess—or in anything, for that matter."

The women fell silent and shut their eyes. Martha kept hers open but found it too upsetting to witness the expressions of great strain or great peace. She closed her eyes and felt herself gradually unclenching. Then Hegwitha hissed, "This is about getting centered," and every muscle tensed again.

After that, Martha waited fretfully until the women raised

their joined hands and cried, "Yo!" and burst out laughing.

"Blessed be," Isis Moonwagon said.

"Blessed be," the women chorused.

Several women glided along the inside of the circle. In (13) their outstretched arms they carried abalone shells from which smoldering incense sent up clouds of smoke. A deserty smell of burning sage drifted over the beach.

And now, it seemed, Martha had progressed from junior high dances to high school parties. She recalled marijuana smoke wafting up from finished basements and the chill of dread she felt going down those carpeted steps. She smoked dope from water pipes along with everyone else, but never got high enough to laugh at the puzzling jokes or to marvel at the farfetched connections everyone thought so amazing.

The sun was setting rapidly. Martha imagined Gretta's parents waiting for her for dinner, keeping warm a comforting pot of veal *paprikás* and dumplings.

Suddenly Martha shivered. Oh dear God, it was autumn. Why did autumn evenings always make her think that the rest of the world was cozy and happy at home or dressing to go to parties to which she wasn't invited?

Four robed women set a card table in front of Isis and, with the feline grace of stagehands, covered it with a red cloth and an array of objects: a shell, a branch, an animal skull, fruit, feathers, candles, statuettes, a blue glass vase stuffed with dried flowers. Bowing her head, Isis joined her hands so her fingertips pointed down. Then she stepped in front of the table, knelt, and scooped up some sand.

"I call upon the Goddess of the west, the Goddess of the earth," she chanted.

In unison the women repeated, "I call upon the Goddess of the west, the Goddess of the earth." Isis tossed the sand into the air, and the women said, "Blessed be."

Isis said, "I salute the Goddess of the east, the Goddess of the water," and waded into the frothy edge of the waves, knelt, and flung up some foam.

"The ocean's freezing," Martha whispered, proud to know one thing Hegwitha didn't. "Plus there's a killer undertow. I'm a pretty strong swimmer, and I lasted about five minutes."

But the cold and the undertow were only part of why Martha had got out of the water so quickly. She'd had a depressing fantasy about accidentally drowning and everyone, including Gretta, assuming she'd killed herself.

Martha said, "Naturally, I was an idiot for thinking I'd found my own private beach, for not knowing that everybody was swimming elsewhere for a reason—"

Hegwitha said, "I love this ceremony, don't you? If men had invented it, the ritual would probably involve dismembering tiny babies and tossing them into the ocean."

"Oh, I don't know . . ." said Martha. "I mean . . ." The awkwardness that made Hegwitha seem supercilious and censorious, together with her great eagerness to be informative and helpful, so intimidated Martha that she could hardly speak.

"Get real," said Hegwitha. "You know you wouldn't have just wandered into a group this size of men."

Isis was waving an eagle feather, saluting the Goddess of air. Finally she raised a fetish that looked like a bandaged drumstick and turned out to be a torch she ignited with a silver lighter. The torch flared up with a startling whoosh. Isis turned to face the north and invoke the Goddess of fire.

Now Isis motioned to the white-robed women, who again picked up the scarecrow dolls and waded into the ocean, along with four more women, each of whom carried in her arms a light balsa-wood canoe. They set down the boats at the edge of the sea and laid the scarecrows in their hulls. The women knelt in unison and gave the boats a push. Isis, still bearing aloft her torch, followed the boats into the ocean.

Soon the soaking hem of her robe dragged against her legs, which, along with the undertow and the resistance of the water, made Isis falter. The crowd barely breathed as she paused, rocking gently with the waves, then regained her balance and trudged farther out.

The balsa boats and their scarecrow passengers had floated beyond her, but Isis pursued them doggedly, plowing through the water, while the breeze played mischievous games with the torch and her hair. There was a flurry among the boat-and-scarecrow bearers, clearly asking themselves and each other if they should go help Isis. But, as if she'd sensed this, Isis turned toward shore, her face a stony gargoyle of rage and concentration. She grasped the torch in both hands. No one took a step.

Her hesitation had given the boats even more of a lead, and once more Isis charged after them into the mounting waves, which by now were waist-high and strong enough to knock her backward. Martha was struck by the zeal with which Isis pursued the boats: courageously, unflinchingly, unworried by how she must look.

Then one of the women cried, "Blessed be," and a murmur went up, "Blessed be," because the waves had died down, and the boats bobbed in place, as if waiting for Isis. With an eerie gull-like shriek, Isis cut through the water, reached out and grabbed the boats, and set the scarecrows aflame with her torch.

As the effigies and then the boats caught fire, a cry went up from the onlookers, the shrill warbling with which Arab women send their men into battle. Perhaps the difficulty of making this noise was what distracted the women and made them slow to realize that the waves had started up again and were tossing the boats in toward Isis, who was dodging and leaping backward to stay clear of the fiery ships.

Once more Isis shrieked, more genuinely than ceremonially. The women gasped as they watched her sink beneath the water. An instant later she resurfaced, a billowing red flower, then vanished and reappeared again, farther out to sea.

Before anyone else seemed to understand that Isis was in real danger, Martha braced herself against the cold and dived into the water. Chilly, unafraid, she swam toward the burning boats. The ocean felt like panels of silk, slipping along her body, and the salt in her mouth and on her skin was stinging and delicious. Only now did she recall how much she loved to swim, the freedom from thought and self-consciousness that was always denied her on land, the sense of having found at last an element where she belonged, and where all that mattered was buoyancy, breath, and forward motion.

Martha swallowed water a few times until she got beyond the waves, which were neither so high nor so strong as they had appeared from shore, nor was Isis so far out to sea as Martha had imagined. Martha found her easily, though she'd floated away from the burning boats. What drew Martha was the red of her robe and the frantic, windmilling splashing, the helicoptering spray and foam of a huge water bird taking off. Then Martha was inside the waterspout, deflecting Isis's punches.

Senior Lifesaving came back to her, and she remembered how in extremis you were permitted to haul off and slug the struggling victim. Each time Isis hit her, Martha wanted to hit her back. Instead she hooked her arm around Isis's neck and towed her in toward shore.

The girls she'd saved in lifesaving class had been compliant and weightless, but Isis was like an elephant that had made up its mind to drown. Soon, though, Isis understood that she was being helped, stopped resisting, and, when Martha looked at her, managed a watery, terrified smile. Isis's teeth were chattering, her hair was plastered to her skull. The red ribbon had slipped off her forehead and dangled around her neck. (17)

By now they were in water so shallow that they had to stand. Martha put a steadying arm around Isis as they waited for a wave to wash over them. All at once the shoals were crowded with running, splashing women, jumping in the water with ecstatic abandon; their joy came from Isis being safe and from the thrill of flinging themselves into the icy sea. Laughing, sputtering, embracing, they surrounded Isis, gently guiding her in toward the beach, gently elbowing Martha away.

Slumped across their shoulders, Isis staggered forward. Gracing them with wan, luminous smiles, she thanked them and told them she loved them. Then all at once she stopped so short that there was an awkward pileup, and she looked around her, theatrically searching the crowd.

Finally, she found Martha and beckoned and stretched out her hand. She made everyone wait until Martha came forward and took her place in line and joined the long column of women marching arm-in-arm out of the sea.

Isis Moonwagon's beach house was a massive shingle-style Victorian, encircled by swirling verandas and spiked with cupolas and turrets. Climbing roses covered the fences, and a vegetable patch bordered the garden path—red chard, collards, dark green kale, Brussels sprouts twisting on giant stalks like the eyeballs of undersea creatures—rioting over the edge of the walkway, luxuriant but controlled.

Interplanted cabbages, lavender, and nasturtium narrowed the path so that the small group who'd come up from the beach had to break into smaller groups to get from the garden gate to the porch. Martha was struck by the grace with which the women avoided minicollisions and oversolicitous stalls, just as she'd been impressed before by the wordless ease with which these women had winnowed themselves from the crowd on the shore.

How unlike the Darwinian scramble of daily life at *Mode*! Every year, the magazine gave a chic, high-profile Christmas party at which, just when the merriment was reaching a crescendo, Martha would spot some celebrity hostess moving from group to group, whispering invitations into the ears of the chosen few, who would later go on together to some marvelous dinner. Sometimes they whispered into ears that in theory were listening to Martha, who was not supposed to mind, just as she was not supposed to mind when *Mode* gave other, still more chic and exclusive parties to which fact checkers were not invited. **(19)**

But nothing remotely like that had happened on the beach. At the moment of leaving (hastened by the fact that everyone was soaked and shivering), no one lingered, unasked and unwanted, on the edge of some inner circle, forcing the chosen to wait until the uninvited caught on. Everyone seemed to belong to some group whose members swiftly agglomerated like atoms drawn by invisible currents of molecular attraction. The only uncertain ones were Martha and Hegwitha, who were standing near Isis when the exodus began and had hesitated until Isis told them to come along.

It was obvious why Martha was included among the women straggling over the sand toward Isis Moonwagon's beach house. She'd saved Isis's life! But why was Hegwitha here? She'd stuck to Martha like a barnacle as soon as Martha came out of the sea, crying, "Martha! Martha! Are you okay?" repeatedly calling her name, proprietary, familiar, and, as far as anyone knew, Martha's dearest friend. There was no way, short of brutality, to explain that they'd just met. Martha knew it was selfish and childish to mind Hegwitha's presence, and, besides, she felt like a larger person for allowing Hegwitha to crawl under the mantle of glory that seemed to have fallen on Martha's shoulders.

Luckily, no one seemed to hold Martha responsible for Hegwitha's perpetual air of injury and smoldering resentment. Nor did anyone object aloud, though a palpable shudder went through the group, when Hegwitha turned her back to the wind and lit a cigarette. In case there was any doubt about the sincerity of Martha and Hegwitha's welcome, Isis waited for them at the start of the garden path and steered them toward the house. But the path proved too narrow for the three of them, and Martha felt guilty for liking it when Hegwitha had to drop back.

Ambling beside Martha, Isis appeared to have made a miraculous recovery from her near drowning. Though her hair and her clothing were dripping, evidently she'd warmed her inner self with her own radiant inner warmth. Her teeth rattled faintly from time to time, but not enough to keep her from saying:

"A genius gardener named Natalie Cornflower comes over from Riverhead. After she finishes weeding, she chants to the plants for an hour. Everything in the garden is nutritious or medicinal. A universe of healing—a lifetime, cradle to grave. Comfrey to ease labor pains and digitalis to . . . well . . . Plant knowledge has always been women's knowledge, from the time of the gynocentric hunter-gatherer societies. Witches were burned because male physicians were so threatened by female healers. Hags on broomsticks was their metaphor for women in the trance states they'd cook up from the kitchen garden." Isis plucked a lavender flower that she crushed under Martha's nose.

The pungent perfume filled Martha first with pleasure and then with envy of Isis's garden and house. Well, what normal person wouldn't covet all this light and beauty and space, especially someone who happened to live in a dank one-bedroom closet where the smell of curry had long ago lost its charm and where she was often awakened at night by the clatter of mice (Martha hoped they were mice) at play in her silverware drawer?

Isis sniffed her fingers, then shook the petals from her hand. "Oh, don't you wish we could just revert to that pre-agricultural stage, when the most essential knowledge was the names of plants, which herbs cured which diseases, natural uppers and downers, and you never doubted the usefulness of each little thing you did! Every woman a doctor without the trauma of medical school! Imagine if we could time-travel back to the matriarchal era when women ran the world and everyone lived in peace!"

"I guess," Martha agreed. Then, because Isis seemed to be waiting for more of a response, she said, "Your house is amazing! I didn't know anyone had so much space on Fire Island."

Iris wrinkled her nose and looked away, giving Martha the impression that she had rudely called attention to something she wasn't supposed to notice—perhaps the discrepancy between Isis's hunter-gatherer dreams and her real estate holdings.

"It's not just *my* house," Isis said frostily. "It's *all* our houses. That is, it's a sacred protected space for those who follow the Goddess. Do you know what we call it?"

"No," admitted Martha.

"We needed a name for the place where we came together to worship. We meditated on how 'seminary' derives, linguistically, from semen—a place where men could go and not waste their semen." Isis shook her head and rolled her eyes, still pink-rimmed from the salt water. "We decided to call it our *ovulary*."

"That's . . . great," Martha said.

"Yes, well," Isis said. "It's amazing what the group mind can do that we'd never imagine alone. So much of our work depends on sharing time and skills. Natalie does the gardening for free. Who can count the hours donated by the women who made those boats and harvest dolls? The only way we can function financially and spiritually is by the nonhierarchical sharing of talent and sacred space."

The women did seem to feel quite at home—to be staying

there, in fact. No one lingered on the porch, waiting for Isis to ask them in. They went directly to their rooms, presumably to change clothes.

"I'll get you two some dry things." Isis hurried away.

"Gosh," said Hegwitha. "Isis is so considerate! She almost drowned, she must be dying to get dry—but she's thinking of our comfort first. I don't think I can smoke in here, do you?"

"No," replied Martha curtly.

"Well, sorry for asking." Hegwitha stalked off without giving Martha a chance to say something conciliatory: cigarette smoke didn't bother *her*, but Isis might not like it . . . Hegwitha stood outside the front door, muttering and smoking.

Martha drifted from the dark baronial foyer into the summery front parlor, with its glossy wood floors, antique kilims, and groves of potted ficus trees and fat-leafed serpentine plants. Tall windows interrupted the spotless white walls with thrilling views of the ocean. Carved tables supported arrangements of basketry, Kashmiri brass, Chinese porcelain. The orchestrated clutter recalled the homes of Victorian adventurers: steamer trunks overflowing with moth-eaten rugs and fake *objets* for which the traveler had been overcharged everywhere on the Grand Tour.

The room's centerpiece was a huge low circular table painted with red-and-black Arabic calligraphy and surrounded by tapestry pillows and sausagelike bolsters: the ideal setting for warring tribal chiefs to eat a sheep's head and talk peace.

Turning, Martha saw Hegwitha inching into the room, then stopping to contemplate a niche draped with a silk piano shawl. In its folds nestled crystals, geodes, seashells, votive figurines: museum-quality African sculptures and pre-Columbian terra-cotta.

"What a great altar," Hegwitha whispered. "What gorgeous, gorgeous stuff." She watched Martha eyeing three large black cats prowling a minihabitat of ornamental grasses in oversize vases. "Don't worry. Many women have been healed of their allergies with the help of the Goddess."

"I'm not allergic!" Martha said, just as Isis reappeared. Over each of her arms was a towel and an embroidered black Bedouin caftan. One robe was much prettier than the other; Martha edged toward that one.

"The fabulous thing about robes," Isis said, "is that one size really does fit all, pregnant and unpregnant, though, of course, those poor women were always pregnant. Often you see robes that have been patched and handed down through generations. Then men came along and gave us unecological Seventh Avenue and the insane idea that we should slash and burn our whole wardrobe twice a year."

"Believe me, I *know!*" Martha exclaimed, hoping to draw attention from her greedy lunge for the better robe. "I work for a fashion magazine." She wished Isis would continue her attack on the fashion industry, so that Martha could reveal herself as a serious person who had given the subject some thought. The reason she could work at *Mode* with anything like a clear conscience was her conviction that fashion wasn't only about infecting women with rampaging insecurities and unruly consumer desires; it also involved creativity, choice, and self-expression and benefited the economy without promoting mayhem and murder. And her job did seem remotely— marginally—worthwhile. She did believe in language, in accuracy, facts, those tiny building blocks of truth . . .

"Oh?" said Isis. "Are you a writer? Many of us are writers. Writers, psychotherapists, artists—or some combination thereof."

"No," Martha admitted. "I'm a fact checker."

Isis looked disappointed but caught herself and took Martha's hands. "I can't thank you enough. I thought I'd had it out there. I was drowning, choking . . . and then I felt the most astonishing peace, and I knew the Goddess was with me. It was very much a rebirth experience. I feel deeply renewed . . .

Well! Aren't we glad this isn't ancient China, where if someone saves your life you practically *belong* to that person? If that were true in New York City, people would never help any-one . . . as opposed to *practically* never. I want you to know how grateful I am. You're welcome to stay with us here unless there's some place you have to be—"

"We'd *love* to!" cried Hegwitha.

Isis awarded each of them a separate lambent smile. "It's always so icky to ask: Are you two . . . together? This is the last place to feel self-conscious about it. As priestesses, we're free to love whomever we wish. Some of us are gay, straight, asexual. I've been celibate for years. I've been working to achieve total omnisexual receptivity, so that just walking around is like having sex with the rocks and trees and plants—"

"No, we're *not* together!" said Martha, so vehemently that Hegwitha and Isis flinched. "I should tell you . . . I didn't even know Hegwitha . . . or anyone . . . I was just hanging out at the beach, and I saw the women gathering, so I decided to come over . . ."

Isis smiled. How absurd of Martha to imagine that *she'd* decided. "Don't we think the Goddess sent you? I don't sup-pose there can be any doubt about that, do you?"

Of course not! Martha shook her head. Then she said she wasn't sure she *could* stay over, she was visiting a friend's parents, she would have to call and—

"Well," Isis interrupted. "We can play that by ear. For now, you two go and find empty rooms. When you're dry and comfy, come have some hot mulled wine."

Isis directed Martha and Hegwitha down a corridor, past

closed doors through which floated an aquatic murmur of voices. At last Martha found an open door and an empty bedroom. Hegwitha slipped in after her.

"No point messing up two rooms," Hegwitha said. "Especially if you're not staying."

"I didn't say I *wasn't* staying," Martha snapped. "I have to make a phone call."

"Whatever," said Hegwitha. She shrugged and turned her back and crossed her arms and lifted her T-shirt. She was facing the mirror, and before Martha could turn away she saw, reflected in the glass, Hegwitha's large pillowy breasts and an immense lumpy scar bunching up the center of her chest, like a pulled seam the length of her rib cage.

Martha slipped on Isis's robe, which capaciously swallowed Martha's body and spit out her head. Before sliding her arms into the sleeves, she reached up under the robe and shucked off her wet shirt and swimsuit.

Hegwitha regarded her with disdain. "I know what kind of girl *you* were. One of the prissy girls who knew how to change in the locker room so nobody saw an inch of skin, while the rest of us tripped on our underpants and flashed the entire gym class."

How repressed and pathetic this made Martha sound: modest, prudish, withholding. And how unfair to be blamed for what wasn't her fault. Some people liked showing their bodies; others simply didn't, and covering up was as natural as blinking in bright light. Summers, during college, Martha's friends had gone skinny-dipping. You were not supposed to be ashamed; you went numb and took off your clothes as if you were at the doctor's, until the water covered you, hid you, and you were safe. You were not supposed to look, though Martha's boyfriends always did—not at her, whom they could see any time, but at other girls. No wonder Martha liked swimming. It was like sex, in a way: a brief respite from self-consciousness—from consciousness altogether!

Dennis had loved to look at Martha, who always found it flattering until the morning she'd awakened to find him staring at her thigh. She craned her neck to see what he was gazing at: a small tangled nest of blue veins that he continued to scrutinize, and they watched together as her white flesh curdled and puckered in front of their eyes.

"In the matriarchies," Hegwitha said, "everyone ran around naked. The fig leaf was a male sky-god invention. Men despise female bodies, they're the ones who have made us ashamed . . ."

But if modesty was a conditioned response for which they could thank the male sky god, why had Hegwitha mocked Martha for wanting to hide her body? And hadn't Isis said that these chafing and all-concealing black caftans were a female creation? Martha lightly struck her forehead to silence the pesky fact checker blithering away behind it.

"What's the matter?" Hegwitha said.

"Nothing," said Martha. "Really. Saving Isis was exhausting, I guess. Even though I'm a pretty good swimmer . . ."

Hegwitha sneered dismissively—and with good reason, thought Martha, embarrassed to have boasted about her athletic ability.

"I must be really out of shape," she said.

"I'll leave you alone," said Hegwitha. "That's obviously what you want."

"No, not at all," lied Martha.

But Hegwitha was already gone.

Martha glanced in the mirror at her pale globule of a face with its cap of iodine-colored hair bubbling up from the neck of her caftan. Then she took a deep breath and left the room and nearly plowed into a woman lurching down the hall on crutches.

Martha had noticed her earlier, coming up from the beach. Sinewy, boyish, with metal-rimmed glasses and steely short hair, arrested at indeterminate age between twenty-five and forty, she wore a baseball cap turned backward, black jeans, and a T-shirt printed with Picasso's portrait of Gertrude Stein. She backed up and shut her bedroom door with the tip of a crutch.

"Gangway," she called to Martha. "One-legged dykes from hell!" She leaned her weight on the crutch and held out her hand. "Good to meet you. I'm Joy."

Martha said, "I'm Martha."

"Right. Gotcha," said Joy.

Joy's eyes followed Martha's to the cast on her leg. "I took a little nap," she explained. "In front of an oncoming train. The train happened to be carrying nuclear waste, the ultimate testosterone breakdown product. Speaking of hormones: it was really heroic, your jumping in to save Isis."

"I don't know about *heroic*," Martha said. Only now did she wonder why she'd reacted first—after all, she was a stranger who'd drifted into this crowd of believers who should have followed Isis blindly through harrowing trials by water and fire. Maybe it was just that: Martha's detachment had freed her to jump into the sea while the others were stuck in the mire of their own fantasies and preconceptions, the history they had to slog through before they could get to the ocean. Or maybe what inhibited them was their jewelry, their jeans and long dresses—whereas Martha had been wearing only a bathing suit and shirt.

"Bullshit," said Joy. "We all saw what happened. But people are going to give you a hard time because you beat them to the punch. You dove in and rescued her while they were standing there scratching their butts. I can afford to say that: there was nothing *I* could do. Plus, having been pretty heroic myself, and with this cast to prove it, I'm not threatened by courage, I can respect it in other women."

"Thanks," said Martha.

"Thank *you*," Joy replied.

Martha was motioning for Joy to precede her down the hall when Joy's door flew open and a willowy young woman appeared, glaring, in the doorway. She had red hair caught in elaborate pre-Raphaelite loops and a pale, tear-streaked face.

"Diana, Martha," Joy said. "Martha, Diana."

"Good to meet you," said Martha.

"I *know* her name is Martha. I was there on the beach today. How stupid do you think I am, Joy? Just because I . . ." Diana's lower lip trembled.

"Sor-ree, babe," Joy said. "Diana thinks every conversation is about her leaving grad school and having a shitty job now like the rest of the world, and everyone assuming she's stupid—"

"Not *everyone*," said Diana. "Just you, Joy."

"Oh!" said Martha. "Diana, what were you studying in grad school?"

"Anthropology," said Diana.

"How interesting," said Martha.

"*Après vous.*" Joy pointed her crutch along the hall.

Making an awkward quarter-turn, Martha continued down the hall, followed by Joy's tapping crutches and, after her, Diana.

In the living room a half-dozen women sat on the pillows around the low round table. They partly stood and smiled when Martha and her new friends walked in.

At that moment a clock chimed. Everything stopped till it struck six. The tall clock was painted with planets, stars, and faux-medieval landscapes.

"Our grandmother clock," Diana said.

Martha ventured into the room, expecting the others to follow, but they stopped in the doorway and left Martha to enter alone. She wandered over toward Isis Moonwagon—the only person she knew by name.

Isis was talking to a substantial woman with a mop of curly gray hair and a flowing pantsuit in blue-and-purple tie-dye.

"Titania, dear," Isis was saying, "we've been through this before. Pollution is pollution, and it makes no difference who puts it in the river, low-caste Hindu women who have been dyeing saris for centuries or a petrochemical plant in Gary, Indiana—"

"*I'm* from Indiana," Martha said.

"Not Gary, certainly?" the tie-dye woman said.

"No," said Martha. "Bloomington."

"Oh," Isis said. "I've lectured there. Were your parents academics?"

"No," said Martha. "My dad sold insurance. I mean, until he died."

"What a terrible job," said Isis. "Trafficking in fear. No one wanting to pay premiums or getting any returns till something devastating happens, and having to deal with everyone's pain for some faceless corporation . . ."

How did Isis know the tragedy of Martha's father's life? People assumed that selling insurance was just a boring job, but they hadn't heard her father at dinner, his nightly litany of bad luck, illness, house fires, and head-on collisions. No wonder he had stopped talking much—and had a heart attack at fifty. He had died on the front lawn, on the riding mower; everyone said it was fortunate that he hadn't been run over but had fallen off before the mower slammed into the hedge. After five years, Martha still couldn't think about his death without experiencing a great shocking jolt of bewilderment, grief, and sorrow. It was awful to lose someone in a way that seemed odd or funny. She almost never told anyone the part about the mower and would certainly not tell these women, who might say that having a coronary while mowing the lawn was the inevitable outcome of typically compulsive, type-A male behavior.

The woman in tie-dye said, "Isis doesn't miss a chance to dump on corporations."

Isis said, "Martha, this is Titania. Titania is the founder and CEO of Love's Body, which, as I'm sure you know, earns a trillion dollars yearly from ecologically sound bubble bath—"

"Not just bubble bath," said Titania. "We put out a whole line of—"

"Martha works for *Mode*," said Isis.

"You *do*?" said Titania. "I think we advertise in *Mode*. That is, I think we used to before the recession set in. Now we mostly stick with the New Age rags whose rates are a bit less inflated."

"I'm just a fact checker, really," said Martha.

"I see," Titania said.

A silence fell. Then Martha asked Isis if she could please use her phone.

"Of course," Isis said. "I'll show you to my study where you can talk in private."

"It doesn't have to be private," Martha said. "I'm just calling my friend's parents."

But Isis was already breezing through the white high-ceilinged rooms until she reached a wood-paneled library lined with shelves of books artfully spaced around niches displaying more geodes, skulls, and figurines. Martha skimmed the spines of the books: anthropology, mythology, women's history, philosophy.

"Academia." Isis sighed. "What a teensy little world and everyone viciously defending their progressively teensier little fiefdoms. My former colleagues still can't get over the fact that a woman with a dual doctorate in social anthropology and philosophy and significant classical Freudian training could have ditched it all for what they imagine as lesbian full-moon orgies, riding naked on a broomstick! (31)

"I got so sick of having to justify my ideas to those phal-locentric Freudian morons who think that female spirituality is a synonym for penis envy. Penis worship, that is. They think we adore their dicks just like they do! Meanwhile the feminists hated me, too, for suggesting that women were anything more than men in drag. Academic feminists have such a warped investment in the sexes being identical except for their repro-ductive organs. As if the womb was nothing more than a baby incubator, as if it didn't connect us to a more cyclical life process. It's not just for lack of opportunity that women don't rape and start wars."

Isis had a confiding manner that assumed you thought just as she did, though from time to time she paused for your opinion, or, more accurately, your concurrence.

Was Martha's opinion being asked? She thought men and women were different. Different bodies, different lives—surely that counted for something? Though women were no less in-telligent, as men so often seemed to believe, even men who knew perfectly well that they weren't supposed to believe this. Martha liked and disliked individual women and men, not entire genders, though it was undeniably true that only men broke your heart, unless of course you were lesbian and gave women an equal chance. Martha's women friends were nicer to her, they seemed to genuinely like her. At worst they were inconsiderate, but never purposely cruel.

She'd be glad to see women running the world, at least

for a change. They could hardly make things worse than they already were! On the other hand, the indignities of daily life at *Mode* suggested that a world run by women might not be heaven on earth.

Isis interpreted Martha's silence as a sign of agreement—perhaps such profound agreement that Martha had lost the power of speech. She said, "It's such a rarity to be around people who understand your work. *Our* work."

But Martha's work, fact checking at *Mode*, was instantly comprehensible. The point was simple clarity, truth in its lowest form, facts, and the first and most obvious fact was that no one liked hearing from Martha: not the librarians she bothered with tedious research questions; not the publicists whose clients a writer had quoted, often wrongly; certainly not the writers themselves, who had gone on to other projects and often hadn't any idea what article Martha meant.

Only Eleanor, Martha's boss, didn't realize how unwelcome Martha's calls were. She saw no reason why Martha shouldn't intrude on someone's private moment to verify some name or date that every schoolchild knew. The best thing about the job was that it taught Martha not to take rejection personally. That is, she'd *thought* it had, until Dennis mused aloud that it might be good for them to start dating other people.

Martha knew which other people he meant: a woman named Lucinda, a strapping, square-jawed preppy girl with thick yellow hair like a doll's. Lucinda and Dennis were doing *Othello* in their acting class. Inspired by Dennis's Othello, Lucinda was pouring the full force of her talent into her Desdemona: three acts of bovine adoration, and then compliantly dying. At an open rehearsal, Martha noticed how much grabbing and pushing it took to smother Desdemona, though in other versions she'd seen, the murder was almost surgical, like etherizing a frog. And of course it had occurred to her that Dennis just wanted to touch Lucinda.

"Are you all right?" said Isis. "You look positively fried."

"I'm fine," Martha said. "Really."

Isis gave Martha's elbow a squeeze. "I'll leave you alone," she said. "Make your call."

Martha watched Isis warring with herself—and losing. "I assume it's a local or credit-card call. I feel vile for even asking. But there have been real nightmares: people calling Seoul, Korea!"

"Calling Korea?" said Martha.

"Well," said Isis. *"Trying."*

"Island Pines," Martha said. "Is that local?"

"Right up the beach," replied Isis. "You could practically do it by tom-tom."

Gretta's mother answered the phone in a high voice, clenched for disaster. Martha's news—that she might stay over with friends—was hardly the catastrophe she'd imagined.

"Good," she said, audibly relieved that she and her husband could have dinner without having to entertain an unsatisfactory substitute daughter. She didn't ask who *were* these friends Martha had just met. She wasn't Martha's mother. And what if she were? Her own daughter was currently engaged in a forty-eight-hour sexual marathon with Xavier.

She said, "We leave the key in the mailbox. Don't worry about waking us. Watch TV, please, if you like."

Martha's vision of herself in Gretta's parents' condo was lit by the icy glow of their TV, flickering like the northern lights. That was what persuaded her to spend the night at Isis's. It would be more uncomfortable and complex, but far less boring and lonely.

In the living room the women had got up from the low Turkish table and were warily circling a buffet of wine and cheese—not the hot mulled wine Isis had promised but California jug. Already, used paper cups were grouped in unsightly arrangements, wine beading up like droplets of blood on their waxy skins.

As Martha filled a cup, a woman behind her whispered, "Cheapo Chianti. Winewise, Isis is still carrying baggage from her graduate student days."

It was Titania, the organic cosmetics tycoon in the tie-dyed pantsuit. "Every time I come here, I bring a case of something good. Nothing special, a modest ten-dollar Chardonnay. And Starling spirits it away, so to speak, and we drink this stomach acid. Have you met Starling, Isis's secretary? Of course, we're all supposed to believe she's just Isis's watchdog, bodyguard, and best friend. I've known Isis forever, but even I wouldn't know the truth if we didn't share an accountant. Though I guess the fact that Isis pays the bills doesn't prove they're lovers. Isis claims to be celibate, but no one ever actually is. Except me. And not by choice, so I'm not boasting.

"Probably Starling saves the good wine for her and Isis to scarf down weeknights. I've brought it up with Isis. She says gallon jugs are more ecological. Don't you hate it when people use the planet to make a point? Ecologically, we should all be drinking out of pig bladders."

Martha drained her cup and poured another.

"Instant migraine," Titania warned, moving into the party.

Martha spotted Hegwitha talking to two women and a girl of about thirteen. One of the women was a lank-haired blonde with a parched marsupial face. The other was older, maternal, squat as a Toltec statue, in a peasant shawl and homespun orange dress, her gray hair parted dead center and pinned up with a silver clip.

The girl was stuffed into a tight white cowboy outfit, satin miniskirt, blouse, fringed vest, a cowboy hat pulled low on her round pretty face. Girls her age didn't dress like that, not the ones Martha saw on the subway, crowds of kids in baggy jeans, faded flannels, and team caps worn backward. This girl had her own style, impossibly defiant, especially at an age when everyone dressed alike, when the impulse was to hide your body, an impulse this girl resisted, though she had the sort of body girls most wanted to hide: large-breasted, with fleshy pink arms and plump knees peeking out from under her shiny skirt. Her lips were fixed in the permanent pout of a surly child whose idea of good behavior was to ignore everyone she could, and annoy and punish the few who insisted on her attention. She was at a stage that Martha recognized right away. And her heart went out to her, though she knew the girl wouldn't want it.

"I work in radiology, at Roosevelt Hospital," Hegwitha was telling the group. "So I was lucky. When I got cancer, I knew all the really good doctors. And even then, they screwed up at first. They sliced me open from stem to stern before they figured out what was wrong."

Martha saw, clear as a photograph, the scar down Hegwitha's chest. Being the only one who had seen it gave her such intimate knowledge, so much shared history with Hegwitha, that they *could* have been old friends. How mean of her to want to distance herself from Hegwitha, especially now that Hegwitha had just revealed this tragic fact about her life.

A brief pause greeted Hegwitha's announcement. Then the girl said, "Cancer. Oh, gross."

Everyone, including Hegwitha, stared at the girl in horror until the lank-haired woman said loudly, "Sonoma! That's the most unenlightened, unconscious, punitive thing I've ever heard. Cancer isn't gross. It's a disease like any other. And it's evil to make cancer victims feel that it's disgusting."

The girl, Sonoma, looked at the ceiling. "Duh, Mom," she said. "Okay. Fine."

"Freya," Hegwitha addressed the blond woman. "This is my friend Martha. And this is Martha's daughter, Sonoma. Oops. I mean *Freya's* daughter, Sonoma."

"I wish," mumbled Sonoma. "Anyone would be better than *Mom*."

"Oh, no! I'm sure I wouldn't be!" What instinct had made Martha defer to this sullen girl's mother? More of the same useless empathy: she could imagine how it would feel to hear your daughter say she'd rather be raised by a stranger. But how could Martha really know? She'd never been able to imagine herself as the mother of a child, not even during one horrific week when she'd thought she might be pregnant, and told Dennis, who'd said it was wonderful news, and then didn't come home for two nights. Martha had been very relieved when her period came. Ever since she'd turned thirty in March, she'd tried not to think about children. The subject was like a precipice, and she wisely avoided the edge.

"And this"—Hegwitha indicated the woman in the Frida Kahlo getup—"is Bernie. Bernie's a therapist."

"Pleased to meet you," said Martha.

"Bernie's short for Bern-is." Bernie rearranged her shawl and gave it a kindly maternal pat. "B-e-r-n-i-s. Originally it was Bernice, but somewhere along in my training I realized what it was costing me to have a name with 'nice' on the end. I felt I had to be nice all the time, so I changed it to *is*. I am. Bernie is. Many of us took new names when we found the Goddess."

Freya snorted. "Titania, for example. Imagine naming yourself after a fairy queen who fell in love with a guy in an ass's head. Though I guess you can't blame the woman after fifty-some years as Maxine."

"Well," said Bernie. "Which one of us hasn't fallen for our share of jackasses?"

"Is Freya your Goddess name?" Martha asked politely.

"Yes, but I was born with it. I didn't have to change it."

"And you, Sonoma?" For a moment, Martha was afraid that Sonoma wouldn't answer and would leave her dangling, humiliated, in front of the other women.

Wondrously, the girl replied. "I was born in Sonoma county. Really original. Right?"

Freya said, "Not born. Conceived. Sonoma's father and I were making a—as it turned out, disastrous—tour of the California vineyards."

Was Sonoma the disaster she meant? Everyone stared at the ground.

"Sonoma, dear," said Freya. "You've already eaten thousands of those little fried crackers."

Sapped by contempt, Sonoma barely had the strength to sigh with exasperation. "Chill, Mom. These crackers aren't half as fattening as the *wine* you're chugging."

"Chugging's overstating it, dear." Freya turned to Martha. "Especially with this wine. I cannot believe the swill Isis serves—and expects us to drink. The toll on our stomachs and livers is bloodcurdling to consider! Naturally, I adore Isis, but the woman is accident-prone. By now there could be a small private army of women who have saved her life. And she always glues herself to her latest savior. Though eventually she discards them when the next lifesaver comes along."

Martha knew she was getting a warning—a warning or insult or both.

Freya said, "I can't count the times she's almost drowned or set herself on fire. If I were Isis, I'd dress exclusively in a lifejacket and asbestos."

"Asbestos is bad for you," Hegwitha said.

"I'm aware of that," said Freya. "You know, I did an installation in Stockholm in 1988. I called it *Fire and Water Women*, and *entre nous* it was half about the Holocaust and half about Isis's brushes with death. Though naturally no one got that—nor did I mean them to."

"Oh, are you an artist?" Martha said.

Freya gave her a weary look. "I'm Freya Wunderlich."

"Oh, *right*," said Martha, as if she had just called up Freya's whole résumé. In fact, she dimly remembered Freya Wunderlich's name, perhaps from a story in *Mode* about why women artists so rarely became rich or famous.

Then suddenly they all felt that silent summons to attention that had energized the crowd of women earlier on the beach. The women returned to the low table and sat cross-legged on pillows as a slight, angular woman flitted about, saying, "All right, ladies. Please. Quiet. Lights out."

"Starling," said Sonoma. "You are such a Nazi."

Starling switched off the overhead light and joined them at the table. Dark, with bright blinky eyes that were at once timid and disapproving, Starling resembled the wife of a witch-burning Salem judge far more than a coven member. Only cruel or stupid parents could have named her with such aptness, though probably, Martha realized, Starling was her Goddess name.

While Martha had been distracted by the bad wine and the strained conversation, someone had set the low table with dozens of stubby white votive candles in glass dishes. A complex system of mirrors and crystals lasered rainbows off the statuettes and bowls of pink roses in water.

"Feel free to put a token on our altar," Isis said. "Anything you want charged up—jewelry, crystals, your car keys." The women dug in their pockets and extracted combs, roots, daggers, stones, onyx eggs. The spontaneous generation of objects reminded Martha of films in which gang members agree to surrender their guns, and an entire arsenal materializes out of nowhere.

Joy put one of her crutches along the edge of the table, and Diana, her redheaded girlfriend, set down what appeared be a terra-cotta hot plate incised with grooves delineating a naked woman's breasts and belly. The women bowed their heads and put their hands over their bellies, a gesture Martha approximated by folding her hands in her lap. She made herself untwist her fingers lest she seem to be wringing her hands. Some of the women shut their eyes, others stared at the table.

Some fresh intensity communicated that this silence was meant to go deeper and signify more than the one on the beach. Martha hoped this didn't mean it would last longer. What was she supposed to be thinking about? Was her mind meant to be empty? It was so unnerving to be peaceful and quiet with strangers.

This silence should have come more readily than the silence on the shore. It should have been easier to avoid getting restless or anxious, easier to concentrate without the distracting roar of the surf or the shouts of swimmers having fun or drowning. But peace did not descend as planned. Martha stared into a large crystal, where a beam of light twisted like the gooey bubbles in a lava lamp. The air felt damp and close. Martha pawed the rough Bedouin robe, unsticking it from her body.

She didn't think she could stand it, being made to keep silent. Who *were* these women to force her to sit here and waste her time with their fruitcake crystals and silly rites and contraband pre-Columbian art? She could be eating veal *paprikás* and watching TV with Gretta's parents! She could just get up and leave and walk out and never see these people again!

Through her mounting irritation and panic, Martha heard Isis say, "The static is incredible. We are all just *buzzed*."

Martha looked around, intrigued to learn that what she'd thought was a personal problem might be a group event.

"Let's try chanting," Isis suggested. "Nothing too heavy."

The women began a nasal, bleating "ma ma ma." Martha couldn't make herself do it; luckily, no one noticed. The drone had the eerie Balkan power of wailing Transylvanian women mourning Vlad the Impaler's death. But the chant kept faltering, and the women seemed tense and inhibited, like partygoers singing "Happy Birthday" without ever quite getting on key.

Suddenly, the phone rang loud—twice, three times—and kept ringing.

"I knew it!" said Isis. "We were waiting for something. That was why we were having trouble silencing and centering." The women made gentle cooing sounds, pleased to find that they'd mistaken their natural ESP for ordinary distraction.

When the ringing didn't stop, Starling cried, "Jesus Christ! Goddamn answering machine never comes through when you need it!" She stood, upsetting a bowl of roses. Water spilled onto the table. A spasm of wiping and blotting accompanied her exit.

No one spoke till Starling returned. "Goddamn travel agent," she said. "He said he knew he could reach us out here, since it's Labor Day weekend. Apparently there's some wrinkle with the four-wheel-drive vehicles for our trip."

What trip? Martha wondered. No one paused to explain. They were all going somewhere together, and Martha wasn't invited. But why would they have asked her along? She'd only just met these women. There was no reason, no reason at all for Martha to feel hurt, nor, for that matter, any reason for Martha to think of herself as so cold and cerebral when she was always getting her feelings hurt by every tiny thing. She was terribly oversensitive, Dennis had often told her, usually just after he'd made some harsh or sadistic remark.

Starling said, "That pig travel agent—"

"There *are* female travel agents," said Joy. "We could have worked with a woman-owned business. A penis is not required equipment to arrange for a four-wheel-drive vehicle."

"Not at all," agreed Titania. "A telephone and a fax are sufficient."

"Maybe Joy should be dealing with it," Diana suggested. "She's the one who's going to be driving."

Joy glared at Diana. "You deal with it," she said.

"Ladies, please," said Bernie. "I'm hearing a little hostility here."

Starling was practically shouting. "That jerk thinks because we're women he can do whatever the hell he wants. I'd like to see him interrupt a *priest* in the middle of mass . . ."

With a rueful smile, Isis offered one limp hand to her friend. The effect on Starling was sudden and dramatic. Her eyes filled with the milky calm of someone coming out of a seizure.

"Well, exactly," Isis said. "Isn't that the point? The male God sends you straight to hell if you whisper in church. But Goddess knows the sacred is *in* the interruptions—the crying baby, the ringing phone, the mail person at the door. Divinity is in the practical: the laundry, the cooking, the cleaning. How much smoother our lives would be if we accepted that, if we could believe the answering machine was broken for a reason, in this case to explain to us why we couldn't get centered."

Everyone stared at Starling, who was smiling shyly, proud that the fit she'd thrown had become the occasion of a spiritual lesson. Martha was impressed by the effortless grace with which Isis had accomplished this, by her kindness to Starling, and by her desire to make someone look better instead of worse.

There was something so soothing about how Isis saw the world! You certainly *would* be happier if you reached a spiritual level which let you see a broken answering machine as a sign from God. Er, Goddess. Martha envied believers their serenity, their faith that an eye was on every sparrow, a hand on every steering wheel as the speedometer crept up past the limit. How jealous she was of the rosaries draped over rearview mirrors and appearing from purses and pockets when an airplane pilot warned, in those confident tones that fooled no one, of turbulence up ahead.

Spiritual comfort and the peace that passeth beyond understanding were not among the options offered by First Lutheran of Bloomington, which Martha had attended sporadically as a child, and where the best one could hope for were the covered-dish suppers. Martha's mother went to church without pleasure or conviction, but as another misguided attempt to "do something as a family." Martha's father came along, grumbling, and fell asleep, often noisily, during Pastor Jensen's sermons. Martha stared at the pastor, unable to hear a word as she warded off comical images of him marching in holiday parades in his Cub Scout leader uniform: the stupid hat, the pointy kerchief, the vast expanse of dimpled knee between his khaki shorts and knee socks. The catch in his throat when he said the word "God" made her skin crawl with embarrassment.

And that was it for religion, except for a month in high school when Martha read *Franny and Zooey* and repeated the Jesus prayer, waiting without the least success to see a blinding light. In college she took a religions course from a German theologian who lectured in a warbling chirp with her eyes shut tight. Martha never believed in God, not even as a girl, and later listened with envy and covetous curiosity to her Catholic friends' merry nostalgia for faked confessions and vicious nuns.

For a few months she'd had a boyfriend who meditated in a spare bedroom, empty but for a poster of an Indian swami in sunglasses and a top hat. At first this seemed exotic but then grew rapidly less charming. Why was she so hard on him? He'd been one of several men who confidently predicted that Martha would always be unhappy because she always had to analyze and dissect every little thing that anyone (by which they meant themselves) happened to do or say. They were right! Why couldn't Martha quit thinking and exchange her niggling trivial doubts for the bliss of total submission, for the blessed certainty and trust in some higher consciousness large enough to do her worrying for her?

What bliss it would be to surrender your griefs, your passions, and your will, to trade them in like an old car for confidence and calm, to become like the Goddess women and float on a cloud of faith that a broken answering machine was a message from your guardian angel sent to teach you heavenly patience and spare you annoying calls that might otherwise ruin your day!

For weeks after Dennis left, Martha called home from work every hour to see if he had phoned, though this made no sense at all; he could have called her at *Mode*. The computer male voice said, "No messages," with what began to sound like triumph. Holding the receiver, Martha had sat very still as prickly shudders of disappointment coursed from her scalp down to her toes . . .

"Okay, forget it," Isis said. "Let's lose the moment of silence. The best thing about priestess ritual," she informed Martha and Hegwitha, "is, if it doesn't work, bag it. There's no rule book, no expectations, and we're writing our own sacred text every minute of our lives."

The women laughed, gravelly caws of relief, and once more Martha was pleasantly surprised to find that her personal insufficiency was, in fact, a collective event.

(44) Isis said, "I'd like to start by welcoming you on this Harvest Night, which by Goddess's grace falls on Labor Day weekend, so we can honor the harvest and our grandmothers who fought for the labor unions. And every woman who has ever been in labor birthing a child—which, the sisters tell me, isn't called labor for nothing."

"You can say that again," Titania agreed.

"Blessed be," chorused the women.

"Goddess," said Isis, "tonight you have sent us two new priestesses." The women smiled at Martha and Hegwitha, genuinely welcoming, though welcome came more easily to some of them than others. It was a stretch for Freya and teary-eyed Diana, but all except Sonoma were trying, and Martha felt grateful and moved. How little it took to make one feel fractionally less unhappy!

"This is not a sorority," Isis went on, "with a torture initiation. No one swallows goldfish or gets naked and streaks town. Nor is it a convent; nobody shaves her head. Nor Esalen, where gangs of balding, paunchy New Age guys think initiation is getting to grope our tits. This is a priestess circle empowered by the feminine, by kindness and awareness of others' feelings."

True, Martha thought, women hadn't invented goldfish-swallowing or war. But women had other cruel rituals and barbed weapons at their disposal. Look at little girls in the schoolyard! And just last week, on the bus, she'd heard a woman telling her friend, "That gray hair looks good on you. I mean it, you look younger. We were all wondering when you would stop dyeing it that toxic dog-doo brown."

"Women," said Isis, "are like the child in 'The Emperor's New Clothes.' We see the truth and say it, no matter what the cost. One of the things we know is, *any* initiation is torture. The double horror of being new—and being put on the spot!

"So let's just go around the circle and say our names. I'm Isis Moonwagon." The women laughed—they knew that!

Isis. Joy. Diana. Starling. Titania. Freya. Sonoma. Bernie. The women introduced themselves, some with shy, retiring smiles, others aggressive or brazen. Luckily Martha knew their names, because she could hardly hear them through the fog of anxiety generated by the prospect of having to say her own.

Hegwitha said, "My name is Randi, but my Goddess name is Hegwitha."

Under the murmurs that greeted this, Martha mumbled, "I'm Martha."

"Beautiful," said Isis. "May the Goddess protect us all. Let's start tonight with the Talking Stick . . ." Several women applauded. Joy whistled through her teeth.

"Like so many of our rituals," Isis said, "the Talking Stick derives from Native American ceremony. It's something we're always mindful of—the indigenous people who lived here before the white man stole their land. In this ritual we pass the Talking Stick, and no one is allowed to talk except the person holding the stick. As long as we have the stick, we can freely share our hopes and fears and dreams. But when we don't, our work is to listen and be caring and not judge."

Not judge, not judge, not judge, Martha thought, repeating it like a mantra until the words melted into gibberish, and maybe that was the point. You gave up fine distinctions that were really just reasons to feel superior, gave up watching from the edge of other people's lives and surrendered and shut your eyes and jumped into the warm gooey center. But wait a minute! Martha made her living by making fine distinctions, and some part of her—a large part of her—thought they should be made.

"First," Isis said, "I'm going to light a little smudge, Little

Sister Sage, the herb Native people use as medicine smoke. Smudge removes the kind of negativity we pick up every day in city traffic. It's a bit smoky—is everyone fine with breathing?"

Martha nodded, and Hegwitha said, "Can I inhale?"

Isis lit the incense: a bundle of twine tied with string. Cupping their palms, the women wafted the smoke toward their faces and hair, greedily sucking in the acrid, smoldering-mattress smell. Then Isis raised a war club decorated with feathers and cloth scraps. "Great Goddess," she prayed, "help us find our voices." She looked around. "Okay. Who wants to start?"

Freya reached for the stick, but Isis whisked it out of her grasp and said, "Let me say one thing."

She held the stick in both hands and bowed her head. "I want to share how lucky I feel for having been saved from drowning. I thought I'd had it out there. I was terrified, choking, and then I felt the most amazing peace, and I knew the Goddess was with me."

It took hearing this a second time for Martha to realize it wasn't true. The panicky woman she'd rescued hadn't found the peace of the Goddess. But why was Martha being so small? Did she want more credit? Recognition for how tough it had been to save the struggling, flailing Isis? Probably Isis was trying to make the others feel better, reassuring them with the good news about her serene near-death moment—while the cold little fact checker, Martha, was insisting she stick to what happened.

"Blessed be," said the women.

Isis surrendered the Talking Stick to Freya, who pressed it to her bosom.

"A miracle occurred this week," Freya said. "My daughter began to menstruate."

Bernie squealed with joy and leaned over to pat Sonoma, who shrank from her touch.

Freya said, "I was shocked by how blown away I was. When she told me, I burst into tears. I was amazed that my daughter's body was a woman's body. And we were women together, with all the mess and hopes and fears."

Martha didn't dare meet anyone's eyes. Already she had realized that she would probably never have much sympathy for Freya. That was why Martha didn't belong in this, or any, religious group—her heart had already turned against some, if not all, of its members. Martha tried to imagine how it would feel to be Freya seeing her daughter grow up. But all she could think of was how it would feel to grow up with a mother like Freya.

"It was like giving birth to her all over again," said Freya. "But with a new sort of joy and pain, an affirmation of the feminine. I felt I was giving birth to myself, to my own re-awakening womanliness—"

"This sucks," said Sonoma. "It's my body."

"Excuse me, dear," said Freya. "I was speaking."

"Sucks," Sonoma repeated. "I can't believe you told them."

"*I* have the Talking Stick," Freya reminded her.

"Sonoma's right," said Bernie. "It's Sonoma's personal stuff. But it's complicated, Sonoma. Because your mom was telling us something about *herself*, not just about you."

"It's my body," Sonoma insisted.

"We know it's your body, Sonoma," said Isis. "And we know your body is an issue between you and your mom that you'll both have to work on. Still you must admit that your mom's weeping because you got your period is better than her bugging you to lose weight and get superthin."

Several women smiled at this. Sonoma wasn't among them.

Isis said, "This should prove that your mom *does* care—"

"Wait! Listen." The women turned and stared: gloomy, silent Diana was speaking. "Lots of indigenous societies have fabulous first-menstruation rituals. Wouldn't it be great if we could do something like that here? Some matrilineal Native American tribes had actual vision quests. At menarche girls go off alone into the desert to meditate and fast until they meet their spirit guide."

"That would suck, too," said Sonoma.

"The weird thing is," Diana continued, "it's kind of why I left graduate school. I kept trying to discuss this with my thesis adviser. I was saying it was so tragic that we had no initiation rites. And he said: We have our rituals. We have kids chugging six-packs and wrecking their cars on prom night."

"Cynical shit," said Titania.

"What an asshole," Hegwitha said.

"Thank you," said Diana, smiling at Hegwitha, and Martha sensed a ripple of jealousy emanating from Joy.

"Well, we do have our initiation rites," Bernie said. "Mine was my dad getting furious when he found out I'd got my period, which meant he couldn't molest me for a couple of days each month. So I started hoarding bloody pads and leaving them in the bathroom so he'd think I had it even when I didn't."

"That never stopped my dad," Starling said. "He kept on, right through."

"Mine, too," said Joy. "That son of a bitch. Afterward I could hear him washing off the blood."

After a silence Diana said, "Sonoma should have a ritual. Something private to mark this new stage and invoke the

Goddess whose blood flows with the cycles of Earth our Mother—"

"No way," Sonoma said.

"You know," Titania mused, "I have a problem with this subject. Sometimes I feel like the gynocentric cultures were saying that we should give up everything and spend a week in the menstrual hut every month."

"I hear you," said Bernie. "And sometimes I agree. Other times I wonder if it's just because I'm menopausal—"

"I rest my case!" said Titania. "We're still calling ourselves menopausal when we're supposed to be crones, wise women, respected for our ancient knowledge. Hah!"

"Freya has the Talking Stick," Isis reminded them. "But first let's finish with Sonoma. Sonoma, this is about what *you* want. Maybe you could have a private ritual. Your period is going to come every month, you'll have to live with it somehow. Not that you need go overboard. In the seventies there was a frenzy for slide shows of dirty tampons and a fairly extremist thing about tasting menstrual blood—"

"Oh, *gross*," said Sonoma, wincing so sharply that Martha recoiled, too. Sonoma knew it was creepy to be spending Labor Day weekend with her mother's uncool friends, discussing menstrual blood. But if she wanted to be cool, why was she dressed like that? Why couldn't she be outrageous in a more conventional way: ripped jeans, green spiked hair, her face pierced in five separate places?

Freya said, "If I have the Talking Stick, why are we still on Sonoma?"

"The thing to remember," said Isis, "is that each month sends us a reminder of our power, the power to give birth—"

"I don't ever want to have kids," said Sonoma. "Everyone knows my generation is the end of the line."

"But you could have a daughter," said Starling.

"Like really great." Sonoma's pink face was like the skin formed by boiling milk, in this case over a bubbling caldron of pure exasperation. It was both touching and frightening to see a girl so young, so angry.

In the silence they heard Joy say to Diana, "Vision quest bullshit. The thing *you* like about it is the fasting for a week."

"Maybe *you* two need the Talking Stick," said Isis.

"I don't know . . ." said Diana.

Joy said, "*I* do," and seized the stick. "Things between Diana and me haven't exactly improved. She quit eating for three days; I caught her slipping her dinner to the dog. I'm sick of the obsessiveness, the excuses about carcinogens, the steamed broccoli meals, no smoking, no drinking, no sex. I'm a Catholic school survivor myself, and it's like I'm back where I started. Catechism, confession—but now the sin is eating instead of sex!"

Isis sighed. "The church had some of us in its stranglehold for years. It imprinted us like ducklings. No matter how we raise our consciousness, it's hard to undo our training: learning to worship the man on the cross, the man in the sky, the man in the confessional who wouldn't be there if girls weren't nasty and dirty. But it's only the sky god who wants us to be ashamed and punish our bodies for our desires. The Goddess wants us to celebrate the holiness in ourselves and in each other."

Once, in bed, Dennis told Martha that men and women would never speak the same language because women saw sex as a sacrament while for guys it was recreation. But wasn't there something holy about love, no matter how misdirected? Love was something to focus on, to give your rapt undivided attention. There had been a time when Martha had only to think about Dennis and the chatter around her would stop, and she would experience the silence and peace she imagined people got in church. Clearly, it was stupid to choose an object of veneration for whom you were interchangeable with a nitwit named Lucinda.

Isis said, "Martha, are you with us? You look positively stricken."

"I'm fine," said Martha, flattered that Isis was paying attention.

Isis said, "Since we're on the subject of food and sex—"

"What other subjects are there?" interrupted Titania.

"What foods do we put on the Goddess's altar?" Isis asked rhetorically. "Think. What are the Goddess's favorite foods?"

"Milk and honey and eggs," said Starling.

"Precisely," answered Isis. Then the women began to laugh—knowing, yet quietly astounded: the way the religious marvel at new evidence of the divine.

The God of First Lutheran's favorite food was macaroni and cheese, with jello-marshmallow salad running a close second. He was a stern but forgiving, reasonable god, very quid pro quo, not a god who made you do penance or starve yourself to death, but neither did He encourage you to celebrate your body.

Isis said, "The Goddess isn't about deprivation. She wants us to recreate the matriarchy, when everyone worshipped Her and lived in peace and gentleness toward one another and the Earth."

"Joy," Diana muttered. "What a fucking misnomer."

"Diana," said Isis. "Please."

Joy stared hostilely at the Talking Stick, not knowing what to do with it when no one made a move to take it.

Starling said, "How come whenever we pass the Talking Stick, it always turns into a bitch session? No one ever wants to take the stick when they have something good to say."

Joy said, "I never understood why it had to be a stick. Why can't it be a Talking Egg?"

"Well, it's tricky," said Bernie, "to share our happy and positive feelings."

"That's how we were brought up," Diana said. "Women aren't programmed to be happy. We're meant to be sacrificial victims—"

"Perhaps one of the new women would like the stick?" Isis said. "Only if you want to. We all know it's scary at first, but like so many scary things, worth it . . ."

Martha shot a glance at Hegwitha, hoping she would demur, and then Martha could refuse as well: they would be in this together. But Hegwitha was already reaching for the stick and only stopped when she saw Martha watching.

"Mind if I go first?" she asked.

"Not at all," said Martha.

Hegwitha pressed the Talking Stick against her chest and concentrated so hard that her face got mottled. Finally she opened her eyes and said, "Maybe it's appropriate that Isis started off talking about almost dying in the ocean because, as some of you know, that's what I want to talk about, too. I've been battling cancer, Hodgkin's, for the last three years . . ."

There were gasps. Then Diana said softly, "How did you find out you had it?"

"I was buttoning my shirt," Hegwitha said. "I felt this lump on my neck."

"Yikes," said Joy.

"Blessed be," said Isis.

"It could happen to anyone," Hegwitha said. "That's why no one can stand to—" Isis and Bernie hugged Hegwitha, who'd begun to cry. Martha felt her own eyes fill with sympathetic tears.

Hegwitha said, "No one wants to know what it's like, waiting for the diagnosis, trying to get through the weekend till some doctor gets the results, waiting in radiology, hour after hour. You'd think it might be less lonely because I work in radiology and know everybody there. But that makes it worse somehow. Whatever control you thought you had is totally taken away . . .

"If you try to keep your spirits up, people tell you you're in denial. I had to quit my first cancer support group because they were all such bitches. And if you try to say, 'Listen, I'm dying, I'm scared,' everyone acts like you're being a wimp . . ." Hegwitha was weeping again. "Everybody pretends to care. But they're really just glad that it's me and not them."

Hold on there! thought Martha. That's not true—but, of course, it was. Better Hegwitha than her. Much better. Besides, the fact of Hegwitha being ill seemed, deceptively, to shrink the odds of the same thing happening to Martha.

"We're here for you," said Isis.

"Let it out, Hegwitha," said Bernie.

Fat tears slipped down Hegwitha's cheeks. Titania, Joy, and Diana wept, too. The rest of the women were silent, white-lipped, and tense.

"I'm in remission," Hegwitha said through her tears. "I've really got to quit smoking."

There was a long silence. "There's nothing to say," began Isis. "Except to remind you, Hegwitha, that this isn't your fault. Goddess religion isn't like phallo-psychiatry, it doesn't try to tell you you're responsible for your cancer. You didn't bring it on yourself, the Goddess has Her reasons. And we'll always be here for you, Hegwitha, any time you need us."

"Thank you," murmured Hegwitha. "I mean it. Thank you."

And she passed the Talking Stick to Martha.

What was Martha supposed to say after Hegwitha's story? Breaking up with your boyfriend was not exactly like dying of cancer. Martha knew that, she knew that. And yet she was so unhappy. Maybe she should tell them that her problems were hardly worth discussing—that is, compared with Hegwitha's. But wouldn't that sound self-congratulatory and make Hegwitha feel even worse?

Martha took the Talking Stick and shut her eyes for what she hoped would pass for a moment of silent prayer. Then she said, "I hate my job. I'm a fact checker at *Mode*, and I'm wasting my life chasing down details I don't care about—"

"A fact checker at *Mode*?" said Starling.

"What qualifies as a fact there?" said Joy. "Like, do blondes have more fun?"

"Face-lift prices. Collagen lawsuits," said Titania. "The price of the new swivel eye pencil and the colors it comes in."

"Exactly," said Martha. "My supervisor, Eleanor, is a maniac and a sadist. She makes me call and check facts any sixth grader would know—"

Martha was gearing up to trash Eleanor when she noticed Isis waving her arms, as if Martha were an airplane she was flagging in for a landing.

"Come on," said Isis. "Tell us what's really bothering you. The Talking Stick knows when you're talking *around* your issues—"

"There isn't anything, not really," Martha said.

Bernie said, "What's his name?"

Titania said, "Ed? Ted? Fred? Rumpelstiltskin?"

"Or *her* name," Joy said. "Polly? Molly? Holly?"

Martha filled her lungs and heard herself say, "Dennis."

Diana said, "Doesn't it make you sick to consider how many women are driven into the arms of the Goddess by some schmuck named Dennis?"

Isis said, "Come on. Hush. Martha has the Talking Stick."

In fact, Martha found that the interruptions had made talking easier—more like conversation, less like ritual confession.

"Who was he?" said Titania. "How did you meet?"

"Who cares?" said Joy. "I mean, really."

"Go on," said Isis.

Martha said, "He's an actor. He fixes appliances for a (55) living. He came to repair my refrigerator. I was in a foul mood, I was missing a day of work. I was shocked when I opened the door. He was so handsome that I was embarrassed. He looked at me when I talked to him, intense but completely unsleazy . . . like he cared deeply, up to a point, what was wrong with my fridge."

What an enormous distance between the sweet, attentive Dennis who'd shown up to fix her refrigerator and the Dennis who suggested she spend more time at the beach. Contemplating it was like standing on the edge of the Grand Canyon, and it left Martha light-headed, deoxygenated, and breathless to take credit or blame for such cataclysmic transformation.

"Go on," Bernie urged.

Martha said, "The entire time he was checking the fridge, I hung around the kitchen. I'd never had so many domestic chores. I washed each dish forty times."

But how could she explain what had seemed like an optical phenomenon: her entire peripheral field had slowly blurred and narrowed down to one bright pinpoint of light, and that pinpoint was Dennis. If she couldn't see, how could she have moved from one room to another? The safest, the only thing to do was to stay near Dennis. It was as if some new gravity were pinning her in the kitchen and she couldn't resist any more than she could have chosen to leave the earth's surface.

Surely these women could understand this most basic human experience, the miracle everyone wanted, this sudden unwilled falling in love. And yet Martha suspected that they all had learned to distrust and fear it. (All except Sonoma, who might think it was disgusting.) And who was to say that they weren't right? Martha should have distrusted it, too, and meekly paid the repair bill and thanked him and gone off to work.

But it was already too late by the time he said her freezer needed defrosting, and his statement hovered in the air like some vile double entendre. They stared at the kitchen floor. Martha noticed a stuck-on parsley leaf right where he was looking.

"I asked if he wanted some coffee," Martha said. "We sat at the kitchen table. It was four in the afternoon before we got up again. I knew that hours were slipping by; it felt dangerous and risky. Blowing off work, shooting the day—I remember his beeper kept beeping. And I was thrilled that a guy being paged would keep on talking to me."

Were they asking themselves why he—why any man—would be so entranced with Martha? Probably they were beyond wondering about anything men might do. Martha wished there were a way of subtly letting them know that Dennis didn't date every girl whose refrigerator he defrosted. "Once he told me that what he liked about me was that I was always right there. Whatever he said, I *got* it, I understood, though women often didn't—"

"Watch out," Titania said. "Watch out when a guy tells you what most women don't get, or what he doesn't like about most women . . . except, of course, for you."

"Men," said Joy. "Their definition of intelligence is when we understand them."

And yet there had been times when she and Dennis were out with his friends, and he would say something smart or funny, and hers was the face he sought out to see if he'd impressed her, if he'd made her laugh. What a distance he'd traveled from loving her for being right there to hating her for being (as he'd said) on some other planet completely. And if she was, hadn't he driven her there, sent her into orbit to escape his perpetual criticisms and the hulking shadow of Lucinda?

"We were together a year," Martha said. "Then he just lost interest. He seemed less happy to see me. I used to think of all the things he didn't do anymore, like hooking my neck in a friendly way when we used to walk down the street." (57)

"You let a guy get you in a headlock?" said Joy. "Serious safety error."

"It didn't seem to matter that I understood what he said. I'd hear him telling other people things he'd already told me. I'd ask myself what I used to do right that I'd started doing wrong. Everything about me began to seem grotesque."

"Like what things?" Bernie asked in her most gently prodding, therapeutic tone.

"I don't know," lied Martha.

One day she'd let herself into Dennis's apartment when he was on the phone. And though Martha liked to believe that she had principles about respecting people's privacy, not listening in on their conversations or opening their mail, the compulsion to eavesdrop was so overwhelming that Martha realized she *did* have the normal human urges that Dennis had been implying she lacked.

Dennis was laughing strangely. It wasn't Dennis's laugh. Then she understood. He was imitating her: a hideous equine snort. Whom was Dennis talking to? She heard him say, "I can't stand it."

Perhaps she was being oversensitive, he was just doing a funny laugh. Actors practiced lots of things besides parodies of their girlfriends. Once she'd heard Dennis describe how he'd watched an old man walk in the rain and had remembered that walk for years until he got the chance to use it. That was when they were first together, and hearing Dennis say that had made her feel quite light-headed with desire and adoration. Imagine: a man who listened and watched with such sweetly empathic attention! But hearing Dennis imitate her had made Martha despise the sound of her own voice . . .

"Like what?" repeated Bernie.

(58) She would tell them the next worst thing. "Finally, I asked him if something was . . . you know, wrong. And he said it was getting old, dating the Little Match Girl."

Sonoma whistled. "Nasty. He *said* that?"

"Sonoma, how do you know about the Little Match Girl?" Freya said. "I'm always stunned when you can access that sort of cultural information."

"Dad read it to me," said Sonoma. "You never once read aloud to me the whole time I was a kid."

Isis clapped her hands. "Please, ladies. Control yourselves. Martha still has the Talking Stick."

"Martha, what did you *hear* when he said that?" asked Bernie.

"What did I hear?" said Martha. Exactly what Dennis had told her: that she was just like that pathetic girl in the fairy tale, always standing out in the snow, looking into windows, spying on warm crowded rooms, parties, family dinners, except that Martha was worse than that, because she secretly believed that it was *better* to be alone, shivering in the cold, and not with loud sweaty people so vulgar they actually wanted to have fun . . .

"What else, Martha?" Isis said.

"Isn't that enough?" said Martha. Although she was new to the group, she was hogging the limelight, making them spend more time on her failed romance than on Hegwitha's illness.

Isis said, "We must remember it's hard for men to love. They weren't brought up to do it, they were brought up *not* to do it. Love aversion therapy. A wire was hooked up to their heart at some point between Boy Scouts and Basic Training, and every time they had a caring thought, they got a teeny electric shock."

"Dennis was loving," Martha said. "He just stopped loving me." How pitiful to defend a man who everyone in the room **(59)** now knew had called her the Little Match Girl.

And then, to Martha's astonishment, tears came into her eyes. As she hid her face in the crook of her arm, hands stroked her hair and shoulders.

Through it all she heard Isis's voice. "Every woman in this room has experienced rejection. The patriarchal culture is *about* rejection. The abusive or absent father, rejecting us, turning his back on us no matter how much we need him. Why would anyone want that hopelessness, that impossible love? What I'd like to know is: Why would anyone choose to suffer like that?"

Isis lifted Martha's damp face and gave her a dazzling smile, then rose to her feet with a grace that made her seem to expand like a genie emerging from the mouth of a bottle.

"I'm going to bed," said Isis. "There's tons of food and wine left. I love you all. I'm exhausted."

In Accatone, the midtown restaurant where Martha met Gretta for lunch, every trick of lighting and decor was employed to make you feel rich and northern Italian. But the syrupy low pinkish light, designed to conceal and excuse, tele-graphed to the whole restaurant that Martha's attempt to be stylish had failed. As she and Gretta followed the pencil-thin hostess to their table, Martha's downtown black, her men's tuxedo jacket, her tights and lace-up ankle boots made her look like a circus hobo foundering in a sea of Armani. Every woman in the room had hair the color of mink or honey, except for Martha, with her nail-scissored shreds of garish skinned-knee orange.

"I'm Enzio," said their waiter, a strikingly handsome per-son of somewhat indeterminate racial origin and gender. He (that much was fairly certain) addressed himself to Gretta and smiled into her eyes, as if they were deeply in love. Would he notice Martha if she were dressed, like Gretta, in perfect fawn-colored cashmere that kept slipping off one plump shoulder?

Martha was wearing the wrong clothes. And what was even worse was that she was wasting her lunch with her friend, worrying about what she was wearing. For someone with such grand ideas about the meaning of fashion, Martha had a lot of trouble just getting dressed in the morning. How perfect that she should wind up at *Mode*, where the attitude toward style was at once superior, ironic, detached, and obsessive. O lucky Goddess women, marching to the beat of a different drummer!

"Martha," Gretta said. "Are you listening? Enzio's just told us the specials."

Already it was Enzio! Gretta's new best friend! One thing to be said for the Goddess women was that they didn't compete for men. In fact, they didn't seem to know that there were any men to compete for. But when had the Goddess group become a source of reassurance, something to put her mind on to make herself feel better? Martha had been planning to ask Gretta for reassurance that her new friendship with the Goddess women didn't mean she'd lost her mind completely.

Since Dennis, Martha had felt like Alice, tumbling down the rabbit hole. But the Goddess women had broken her fall or at least distracted her enough so that hours might go by, precious intervals during which she almost forgot that she was falling. These past weeks were the first time that Martha had ever felt included, gathered into an inner circle. She was dazzled by the speed with which she'd been accepted. It was so flattering, so pleasant to be taken up by a community that it seemed ungrateful to wonder if it was a group you wanted to join. She liked it that the women—especially Isis—seemed to want her around, though she recognized disturbing echos of the mind-control techniques that suckered unstable teens into cults. But the Goddess women weren't Moonies or Hare Krishnas. They were Jungian therapists, writers, scientists, academics . . .

"Earth to Martha," said Gretta. "What is *with* you today?"

"What are you having?" said Martha.

"The pasta with pine nuts and sun-dried tomatoes," said Gretta. "The grilled vegetables. *And* the green bean salad."

"Make that two," said Martha.

"Two it is," Enzio told Gretta.

"And bring that wine now, please," said Gretta.

"Pronto." Enzio danced away, turning to wink at Gretta.

"This is something new," said Gretta. "Some kind of foreign-guy charisma. It must have something to do with Xavier. Something's rubbing off."

"What's the matter?" Martha said. "You look sort of tense."

"Oh, nothing," Gretta answered. Enzio brought her a glass of wine and grudgingly gave one to Martha.

Gretta took three large gulps and then told Martha a story about how they'd gone to a party last week, and Xavier had spent the evening flirting with another woman. It was a very long story and contained many details about the party and the woman, and many pauses during which Gretta waited for Martha to say that Xavier really did love her, but he was just being Xavier. Finally Gretta paused and said, "So how are the Wicca women?"

"Not Wicca women," Martha said. "Goddess worshippers."

"Same difference," said Gretta.

"Not really," said Martha. "They're not really such flakes. Listen, I stopped at a bookstore, and there was a huge selection of Goddess books."

Martha knew she was signaling Gretta that Goddess worship was a happening thing, so Gretta wouldn't think that it was just Martha and one lone coven of crazies. This was how Martha used to convince her mother that something was all right: lots of people did it, especially popular kids. It was also how *Mode* decided that a subject had interest and value. The right people were doing it, and doing it right this minute.

Gretta lunged her empty wine glass at a passing waiter, not theirs. "Goddess books are out of my department, my sub-department, and any sub-subdepartment I could imagine getting into." Gretta was assistant publicity director at a publishing house. Every Monday—for as long as they didn't catch her, she said—she took Martha to lunch.

Martha said, "Isis has five books in print. Bernie's written a big trade paperback about Jungian archetypes. I even found Freya's overproduced coffee-table book about the Goddess in art history, culminating in Freya's work."

"Oh, Lord," said Gretta. "Lord, oh Lord. How can you read that dreck?"

"Come on," said Martha. "It's interesting, sort of. Don't you wonder what the world would be like if women ran it? The Goddess women say we'd be nicer and more loving. But when you mention Margaret Thatcher or Indira Gandhi, they say: Those are women with male values, and we can't know what we'll do until we evolve past that. But what if they're right? How could things be any more screwed up than they are right now?"

Why was Martha making the Goddess women sound like a bunch of philosophy graduate students and leaving out the embarrassing rituals, the Talking Stick and so forth, the truly bizarre discussions of whether rapists deserve to be hexed, the charged allusions to some ritual with a pomegranate and a dagger? Martha had plenty of doubts about their corny rites and wacky historical notions. But to listen to Martha defending them to Gretta, anyone would have thought that she was just like Hegwitha, happy to be accepted, without reservations or doubts, and with a total, unwavering faith in a kindly nurturant Goddess.

"They're not so bad," said Martha. "They're kind of smart. They're strange. They seem to like me."

"That's pathetic," said Gretta. "Lots of people like you. I like you."

"Name someone else," said Martha. Was she hoping that Gretta would, despite everything, say Dennis?

"My parents," said Gretta. "They said to tell you that they really liked your visit."

Was Gretta lying? Had her parents lied? Martha said, "I felt so badly for them. They were so sweet but so terribly lonely."

Martha stopped. She'd seen Gretta flinch, and she was instantly sorry. What was the use of empathy if it came after the fact, too late to prevent you from hurting your best friend? What had Gretta done to deserve being made to feel guilty about her parents? Poor Gretta was the only person Martha knew well enough to treat badly—not counting Martha's mother, whom she hardly saw and who was, in any case, too fragile to withstand the mildest abuse.

Enzio appeared out of nowhere, and now Martha was grateful as he chivalrously offered Gretta her vegetables and flung Martha's across the table.

"They're mostly nice to each other," Martha said. "The Goddess women, I mean."

"*We're* nice to each other," Gretta said. "Nicer than guys are to us. With the exception of Xavier, who can be very nice."

"We're not the issue," Martha said. "And neither is Xavier."

"How refreshing," said Gretta. "As far as Xavier's concerned, Xavier is always the issue."

"With Dennis—" said Martha.

"Oh, spare me." Gretta held up one hand to silence Martha till the waiter had finished sprinkling their plates with pepper. After he left she counted the items of food on her dish.

"It's a good thing we each got our own salads and grilled vegetables. Otherwise we'd have got exactly three *haricot verts* apiece. Some *sous-chef* back there is counting. I thought pricey starvation went out with the eighties, and the nineties were about meat loaf, mashed potatoes, and gravy. God, don't you hate those places that pretend to be like a diner, or Mom's, except organic and very expensive?"

Martha bit through the creamy eggplant flesh to the oily succulent skin. "Of course, the Goddess women are nuts on the subject of food. Freya and Sonoma struggle over every bite Sonoma eats; Joy's always on Diana's back about her anorexia; Titania says Isis has graduate-student food-and-wine tastes . . ."

"Titania?" Gretta snapped up a green bean thin as a blade of grass. "Which one is she? Which reminds me: who are we today? For the purposes of today's Amex receipt, you are: Editor, *Mode*."

Martha hated being reminded that she wasn't an editor. She wished Gretta could take her out to lunch without playing this game of figuring out what sort of business expense Martha could pass for that day. She resented being made to feel compelled to work for her food.

"I heard a joke," she said.

"Goody," Gretta said.

"What do you do when a pit bull humps your leg?"

"Tell me," said Gretta.

"Fake orgasm," Martha said.

Martha waited for Gretta's loony laugh. "That's funny," Gretta said coolly. "Is that New Age feminist-separatist witch-goddess humor?"

Martha supposed that's what it was and liked the joke a little less. She'd heard it in Joy's minivan on the way to Isis's apartment.

Every Thursday evening Joy picked up the women in her

old VW van with its bumper sticker MY OTHER CAR IS A BROOM-STICK. The trip started at Joy and Diana's apartment in Park Slope, stopped in Brooklyn Heights for Freya and Sonoma, on West Eleventh for Bernie, Twenty-eighth and Lex for Martha, and then snaked around the Upper West Side, where the others lived, before winding up at Isis's West Seventy-sixth Street brownstone floor-through.

The joke about the pit bull was funnier in the van, in the dark, in the rain, in the company of women who were either gay or celibate by default or choice. Some of them actively hated men, others had just given up, and with blighted affection or genuine rancor, they joked about the male body and brain.

Did Gretta think that laughing at the joke would be disloyal to Xavier? When Martha fell in love with Dennis, Gretta had been between boyfriends. Now Martha wished she'd gloated less and been more sympathetic. One thing she remembered about love was that it narrowed the population to two: two lone humans on a planet of unfeeling robots. Once, when they'd first got together, Dennis and Martha spent a country weekend with friends and, when their hostess stepped out, they made love all over the house, ending up on the living room couch. Well, not friends, exactly: their hostess was Dennis's former girlfriend.

Now that Martha was no longer in love—correction, no longer loved—her higher sympathies had returned, working overtime and retroactively back to consider how Gretta must have felt when Martha had just met Dennis. No wonder the Goddess women had no patience for romantic passion. It was like a cult of two, and one had to be deprogrammed.

"I don't know," said Martha. "The Goddess women make me feel less miserable. Even about Dennis . . ."

"Dennis Dennis Dennis," said Gretta.

Martha had broken up with men, she should know better

by now. But in this case repeated exposure had failed to make Martha immune; on the contrary, it left her more vulnerable and more gravely ill. There were nights when she lay awake, thinking of Dennis and weeping. And Gretta was tired of hearing about it . . . (67)

"At this Goddess meeting the other week, I brought up the subject of Dennis, and Isis said how crazy it was to choose to feel so much pain when it was so much smarter to be with friends who valued and appreciated you. She asked, Why would anyone *want* to suffer like that? And the minute she said that, it just made so much sense."

In fact, when Martha awoke at night, the clean simplicity of that question sliced through the mists of regret, if only for a minute, till the fog rolled in again. Still, in that brief clearing, Martha could sometimes fall asleep. It was better than Valium, with its guilt-inducing visions of prescription-drug dependence.

"I've been telling you that for years," Gretta said.

"Months," Martha corrected her.

"Months," said Gretta. "Where's Enzio? Are we having dessert?"

Martha said, "The Goddess women even help me deal with Eleanor."

Gretta gave a little shudder and speared a last thin oval of grilled zucchini remaining on her plate. Her feelings about Martha's boss mirrored her attitude toward Dennis. Martha's complaints were justified—but really, enough was enough.

"Yesterday Eleanor made me call a writer and ask where he'd got the idea that our ordinary social exchanges were like baboon dominance rituals. The writer said, 'It's my opinion. Just say it's my opinion.' "

"Oh, humiliating!" said Gretta.

"I said I'd figured that, I was just checking. Eleanor was standing over me while I made the call. Usually I'd have wanted to kill her, but now I looked up at Eleanor's face . . ."

Eleanor's husband was leaving her after a long marriage; a teenage son was in a pricey boarding-school dry-out clinic. "I saw that Eleanor was in pain. And I understood that her making me call was her primitive magic, her way of imposing order on the chaos around her."

"This is nothing new," said Gretta. "You've always had sympathy for Eleanor. Too much sympathy, actually. Lack of sympathy is not your problem. Too much sympathy is your problem. You've got so much sympathy for Dennis that you would be the first to explain why he *had* to treat you like shit."

Startled, Martha sat up straight. She couldn't remember telling Gretta about those white nights when just before dawn she realized that Dennis was right: anyone would have gotten sick of Martha's plodding fact-checker's soul, her chilly cerebral remove, her skinny aging body, the cocker-spaniel eagerness with which she had listened, practically panting, to Dennis's every word, her hypersensitivity to imagined slights, her braying equine laugh. Not once, with the Goddess women, had her laugh sounded like a snort. Long ago, Martha's mother advised her that whenever she saw her friends, afterward she should ask herself, Did she feel better or worse? That was a simple formula to tell her who her real friends were. Martha thought of her mother, drinking vodka, watching TV, the whispery husk of the energetic woman who used to tuck her into bed . . .

"Martha?" said Gretta. "Are you okay?"

"Oh, I don't know," Martha said. "Maybe none of it makes any sense. But maybe that's the point. Isis says the first step is accepting the irrational, embracing things that don't add up."

"That would be a stretch for you," Gretta said. "You're not a fact checker for nothing. And, frankly, I'm not sure it's a stretch I want to see you make."

"Maybe I want to," Martha said. "All I know is, when I looked at Eleanor's face, I saw that she was suffering. I thought of the Goddess women and how damaged they are. Joy, Bernie, and Starling were abused as kids. I always doubt the statistics, but that's three out of ten. Hegwitha's got cancer. Bernie's husband died five years ago, and she's still grieving. Titania's daughter won't talk to her. Freya and Sonoma despise each other—"

"Well," said Gretta, "you're not exactly dealing with an average cross-section of the female population."

Martha said, "The Goddess tells them it's okay, that they're connected to something outside themselves—"

"*Crème brûlée*," said Gretta. "Or, wait. I'll settle for the *tiramisu*. Where is the waiter, anyway? Isn't that typical of men? First the guy's halfway down my throat and then he disappears."

"What do you think?" said Martha. "About this Goddess thing? These women?" But why was she asking Gretta? She hadn't told her enough of the truth for her to have an informed opinion. Anyway, what *was* the truth? Martha's impressions of the Goddess women were like a column of figures, dauntingly long and complex; each time Martha added them up, the total was always different.

"Well . . ." said Gretta. "Anything that helps you make it through the day." It was the tone a person takes when a friend's mind can't be changed and the wisest course is to show good will and gracefully change the subject. Gretta scooped a forkful of tiny carrots onto Martha's plate—a gesture in which Martha recognized the distillation of all Gretta's love and concern.

"Come on, hon," she said. "All you have to do is survive a few months till you fall in love with someone else. If you've got to go through some cult thing, fine. If it helps you, fine. **(70)** Just promise me not to get into anything seriously weirder than this."

But that night, on the way to Isis's for the Witches' Sabbath, weirdness thrummed with an aboriginal twang beneath Joy's van's many problem noises. One by one the women climbed in the van, said hello and blessed be, then hunched their shoulders and lowered their heads and burrowed under their hair.

No wonder they wanted to hide! They had gone to impressive lengths to make themselves look frightful. Witches' Sabbath, said Isis, was a celebration of the inner darkness that women of all ages shared with the ancient hags and crones: a night on which to remember their dead, to honor the witches burned at the stake, and to have their feelings about the dead and dying. Martha had asked Hegwitha how often they held Witches' Sabbaths. Hegwitha referred her to Starling, who said, "I don't know. When we need to."

An anticipatory buzz had grown steadily in advance of the evening. Isis had urged them to be creative in turning themselves into witches, smearing hag paint on their faces, obliterating their vanity, mocking the culture that valorized male standards of feminine beauty. So now, as each woman got into the van, there was considerable rubbernecking to see how far she had gone in her pursuit of hagdom and cronehood.

Sonoma's makeup job was pure rock-and-roll science fiction. Bernie and Titania had streaked charcoal on their foreheads and cheeks. Diana's face was painted in some femme apotheosis: part Betty Boop, part Glinda, the Good Witch of the North. Joy had a furry beard and mustache. Freya wore a skull mask and a hooded cloak and said, "I'm Death from an early Bergman film."

Martha had used pale powder and black smudgy rings of kohl, and in her bathroom mirror appeared dismayingly unchanged except that her teeth looked yellow. So what! It felt good to look so bad, liberating and subversive, after years spent fretting about her clothes and face and hair, years of thinking she looked all wrong—even for lunch with Gretta!

On Amsterdam and Ninetieth, the van stopped for Hegwitha. The roof light went on when she got in, and the women gasped. Hegwitha had painted her entire face an opaque neon green.

Diana said, "Hegwitha, you win the prize."

"Thanks, Diana," Hegwitha said shyly.

Starling answered Isis's door in black jeans and a black T-shirt. Entering the dark living room, Martha saw a circle of small low tables, on each of which a candle burned inside a translucent, convincingly lifesized, but not, she hoped, authentic, human skull.

"Welcome, witch sisters." Isis emerged from the gloom in a flowing black velvet robe with a hood, a garment that could have been amicably shared by Dracula and Scarlett O'Hara. Her hag paint was dramatic and glamorous: white rice powder and Kabuki-like swirls of pink-and-purple eye shadow.

There was an audible intake of breath. "Blessed be," someone said.

Tonight there was no time for chat; the women got down to business. Each knelt on a cushion in front of a skull. On each table was a vintage cardboard matchbox painted with Turkish harem girls. Martha waited to see what the others did, then knelt in front of a skull which no one had chosen and which seemed to be plaintively eyeing her. The women picked up their matchboxes. Martha did the same.

"Night of death, night of darkness," Isis intoned. The women blew out their candles.

"In cavelike darkness . . ." Isis began.

Martha recalled how, as a child, she'd gone to Virginia with her parents and toured a cave hung with eerily lit, dripping phalluses made of rock. Near the end of the tour, their guide instructed them to hold their hands near their faces and then extinguished all the lights, and (this was the point of the exercise) they couldn't see their hands. The blackness lasted long enough for Martha to fear they'd been left there forever. By comparison, Isis's apartment was reassuringly bright: there were streetlights outside, a faint kitchen glow, a blinking answering machine.

"Now," said Isis, "we will each light our candle to the dead spirit we want to honor."

The women lit their candles quickly; they'd given the subject some thought. It took Martha a while to decide to light hers to her father. Five years had passed since Martha's mother phoned to say he was dead. It wasn't till Martha came home for the funeral that she heard about the lawn mower. At the time, Martha had thought that grief was something she couldn't live with. But now, though the memory of him could still make her briefly quit breathing, that sticking pain was mostly replaced by a dull intermittent ache. Still, whenever Dennis had been mean to her, she'd missed her father's love and protection. Why hadn't his spirit lurked nearby, making Dennis be nice?

She stared into the glowing eyes of the skull: crockery cobwebbed with hairline cracks, the sort of object one might find at the bottom of a fish tank.

How much time had passed? Minutes? Hours? Starling turned on the lights.

Isis said, "Listen, ladies! I actually contacted the spirit of Cleopatra and heard all sorts of yummy stuff about the Goddess Queens of Egypt."

"Oh, Isis," said Joy, "that's so sickeningly positive. I've always thought Witches' Sabbath shouldn't be about dead heroines but about people who should be dead, or if they are dead, should stay that way."

"Joy," said Bernie, "that's negative magic!"

"I guess I feel closer to the dead," said Hegwitha, her green face glowing, "being closer to death myself."

"Beautiful," said Diana.

Martha was annoyed at Hegwitha for always using her illness to turn conversations to herself and smooth over troublesome rough spots. Then she was annoyed at herself for feeling that way about Hegwitha. She liked Hegwitha, or anyway admired her for her resilience and for how bravely she elbowed her way through this thorny patch in her life.

"I lit my candle to Jim Morrison," volunteered Sonoma.

"Jim Morrison?" cried Freya. "Don't you get it at *all*?"

"Get what?" said Sonoma.

"That the Witches' Sabbath is about our inner darkness and communicating with the spirits of the witches who preceded us."

"Oh, *well*," drawled Sonoma. "Jim Morrison is dead, and he was pretty satanic. Anyway, I didn't light it to Jim Morrison. I lied. I lit it about my dad."

"You're lying now," said Freya. "You're just saying that to pull my chain. Anyway, your dad is alive. Theoretically."

"Yeah, right," said Sonoma.

"Fathers!" said Joy. "They'd all be better off dead—"

"Men in general," said Hegwitha. "The male of the species may turn out to be a bad idea that the human race can still evolve beyond—"

"I lit my candle to Stan," said Bernie. Stan was Bernie's dead husband; he'd been a therapist, like Bernie. "And I could feel Stan telling me it was okay to let go. So if it's all right with the rest of you, I'd like us to quit trashing men for a minute, considering—"

"Ladies! Ladies!" cried Isis. "It's always a heavy occasion. I think we need a cleansing fire to purge the demonic residue that's clinging to us from brushing so close to our dead."

"In the apartment?" said Starling. "Isis, not indoors . . ."

Isis went to the kitchen and returned with a metal wok. She began tearing scraps from a ream of copy paper and handed them out along with a tray of pencils. "I want everyone to write down the names of the good and evil dead, the loved and hated dead. Let's put them all in the fire that purifies and destroys so it can burn off the negativity and bring the loving dead closer . . ."

By now the women were scribbling and tearing. Whose names were they writing? Martha couldn't summon the name of one dead person except, of course, her father, and that was too serious for this: too important for burning copy paper in a wok. Her father's death had made her realize she didn't believe in God. There was no higher power to comfort her. There was no order, no plan, no reason for a good man to die on his riding mower.

The wok was overflowing when Isis lit the scraps. Within seconds, the flames shot out of control. Why didn't the others stop Isis before she got anywhere near fire or water? Starling ran for a bucket and sloshed water over the fire. A plume of acrid smoke spiraled up.

"Blessed be," said the women.

Martha contemplated what Freya had said about Isis always having to be rescued and promptly attaching herself to whomever had saved her last. Probably Starling had saved her too many times for it to count. Were Starling and Isis lovers? It was hard to tell, as it was with everything concerning Isis's sexuality. Maybe Isis did have sex with the rocks and trees. In any case, there was a sexual charge in how she bestowed her attention, attention she often focused now, flatteringly, on Martha.

"Thank you, Starling," said Isis. Wisps of black debris from the burning scraps fluttered around her head.

Ever since she was a girl, Martha could never enter a dark room without closing her eyes and keeping them shut until she'd turned on the light. What was she afraid of seeing? Or what was she hoping to see? What ax murderers or malevolent ghosts was she politely allowing to leave?

Tonight (it had been almost a week since the Witches' Sabbath) Martha returned from a perfectly grisly and ordinary day at *Mode* and knew exactly what she would rather not see, here in her own apartment: the squalor, the dirty clothes, the half-empty teacups, each with its pale bloated lemon slice floating like a dead fish in a tank. Martha's decor reminded her of films in which the set telegraphs the fact that a lonely-guy substance-abusing cop is toughing out a messy divorce.

For a long time she'd existed with the barest essentials: cooking equipment, chairs, a table, the futon she could jettison at a moment's notice, which meant—though she would have insisted that this was *not* what it meant—an invitation from a suitable man to relocate elsewhere. But in recent years, Martha's mother had been divesting herself of possessions in preparation for her death, although she was in good health and might live on for decades. Martha's apartment began to fill with items of Fifties decor—two tall orange ceramic lamps in the shape of elongated cats, pulled like taffy; segmented lazy Susans for parties Martha would never give; kidney-shaped ashtrays so essential for the nonsmoker—articles that might have been newly chic but for their contaminating association with Martha's childhood.

At first Martha kept these objects safely contained in packing crates, but Dennis had discovered them and gleefully unwrapped them. With Dennis around, they'd had no power to harm her. But as soon as he left, the ceramic cats had regrown their claws: memento mori, grim reminders of time passed and passing.

The apartment smelled of curry, a spice Martha used to love, but which over time had become a reproachful message from her neighbors, a comment on Martha's rootless solitude and failure to have clamorous children for whom to cook hot vegetarian meals. Reflexively, Martha turned on the TV and caught several minutes of a documentary about a professional magician dedicated to exposing bogus healers and psychics. She watched long enough to hear the magician say, "I came to see that I would have to live without the comforts of faith." Then Martha switched off the television and stared at the empty screen.

Just at that moment, the phone rang.

"Martha," said Isis. "Have you eaten? Let's meet near my place, in an hour."

Martha and Isis met for dinner at Sell Grit! on Columbus in the Eighties. Well-scrubbed beaming waitresses carried platters of mashed potatoes and gravy, biscuits, organic chicken, and menus that vouched for the wholesomeness of the chicken's entire life. Country kitchens throughout the heartland had been raided for the decor: bare wood, gingham, oak hutches, homespun napkins the size of dishcloths, thick crockery of a mossy, unappetizing gray.

The waitresses all knew Isis and her dietary guidelines, more complex and purer than those of the restaurant itself: no salt, no wheat, no dairy, tight restrictions on glutens. Martha ordered the corn-fed baked chicken, whipped potatoes, and gravy.

Isis said, "Many women have been healed of allergies by the Goddess. But not, unfortunately, me. I assume it's karma, punishment for when I used to think that allergies were a delusion of hypochondriacal pussies. This was before I became deathly sensitive to absolutely everything good.

"Of course, by then academia had made hamburger of my immune system, turned my body into Disneyland for every virus that came along. Thank the Goddess that this was before HIV! For me, the sexual revolution coincided with the energy crisis. I didn't have the energy to turn the wrong men down, I mean wormy little *graduate students* at MLA conventions."

Martha couldn't help thinking she'd never had that problem: too many men desiring her and having to reject them. But these grumpy ruminations were mediated by her pleasure at the fact that Isis had actually called her and invited her out to dinner. She poked a stalk of celery into the spicy peanut dip.

"By the time your generation came along," Isis said, "desire was no longer a concept. I find now that I can get hotter sitting alone in a room and concentrating on moving my kundalini up through the chakras. It's what the women saints knew, except they thought they needed Jesus. Mental sex with a deity is so much better than sex with mortals—healthier, always available, less messy in every way." Isis laughed her abandoned laugh: musical and throaty.

What if Gretta or Dennis met Isis? What a lunatic they

would think her with her spacey affectations, her fluting voice and relentless eye contact. So what! Lots of people would envy Martha at this moment! Every woman on the beach that day at Fire Island would give her lucky crystal for dinner *a deux* with Isis.

Well, it was understandable to want to be with Isis. Though the Goddess movement was in theory nonhierarchical, Isis was the leader of a growing organization; at one meeting Starling had announced that ten thousand women were on their current mailing list. There was no denying the draw of celebrity, even if one's fame was limited to the New Age shamaness population.

But finally, Isis's appeal had less to do with position and power than with her simultaneously endearing and maddening personality, with the alternating currents of intimacy and distance, the fluctuations of presence and absence with which she drew Martha in. Half the time she paid Martha no attention at all, causing her to worry that she might somehow have lost Isis's friendship, a possibility that affected her with a sense of loss so profound that she began to think she cared about Isis far more than she'd suspected. At other times, Isis showed an intensely seductive talent for convincing Martha that she had seen into her secret depths and admired what she saw there. Isis said things about her that were so flattering and (Martha hoped) so accurate that Martha could only conclude that Isis was acutely perceptive, perhaps even psychic. Isis said that Martha was a rare being: cool-headed, concerned with facts, and at the same time empathic in the extreme.

A few of the women seemed jealous of Martha's new friendship with Isis. More than once, Starling had echoed what Freya said that first evening about Isis attaching herself to whomever had just rescued her from danger. (Starling told Martha she'd met Isis at an academic conference, over a buffet table of chafing dishes warmed by gas burners, one of which set fire to Isis's blouse. With unashamed nostalgia, Starling described how she'd wrapped her jacket around Isis's smoldering sleeve.) Perhaps that did explain Isis's otherwise inexplicable interest in Martha, and the fact that Martha and Hegwitha had been so swiftly taken up by this privileged coterie of superstar Goddess worshippers.

But they weren't all superstars. Diana was a grad-school dropout, Joy an environmental activist with day jobs as a file clerk and a hardware-store cashier. Yet Diana was said to be very smart; Joy was capable, a hothead: qualities the older women seemed to prize and encourage. The principles of affinity operative here were too deep-rooted and knotty for Martha to untangle. Perhaps the group was simply a warm amoebalike blob that had engulfed and digested Martha and Hegwitha.

Isis's gaze tracked a celery stalk up to Martha's mouth and watched as Martha hesitated, trying to forestall or avoid the inevitably loud, awkward crunch. Isis turned away with a shudder, as if from a decapitation. Oh, unfair! Martha hadn't wanted the celery in the first place. She was eating it not from hunger but to fill a conversational void.

Isis said, "It's not as if we all aren't ga-ga about food. What the women in our group *won't* eat would feed the entire Third World. It's the chief torture implement with which Freya punishes Sonoma, and Diana's an expert at using her eating disorder to make mincemeat out of Joy."

Martha said, "I was just telling my friend about that at lunch the other day."

Isis's delicate wince made it clear that she didn't want to know about this friend to whom Martha gossiped about the Goddess women's dietary neuroses.

"Meanwhile," Isis went on, "Titania's convinced that if

she'd spent less time on her megabuck cosmetics business and more time making nutritious home-cooked meals for her daughter, the kid wouldn't have joined the Moonies and run away to Korea."

"How awful for Titania!" said Martha. "I knew she had trouble with her daughter, but I didn't know what it was."

"Awful?" Isis said. "I suppose . . . You know, it's hard for me to think of her as Titania. I still think of her as Maxine. Oh, gosh. Is the food here already?"

"Stress Reduction Technique Number One," said the waitress. "We try to feed you before you get cranky." Did she mean customers in general or Isis in particular?

"Cranky . . ." Isis eyed Martha's plate. "It would make *me* cranky to wonder when that chicken was roasted. Presumably not in the blink of an eye since we placed our order." Isis had ordered something with mustard greens or kale, slimier and more seaweedlike than one would have expected from a restaurant so solidly geared to a picky ten-year-old's food tastes.

Martha's first mouthful of mashed potatoes felt like a soothing hand on her brow. It was stunning, the power of food to comfort and console, even though, like so much else, it was ultimately unreliable. When things were going seriously wrong, even food could turn nasty.

The last time Martha had dinner with Dennis, she had ordered gnocchi, a dish she would never have considered had she known what the evening would bring. They were in the neighborhood Italian place they'd frequented when they'd first fallen in love, when the romantic dimness made for a smoother transition, going there straight from bed. They'd continued to eat there when they couldn't think of anywhere else, long after it became irritating to be unable to read the menu. By then Martha was looking for things to be irritated by, particularly things about Dennis: the officious way he ordered pasta, the way he seemed to think that his good looks gave him carte blanche to let his hair get greasy.

If she'd known what he had to say that night, she wouldn't have gotten gnocchi, gummy little pillows that would turn to glue in her mouth and make the task of swallowing seem suddenly Herculean. Though perhaps she *did* know. Why else would she have started off talking about a piece they were doing at *Mode* about the former girlfriends of convicted serial killers.

Martha said, "There was one killer whose modus operandi was to empty the joint checking account and then ask his girlfriend to dinner. Twelve of his fourteen girlfriends were never heard from again."

Dennis took a sip of wine. The flickering candlelight slalomed down the planes of his handsome face.

"Well," he said, "compared to that, I guess this isn't so bad."

"What do you mean *this*?" said Martha.

Dennis gulped the rest of his wine. He seemed genuinely distraught, though with an actor one never knew. He took a deep soap-operatic breath.

"It's not working out," he said.

"What do you mean *it*?" Martha said.

"I mean us," said Dennis.

No wonder Dennis had asked her to meet him at Nino's! Didn't one always hear that tense conversations with volatile lovers should occur in restaurants and other public venues so the presence of other people would have a calming or shaming effect in case he or she began to scream or make menacing jabs with a steak knife?

"I'm not hungry," Martha said. "Do you think I can send back my dinner?"

"No," Dennis said. "It's too late for that, too."

Why couldn't Dennis have told her before she ordered dinner? No matter how much she muscled down, the gnocchi sat there, undiminished, winning a battle to the death between her and potato pasta. Each time she swallowed a mouthful, three gnocchi took its place.

Maybe the gnocchi were on her side, keeping her mouth glued shut. Because as soon as she'd got the last bit of starch unstuck from her palate, she started talking, begging, coming up with reasons and microadjustments that would enable her and Dennis to stay together forever. She felt as if Dennis were a brick wall she kept running into. Though maybe she only thought that because the restaurant had brick walls—white brick walls that, in the past, she and Dennis could make vanish by staring into each other's eyes until the room went out of focus . . .

"It's not Titania's fault," Isis was saying. "Nor is it Freya's, exactly. Patriarchy turns the mother-daughter bond into the relation between the seasoned jailbird and the first-time offender, hardened prisoners showing new convicts the ropes of the penal system—and in the process allowing the system to continue. Chinese mothers bind their daughters' feet. In Africa it's the mothers who do the clitoridectomies. I'm sure you've noticed it's impossible to watch TV without Barbara Walters blabbing on about female circumcision. For most American men the big news is that women have a clitoris to begin with. For millennia Mom's been the gal in charge of removing your pleasure button—is it any wonder it's not a relationship of great trust? What about your mother, Martha? Are you close? Do you get along?

Martha didn't want to think about her mother. It had much the same effect on her as thinking about Dennis, although her mother and Dennis weren't at all alike. Martha wasn't one of those women who suddenly realize that the men they love are their moms in drag! Dennis was mean and shallow, Martha's mother was just a mess. When Martha called her mother, they talked doctors, arthritis, TV, money, what the doctor said, what Donahue said, what was on sale at the Pic-Way, what Martha's dad's death benefits would and wouldn't cover. Martha's mother had nothing in common with Dennis except for a remarkably similar knack for making Martha feel tragic, paralyzed, doomed, and hopeless.

"She's in Ohio," Martha said. "I hardly see her—"

"The Midwest?" said Isis. "You come from the Midwest? I don't know why I thought . . . I had the impression that you were visiting your parents on Fire Island. What a sparrowlike little person you are, Martha. Look how you're watching me. That quality of watching—it's one of the things about yourself that you undervalue. You think it's one of your worst traits, but in fact it's among your best."

Knocked breathless by the accuracy (she hoped) of Isis's assessment, Martha could only mumble, "Oh, no, those were my *friend*'s parents who live on Fire Island." Immediately she felt that she had somehow disappointed Isis—which, as usual, sharpened her craving for Isis's approval and eradicated any lingering doubts about her eccentricities.

"What was I saying?" Isis asked.

Martha tensed. Was this a test? She said, "You were talking about female circumcision. How your own mother did it."

"Well, not *my* own mother," said Isis. "One's own mother. Isn't it interesting how we segued from the subject of food to the subject of mothers and sex? Anyway . . . we're just now getting a glimpse of the outer limits of diet, way beyond mood and you are what you eat and getting or not getting cancer. I met this great Romanian nutritionist at the World Healing Conference and happened to mention to her that I was terribly accident-prone.

"The dietician gave me a fabulous book about gluten's

effect on the pineal gland, which scientists associate with clair-voyance and ESP. Not only was I screwing up my neurotrans-mitters, I was burning down my psychic telephone lines to the future—say, the moment when the hem of my robe would catch in the ritual fire. Since I changed my diet—it's been almost two years—I've not only been thinner and felt better, I've actually been safer!"

Had Isis forgotten that Martha had saved her from drown-ing? Sometimes she seemed not to recall where they'd met—that short but nasty paddle in the freezing Atlantic. And should this make Martha feel unappreciated, or hopeful? If Isis didn't remember, it couldn't be why she liked Martha.

"Isn't that what everyone wants?" Isis asked. "To feel protected? Guided? My favorite holy picture, when I was girl, was the angel watching over those two kids like some kind of weird winged nanny. The children about to cross a broken bridge and the angel pulling them back. Of course, this was before the night when all that changed forever, and my child-hood guardian angel was reborn as the Goddess. It's no wonder so many ex-Catholics wind up in the Goddess movement. Take that blue robe off Mary and what are we looking at?"

"The Goddess?" Martha ventured.

"Well, obviously," Isis said. "And the experience of the miraculous is the same with both. Or at least as I experienced it on that incredible night."

There was no way for Martha not to ask, "What incredible night?"

Isis smiled. "The night I discovered my spiritual nature, which had been concealed from me for my first thirty years. Let's face it, ours is not a culture in which a girl's parents consecrate her at birth to the service of the Goddess.

"I was your basic control-freak, a promiscuous, over-achieving Catholic academic. I'd gone from Fordham to a lectureship at New Haven, and my first book, *Freud, Jesus, and Matriarchy*, had gotten gobs of attention. Even the media had got into the controversy, which was less about my ideas than a titillating mix of religion, gender, and sex. My academic (87) career went into overdrive; I wasn't prepared to be famous for all the wrong reasons. Plus I was in personal crisis, stranded between love affairs, which at that point meant I'd been chaste for about two seconds . . . Anyway, I was asked to take part in that infamous Washington panel on women and the patriarchal paradigm."

"Infamous?" said Martha.

Isis's lips formed the rippling, mindless smile of a Botticelli angel. "When they sent Daniel into the lion's den, at least they had the decency not to call it a panel. This one was held in the ballroom of a huge D.C. hotel. The minute I entered I was assaulted by waves of hatred, five hundred old-boy academics whetting their knives and licking their chops. Somehow I managed to find my seat at the seminar table, between a priest, a heavy-duty feminist theorist, and a bigshot Freudian, all of whom had already dismissed my work as garbage."

Martha tried to look properly sympathetic and pained, although at that instant she was nearly ecstatic with pleasure in her meal: the sweet-salty crispness of the chicken skin, the airy whipped potatoes, her forays into the side dishes of sweet corn, coleslaw, and creamed spinach.

"What *was* your work then?" Martha asked, regretting it at once. "I mean, remind me . . . Sorry, I've forgotten . . . My memory . . ."

Isis waved away Martha's apology. Why should Martha be held responsible for the details of Isis's former life?

"Goodness," said Isis, "it seems so remedial now. I pushed the envelope of the feminist critique of Freud and Christian culture. The shrink thought it was preposterous to see Freud's work in the context of the lost matriarchal societies. The feminist had an investment in women not being witches—in our being regular guys who would make great department chairs. The priest thought I was going straight to hell for reading the church fathers as the psychotic misogynists they were; later he dismembered me in a scholarly Catholic journal.

"As I sat down, all three gave me eat-shit grins. I arranged my water glass and my pen, and then discovered I couldn't lift my head, couldn't look at the audience or my fellow panelists. Suddenly I felt . . . well, a *force* jerking me out of my chair and carrying me from the room.

"The hotel was built on a mountain in the middle of Chevy Chase: billion-dollar landscaping, scary but probably safe. The night was out of a horror film: full moon, fast-moving clouds. I remember thinking I'd become so mired in academia that here was this gorgeous moon, and I hadn't noticed . . . And that was more or less the last thing I remember thinking."

Isis contemplated her seaweed, then pushed away her plate. "I somehow feel compelled to say: I am not a psychotic. I know I sound like Richard Nixon. But I do worry that people may think I'm nuts when I try to describe that night."

Martha hoped her smile conveyed her faith in Isis's sanity. Isis seemed encouraged and took a deep breath and went on:

"I know it contradicts our patriarchal, Judeo-Christian notions of causality when I say that on that night, in the middle of the American Society of Academic Psychologists convention, in Washington, D.C., I looked up at the sky and saw . . . what I thought was a comet. But soon I realized it wasn't a comet at all. It was . . . a woman in white, flying across the sky in a chariot pulled by winged white horses."

"Whoa," said Martha. For the first time it crossed her mind that Isis might be clinically insane. Well, she might be a lunatic, but she ran an entire movement, had people taking care of her, owned an Upper West Side floor-through and a house on Fire Island, all apparently without any need to go out and work for a living. Isis had power, money, friends, a great place—places—to live, while Martha had a lousy job, a cramped and grimy apartment. So really, you might ask yourself: Which one of them was crazy?

"It was a brilliant vision," said Isis, "and at the same time so ordinary it could have been the Goodyear blimp over the Astrodome. But I knew it was the Goddess: Astarte or Diana. And this was before I'd heard a word about Goddess worship! I myself don't believe it. I just know what I saw.

"I knew how I'd been primed for revelation—years of Catholic education. But I also knew that this was real. My life would never be the same. I didn't have to go back to that seminar room. Or sit on that panel. The consensus in academia is that I suffered a nervous breakdown, psychosis being the only reason to give up tenure-track and a cost-sharing retirement plan. And for the record: my Astarte book has sold one hundred thousand copies more than *Freud, Jesus, and Matriarchy!*

"The Goddess was ready to enter my life, and I had to make room. I steeped myself in Goddess lore and religion, from the early Mithraic and Cretan cults to the European Wicca faith; the persecutions that drove matriarchy underground and allowed the rape of Mother Earth; the change from worshipping the female principle to blindly adoring the phallus—" Isis smiled at Martha. "Have I got kelp on my teeth?"

Martha shook her head no, and Isis said, "Speaking of making room . . . are you having dessert? Go on. It's my treat. I know you can't afford it."

Martha almost protested that she *could* afford it, though the prices on the menu were many times what she was willing to pay for apple-blueberry crisp. How typical of Isis to graciously buy her dinner and temper her generosity by referring to Martha's relative poverty. That mix of kindness and smallness, of compassion and meanness—it did seem to run through the Goddess group in unusually high concentrations. But why should that surprise her? Didn't Martha contain all that in herself? And weren't things always complicated when money was involved? Gretta never let Martha forget who had the expense account.

"Go on," Isis urged. "Order the hot fudge sundae, the gooey treat your child self wanted and wasn't allowed to have. It's so important to give our former selves what they were denied."

Frankly, Martha's adult self wanted the peach pie with brandy sauce. Nonetheless she heard herself order the hot fudge sundae that her child self could have had any time it wanted. Her parents had been indulgent with her, when they could afford it.

Martha's mother had been a good cook, but her father's nightly litany of recompensable or unrecompensable death and disaster had leached all the flavor out of the food. Her father had been a depressive. Martha saw that now. Could he have intuited that he would soon be dead on a riding mower? Depression was hereditary. Everyone knew that. Maybe Martha's existence—her job, her romantic troubles, Dennis, her involvement with the Goddess women—was nothing more than a case of predetermination by DNA. Given the choice, Martha would rather believe in Isis and her vision than in that grim reductive version of life.

Sipping her chamomile tea, Isis watched Martha mine the volcanic eruption of whipped cream, nuts, and syrup. She beamed at her like a mother—not a punishing mother, not Freya, but a loving mother who wants only to see her child enjoy dessert.

"You know what I'm saying," Isis said. "That's what's so appealing about you, Martha. A person need only *look* at you to know you understand."

The startling echo of Dennis made Martha put down her (91) spoon and suddenly see her sundae for the inedible joke that it was. Hadn't Martha reported in a Goddess meeting that Dennis used to say that? Yet Isis must have forgotten the context in which she'd heard it and believed that she was the first to make this observation—another shining trophy retrieved from the wreckage of Martha's psyche.

The women had returned to Fire Island to celebrate the autumnal equinox. Just the inner circle this time, they'd come back to the beach to participate in a ritual involving much antiphonal chanting about preparing for the coming dark by embracing the darkness within them.

"What season is coming?" Isis intoned.

"The season of shadows," chanted the women.

"Where are the shadows?" sang Isis.

"Within us," chanted the women.

"Goddess of darkness," Isis prayed, "find us in your cave."

The landscape had changed appallingly over the past weeks. Shivering in the clammy salt air, Martha felt as if she were visiting a beloved invalid who'd taken a horrid turn for the worse. The vegetation looked stepped-on, brownish, jellied, translucent. Who would believe that sane people once swam in that inky sea?

Isis turned from the ocean to the celebrants on shore. "The season of grief is coming, the melancholy time. We must accept the sadness but not let sorrow overwhelm us."

Overhead, a vee of geese honked concurringly. Really,

thought Martha, trying to keep up one's spirits would be like grabbing a broom and trying to sweep the waves back into the sea.

Perhaps that was why the service seemed rushed. Maybe the women were eager to return to the warmth of the house and get on with the more cheering reason they'd come—to discuss their upcoming retreat, their timely escape from the autumn chill to the Arizona desert. They were all going to study with Maria Aquilo, a Native American medicine woman and healer Isis had met at a conference in Bolinas.

Back at Isis's beach house, Martha ducked into the bathroom. By the time she rejoined the group, Isis was telling yet another story about the wonders she'd seen Maria Aquilo perform:

"A group of conference faculty went up a mountain for a picnic. After lunch we were talking, and suddenly Maria started making this turkey grumble. Everyone fell silent as we tried to figure out what she was doing. And then, out of nowhere—four eagles appeared in the sky! They swooped in and circled overhead. Everyone was blown away, but Maria acted like it was some party trick every Native healer can do, nothing compared to the wild stuff that goes on when they have chanting and sweat lodge. The sad thing was: Maria had been sort of dating Johnny Red Bear, this cute young shaman from Vancouver. But when she called the eagles it freaked him out, and soon after that they broke up."

"Competitive," said Titania.

"Just like a guy," said Starling.

Bernie said, "It gives me chills to think we'll be learning medicine ways from Maria, who lives so much closer to a culture that still has female goddess and spirit figures—Spider Woman, Changing Woman, Clay Lady, Buffalo Calf Woman."

Hegwitha said, "I've been reading up on Native American

myths. That bibliography you gave us is really helpful, Diana."

Martha dreaded this conversation. She hardly knew where to look when the subject of the trip to Tucson arose. If she (94) asked to come along, as Hegwitha had, she would be perfectly welcome. But Martha hadn't been invited outright, and something kept her from asking. She supposed it was the memory of those gloomy Sundays when Dennis would pick up the Sunday travel section and say, I'd like to go to Bali or Copenhagen or Prague, never once using the first-person plural, never including Martha, until Martha bleated pathetically, Hey, can I come, too?

It was comforting to consider the nightmare of group travel: constant friction, Byzantine complications, everyone's whims, fears, hurt feelings. Imagine walking into a desert truck stop with a dozen Goddess women, half of them dressed like Mama Cass and all with bizarre dietary restrictions.

Already there was tension about what the retreat would involve. This much was agreed on: They would fly into Tucson, where they'd lease a four-wheel-drive van from the dread travel agent, Pete, the Marlboro man with the penchant for phoning in the midst of priestess rites. Then they'd head for the desert where Maria Aquilo lived. There was less consensus about how much time they would spend in Tucson.

Titania said, "What did we decide about Tucson?"

Groaning, the women dutifully geared up for the unavoidable discussion, tedious but integral to the democratic process.

Bernie, who'd been to Tucson, thought that two days weren't enough. "Tucson's a marvelous city with a rich multicultural mix that we, as Eastern canyon-dwellers, could learn an enormous amount from."

Joy said, "Oh, Bernie, only a liberal could imagine that there was real multiculturalism in *any* American city."

Freya said, "The Tucson Art Museum offered me a show. I was terribly overcommitted. I had to turn them down."

Sonoma said, "I can't stand how you're always bragging about things you had to turn down. Why don't you tell the truth, Mom? You turned them down because you thought Phoenix was the happening city in Arizona, and when you found out it was Tucson you had a total fit."

"Oh ha ha," said Freya mirthlessly, and as Martha watched, a tiny twitch of satisfaction tugged at Sonoma's impassive face. So childish in so many ways, Sonoma was prodigiously adult in her ability to wound her mother with weapons sharpened in self-defense over the course of a lifelong struggle.

"What I can't understand," said Diana, "is how we can talk about returning to earth religion, leaving city religion, and not only do we live in the city but we're spending our retreat time hanging around *another* city."

"Trust me," said Starling. "We'll be spending most of it out—*way out*—in the desert."

"Speaking of spending," said Titania, "and of being out in the desert . . . am I the only one concerned about our lodgings? Considering what we're shelling out, there should be some assurance that our adorable rustic hogans will have indoor plumbing. I wish this didn't feel like an age thing. When I was your age, Sonoma, it was easier to put up with discomfort."

But Sonoma was the last one to forgo her creature comforts. "No bathrooms? What is this? Mom? No way. I'm not going."

"I'm as old as you are, Titania, dear," Bernie offered.

"Hardly," said Titania. "There is a universe of difference between fifty-eight and fifty-two."

"Who's counting?" said Bernie. "And besides, Titania,

are you saying I should feel guilty for being six years younger?"

"Navajos live in hogans," said Joy. "Maria is a Papago. And what do earth wisdom and medicine have to do with plumbing?"

"Well, actually," said Freya, "didn't Ram Dass have that guru, that Brooklyn housewife who was in the bathtub practicing her reducing-class yogic-breathing exercises, and she overdid it and had a vision of a sweet little Indian man sitting on the toilet? In that case, I think, enlightenment was closely allied with plumbing."

"Speaking of visions . . ." said Diana.

Joy rolled her eyes. They all knew what was coming next. From the start, the most rancorous contention had surrounded the question of whether the retreat would include time for solo vision quests, for going into the desert alone and contacting their spirit helpers.

Diana said, "I can't think of anything more important than a real aloneness experience, than communion with Mother Earth, gazing into the mirror of nature, praying for a vision."

"In the Sonoran Desert?" said Titania. "This is not Fire Island, Diana. This is cactus. Scorpions. Rattlesnakes. This is walking up the wrong arroyo and dying of flash floods and thirst and starvation."

"Serial killers," said Joy.

"You're not kidding," said Starling. "The whole Southwest is full of crazed drifters with private arsenals."

"What's wrong with snakes?" said Diana. "They were important symbols in the ancient Goddess religions. The matriarchy embraced all of nature and didn't privilege one creature above another."

"That's right," said Hegwitha. "It was patriarchy that gave the snake a bad rap because of men's neurotic conflict about their penises."

"Penis," said Joy. "Singular. Martha, you're awfully quiet."

"I don't mind the idea of snakes," Martha said. "I just don't want them near me."

Sonoma said, "I wouldn't go out in the desert alone. Not for a million bucks."

"No one's asking you to," said Freya. "In fact, you're not allowed to, young lady."

"Not allowed by who?" growled Sonoma.

"By *whom*," corrected Freya.

"It would be great for Sonoma," said Diana. "A menstruation ritual vision quest. When a Papago girl comes into her moon time she goes to what they call a little house, and the grandmothers educate her in female magic, and the village dances all night."

"Diana, darling," said Titania. "We've been over this ad nauseam. That Papago girl doesn't go to the little house just to learn female magic. She goes away so the sight of her won't make all the husbands impotent and sour the milk and ruin the crops."

"Titania's right!" said Bernie, with a conciliatory smile meant to smooth over their little tiff on the subject of age.

Freya said, "Some tribes bury pubescent girls in pits of hot stones for three days. I did a lot of reading about this when I did my *Biocycle-Sphere Menstrual Hut* installation in Edinburgh."

"Not the Navajos," said Diana. "They have a four-day party."

"When you have a daughter," said Freya, "*you* send her into the desert."

What personal stake did Diana have in Sonoma's vision quest? Why did she keep mentioning it, though Sonoma showed no interest and grew more sullen than usual when Diana brought it up?

"Can we stop harping on this?" said Sonoma. "I am *not* going out in the desert."

"Diana's projecting," Joy said. "She's the one who wants to do the vision solo. She wants to go into the wilderness where she doesn't have to eat for three days and no one will criticize her and she can feel good about it."

"Stop it, Joy," said Diana. "You know, Goddess worship is supposed to be so nonhierarchical, but when real decisions have to be made around here it's always Isis and sometimes Starling. If they want to do a solo, the rest of us will do solos, too. And if they don't . . ."

Hegwitha leaned forward. From that first day on the beach, Martha had noticed that questions of power and hierarchy were of great interest to Hegwitha, who often seemed to be weighing her ideals of a purely egalitarian Goddess-centered society against the more practical exigencies of life in New York and Fire Island. The nearness of death had done nothing to help her transcend all that. But who could say how anyone would or should act in Hegwitha's situation?

"*Reisefieber*," said Isis.

"Excuse me?" Starling said.

"*Reisefieber*," Isis repeated. "Travel anxiety. Freud coined the term. One of the very rare occasions on which he got it right. It was based on his observation that everyone gets nervous before a trip, because every journey is linked in our minds to the final journey of death."

"Air travel especially," Titania said.

Isis said, "Katherine Mansfield wrote in her journals that whenever she left for a journey she would get her house in order as if she were never coming back."

"Cool," said Sonoma.

"That's so beautiful," Bernie said.

"A little morbid, if you ask me," said Joy.

"I don't know," said Isis. "The point is, we don't have to struggle about vision work now. There will definitely be alone time. No one's going to make anyone stay with the group every minute. But Maria has so much to teach us, our time with her will seem too short, and we won't want to go off and miss this great opportunity. If the rest of you had met Maria, you'd know what I mean. Anyway, Goddess religion was never about individual vision so much as about the collective healing power of the group."

"That's fine for you to say, Isis," said Diana. "You've already had your vision."

"Yes, well." Isis sighed. "We're not in competition about this. And the vision experience can be overrated. I realize I've said this before, but when I saw the Goddess in her chariot over the ASAP convention, it seemed somehow so ordinary, so integrated with the rest of life, it could have been the Goodyear blimp—"

"That reminds me," interrupted Freya, "I heard the funniest story. There's this immensely overweight woman sculptor—you'd recognize the name. She was working in her garden, and she heard some workmen across the way saying: Look at the Goodyear blimp! She ran inside and got her husband, and he came out, all set to punch out the workmen for insulting his wife. But just then he looked up at the sky—"

"And saw the Goodyear blimp," said Titania. "Fabulous. I love it."

Sonoma said, "Why are you always telling fat stories? Why can't you do anything but torture me about my weight?"

"I'm sorry, Sonoma," said Freya. "I thought it was a funny story." To the other women, she said, "Her father had no sense of humor either."

"Look who's talking," said Sonoma. "Laugh-a-minute."

"Sisters," said Isis, "be kind to each other. Please."

Joy said, "I know this trip will heal us in important ways. Just getting out of the city, back to the natural world—or as close to natural as the lack of ozone allows. And being around

wise women who live in harmony with Turtle Earth, women respected in their tribal cultures, passing wisdom from mother to daughter. How could that not be good for Freya and Sonoma? And for me and Diana, to be around women living together—"

Diana said, "Joy makes Native American religion sound like couples therapy."

"I don't," said Joy. "You know I'm not into couples therapy. You always find the thing I hate most and tell me that's what I'm into."

Isis said, "If you'd met Maria you'd know that anything is possible. There were people at Bolinas who swore that they'd seen her turn *into* an eagle, which of course is her spirit guide and the sacred name of her clan. She is so charismatic! You want to throw yourself at her feet. The first time I met her she told me that for a thousand years before the coming of the white man, her people had a song, and its lyrics said the white men would come and kill the earth, and Native people would not be able to stop it. Needless to say, I just nose-dived into a pit of white-woman guilt. But Maria said the most liberating thing. She said, 'Were you at Little Big Horn, Isis? Why should *you* feel guilty?'

"After that I felt completely empowered, capable of anything. This was at the '89 Bolinas Conference on Earth and Spirituality. After I met Maria, I volunteered to teach a second Goddess workshop for free."

Bernie said, "We don't doubt that Maria's terrific. But I worry that some of us may be bringing unrealistic expectations to this trip."

Joy said, "*That's* therapy talk."

Isis said, "No, really. I'm glad Bernie brought it up. Maybe we should go around the room and share the expectations we're bringing to this journey. We could use the Talking Stick."

"The Talking Stick!" cried the women. They were always so glad for a chance to use religious paraphernalia—the sweet enthusiasm of little girls deciding to bring out their favorite dolls. Sometimes when they did visualizations, nurturing their inner children or vision-traveling as a group to some sacred Aegean temple, they reminded Martha of children closing their eyes and playing pretend.

Isis took the stick first. "I'm looking forward to having time to learn from Maria, to absorb her magic and wisdom and make it my own."

"Blessed be," said the women.

Isis passed the stick to Joy, who said, "I guess I already said what I thought this trip is going to be about."

"Say it again," said Isis.

"Well, about Maria," said Joy. "And also about healing —especially for me and Diana." Hastily she handed the Talking Stick to Bernie.

Bernie said, "I love Tucson. And the desert. And there's always so much to be learned from Native American cultures."

Diana took the Talking Stick and said, "Well. To learn from Maria. And to learn from the desert and solitude and nature."

She gave the stick to Freya, who said, "For me there is always the hope of finding something to use in my art."

When Titania got the stick, she smiled and shook her head. "I usually know what I want," she said. "But I am trying to go slower in my life journey. I have no expectations about what I want from this trip."

The women applauded decorously. "Good attitude!" said Bernie.

Sonoma took the stick and held it. There was something lethal, Martha thought, about the stubbornness of children who knew that time is their secret weapon and that they can outwait and outlast the most patient adult.

"I don't know," Sonoma said. "I'm going because Mom's going, I guess."

"Is that all?" said Freya. "Because if that's all, we can find someone for you to stay with. Don't you have *any* thoughts about this? Most likely you are the only lucky girl in your class missing a week of school to go to one of the most beautiful parts of America."

"I *like* school," said Sonoma.

"That's the first time I've heard *that*," said Freya. "Well, you can stay home if you wish."

Sonoma was silent for a few moments. "The desert could be cool," she said. "I'll go."

"Thank you kindly!" said Freya.

When Hegwitha's turn came, she said, "I'd be lying if I didn't say I was hoping to discover some magic cactus or desert weed—the Native American cancer cure. Beyond that, it always helps me to get back into nature and get in touch with something that will be here after I'm gone."

Finally it was Martha's turn. Did they take it for granted that she was going? It was harder for her—she wasn't like them, a self-employed therapist or artist or writer who could just cancel clients or put the newest creative project on hold. She said, "I'm not sure what I'm supposed to expect. I mean, considering I'm not going."

"You're *not*?" chorused the women.

So the women had assumed she was coming along. It would seem petty and silly to say that no one had asked her.

"The money . . ." murmured Martha. "Besides, I don't know if I can take time from work . . ."

"The money is a nonissue," said Isis. "In cases of genuine need, we can draw on our Astarte Travel Scholarship Fund. And as for the time off from work . . . Well, the Goddess will have to arrange it!"

But perhaps the Goddess knew that Martha was only pretending to believe in Her and therefore refused to help persuade Eleanor, Martha's boss, to overlook the fact that Martha had six more months of hard time at *Mode* to be eligible for a week's parole. Martha had never felt less divinely guided as she began her feeble petition with a half-dozen excellent reasons why Eleanor should say no.

As Martha spoke, Eleanor's face seemed to grow a sort of protective caul, a film that might be gruesomely torn by the slightest tic. From behind this unstable crust, Eleanor watched Martha struggling to explain why she needed to go to a private . . . seminar . . . with a Native American medicine woman. How insane of Martha to have imagined that the truth would set her free! She should have invented a sick parent or some grave condition requiring expensive diagnostic tests; she'd heard enough from Hegwitha to fake a full-body medical workup.

In the fluorescent glare of Eleanor's cubicle-office, Martha saw her association with the Goddess group for the walking nervous breakdown it was. The Goddess women and the *Mode* staff might have been warring armies or competing football teams identifiable by their uniforms: the *Mode* army in black miniskirts, Lycra, and clunky shoes; the Goddess team in tie-dye, paisley, beads, and tinsel headbands.

Though someone had once assigned—and killed—the piece on Goddess worship, the young *Mode* staffers probably didn't know that Goddess religion existed. Sometimes, just to experience a twinge of humiliation, Martha imagined telling the art-department girls what Isis and her friends believed. The basic concept of matriarchy might not seem so exotic: *Mode*, after all, was a misogynist's nightmare of a matriarchal society. But the Goddess women would say that the editors at *Mode* had embraced corrupt male values, while the ancient matriarchies were based on tender loving care. Goddess civilization was nonhierarchical, whereas the *Mode* masthead was as stratified as the angels in *Paradise Lost*. In the matriarchies, you could change your job at will, and if you needed a week off to consult the oracle at Delphi . . .

"Arizona?" said Eleanor. "What area code is that?"

"What *area code*?" said Martha.

"Oh, never mind," said Eleanor. "I don't think it's going to work out."

"You're right," said Martha. "It's impossible. I really shouldn't go. It would be tough to have one less fact checker around right before the issue closes—"

Eleanor sighed. "When I said I didn't think it was going to work out, what I meant by *it* was *you*. I meant you, at *Mode*."

"Me?" said Martha. When had they progressed from talking about vacation to talking about *her*? She'd had this experience with men: some boundary was crossed and, before you knew it, an abstract conversation escalated into a personal assault. Was Eleanor firing her? Was this happening? Couldn't they just slink back to the start of the discussion when Martha had no vacation but still had a job?

"I've tried," said Eleanor. "You have no idea how I've tried. To overlook your . . . attitude and your total . . . contempt. Your acting from the very first day as if you're too good for this job. Do you think I don't see you smirking when I ask you to check things that legally must be followed up?"

"Legally?" said Martha.

"There you go again," Eleanor said.

"I'm sorry," said Martha.

"I'm sorry, too," Eleanor said. "I am. Needless to say, you **(105)** can feel free to use me as a reference."

"Statistically," said Titania, "driving to the airport is the most dangerous part."

"Psychically or physically?" asked Bernie.

"Both, obviously," answered Starling.

The women were stuck in traffic on the Long Island Expressway. For half an hour they'd inched forward at an exasperating pace that they'd come to appreciate now that they had stopped moving entirely. Joy slumped down in the driver's seat and propped her cast against the door. She slid in a tape, and country music blared until Diana turned it down.

"In-*sane*!" said Hegwitha.

"Starling, dear, how much time do we have?" Isis had asked this same question every few minutes.

"Hours and hours," Starling replied. "For which you can thank me."

"The reason driving's more dangerous," Joy said, "is that on the road your life is in the hands of a million assholes but when you're finally up in the air you're just at the mercy of one."

"That's if you just count the pilot and not the million assholes who built the plane," said Titania.

Joy said, "Or if you count the lightning or solar flares that can hit it." She turned the music up again.

Diana jabbed the button that lowered the volume, then said, "Fuck you, Joy. Just fuck you."

Isis said, "We have to make an effort not to let ourselves get sucked into the negativity of being stuck in traffic."

Bernie said, "I think we all know that Diana's anger is not about the traffic."

Earlier, as each woman entered the van, Joy had announced that she and Diana had broken up last night but had both decided to come on the trip because they hadn't yet figured out who they were in their separate lives.

Now Joy said, "I think we can handle this if we stay up-front and center about it."

Isis said, "With the help of the Goddess."

"Of course," Diana said.

Martha had learned to ignore the sounds of Joy and Diana bickering, the way children screen out their parents' front-seat quarrels when they are stuck in traffic, or lost. But their sniping wasn't what Martha wanted to hear now, during what might prove to be her last few hours on earth.

Though Martha hadn't traveled much, she considered herself a confident flier, meaning she didn't dig in her heels and refuse to get on the plane. But at some point during every trip to the airport, she knew she was going to die. Were the others thinking this, too? It would have seemed hostile to ask. Instead she tried to calm herself with Titania's statistic: if she survived this car trip, the riskiest part was behind her. But how could any sensible person believe that sitting still in traffic was as perilous as flying thirty thousand feet up in the air?

Martha said, "Do you think they mean that driving in general is more hazardous than flying, or do they mean driving to the airport in particular? Is driving to the airport more dangerous than normal driving?"

"I hope to hell it isn't," said Hegwitha, who along with Martha, was riding on the floor in back, hunkered down with the luggage. It was the only way that all of them and their possessions could fit into Joy's van. Freya and Sonoma had elected to meet them at the airport.

"Me, too," said Martha. "Or we're dead meat. This has got to be the most unsafe place in the van."

"We're lucky to be here," Hegwitha reminded her. "We should be thanking the Goddess that we were invited along."

After that Martha was unable to think of anything to say.

It was weirdly intimate, riding with the luggage. Just seeing the women's baggage had seemed deeply revealing, rather like the first time one sees a friend in a bathing suit, exposing so much more than flesh. The choice of a suit—or a suitcase—hinted at a secret life involving matters like self-image, money, and shopping decisions. Each woman had had to decide how she wanted to carry her clothes. And what a range there was, from Joy's sturdy all-terrain camping gear to Titania's elegant satchels! Even stalled in traffic, Martha found this touching, and through a haze of goodwill she heard Isis clap her hands.

"Let's chant," Isis said, "and direct our Goddess energy toward getting this traffic moving."

The women closed their eyes, and a soft "ma ma ma" began, a whirring that turned into cheers when Joy hit the gas. Soon they started seeing signs with heartening pictographs of airplanes. They had crossed a subtle divide beyond which their anxiety about flying was less severe than their fear of missing the exit. In unison they read the lists matching airlines with terminals and at last called out triumphantly, "Terminal number 3!"

"Lucky number," said Hegwitha.

As they pulled onto the ramp leading to the departure

area, Titania said, "I'm glad they no longer have curbside check-in. That's one thing for which we can thank Saddam Hussein. You felt silly for not surrendering your baggage. But you knew there wasn't a chance of your stuff making it onto the plane."

Starling said, "No one's luggage is going to get lost." She herself had surprisingly good bags—handsome, burnished brown leather, masculine and expensive. Starling was full of surprises today. It was impressive to witness the crisp precision with which she directed Joy up to the curb and supervised the unloading of the van.

From the start it was understood that Starling would not only make the travel arrangements but carry—and be responsible for—everyone's tickets. She liked to say she had been raised for this; she was a military brat. And her competence let Isis, normally so in control, slip into the role of a dreamy child on a family vacation.

Now Commander Starling steered them through the gantlet of distracted travelers and up to the ticket counter, with its long lines of nervous wrecks and dispirited footdraggers.

"Relax," she said. "We have to wait for Joy to park the car."

"How much time do we have?" asked Isis.

"Hours and hours," said Starling. "We've got it made. Where are Freya and Sonoma?"

At last they reached the counter, and Starling surrendered their tickets while they placed their luggage on the scale. A woman with owlish spectacles typed something into the computer, waited, frowned at the monitor, typed more, frowned again.

Starling said, "Is there a problem?"

"Not really," said the woman, furiously typing. When the

screen scrolled up, she said, "Damn," and then, "Excuse me a minute." Clasping their tickets against her chest, she vanished through a door. A man behind them in line said loudly, "Jesus Christ, can you believe this?"

"Move it, jerk," Joy said, pushing through to join them.

"You made it!" said Bernie. "Wonderful!"

"Blessed be," said the women.

"Now all we need is Freya and Sonoma," Starling said.

"And our tickets back," said Isis.

Just then, the ticket agent reappeared, clearly relieved but feeling that it would be unprofessional to show it. "It's all straightened out. Your flight leaves from Terminal 4."

"Terminal 4?" said Starling. "This is Terminal 3."

"I'm aware of that," said the woman. "It's just one terminal over. You can hop the shuttle bus that runs every ten minutes."

Diana moaned. "I didn't see a Terminal 4 when we came into the airport."

Joy said, "They wouldn't be sending us to Terminal 4 if there wasn't a Terminal 4."

Bernie said, "Couldn't the plane just stop by here on its way out and pick us up?"

"This is outrageous!" said Starling.

"It's a charter flight," the woman explained. Was there disdain in her voice? It was so hard to distinguish contempt from ordinary business manners.

"I'm exhausted," said Diana, "and the trip hasn't even begun."

"It's begun," said Bernie. "Be with us here now."

"Maybe if you'd eaten breakfast, Diana," said Joy, "you wouldn't be so wiped out."

"You're not my mother," Diana said. "You're not even my lover."

"Would you stop saying that?" said Joy.

"Excuse me," said the ticket clerk. "Other people are waiting." Starling moved the group to one side, where they stood, looking worriedly for the exit.

"Do you think this would be happening if we were a group of men?" demanded Hegwitha. "Do you think for one minute that they would be treating men like this?"

"Oh, dear," said Isis. "This doesn't give me a good feeling about the trip."

As they shuffled toward the door, Joy said, "There's not a chance in hell that Freya and Sonoma will find us."

Titania said, "If Freya can direct the transportation of a major installation from Long Island City to Helsinki, she can get her daughter and a suitcase to the right terminal at La Guardia."

The shuttle bus stopped and picked them up. None of the women sat down.

"Terminal 4!" said the driver, as he let them off in front of what appeared to be a construction site.

"Is this a *passenger* terminal?" said Bernie.

"I knew it," said Starling. "That bastard travel agent booked us on a cargo plane."

"UPS," Hegwitha said giddily. "We're flying UPS!"

"In fucking puppy carriers," said Joy.

It did seem to be a passenger terminal of a stripped-down, no-frills sort: no carpet, no banks of phones, no dim bar full of shady characters—nor the cheering distraction of news-stands and souvenir shops.

"Where do we buy *magazines*?" cried Titania. "I can't fly without magazines!"

"There'll be magazines on the plane," Starling said un-certainly.

"The Sears Roebuck catalogue," said Joy. "On a string in the crapper."

Hand-written signs directed them through labyrinthine

half-finished corridors, snowy with Sheetrock dust. For once, Hegwitha left Martha's side to walk up ahead with Diana. As they crossed a rubble-strewn lobby, Martha found herself be-

side Titania.

"Observe," Titania said. "None of the men give us a second glance. A group of women traveling together is not of interest, except, I suppose, a group of hookers or movie stars or models. A twelve-thousand-dollar face-lift for nothing—oh, it's so unfair!"

But, in fact, men were looking at them and immediately looking away, which was arguably worse than not being noticed at all. Was it the fact that they were a group, or was it the kind of group they were: instantly recognizable mental-case feminist man-haters? Martha felt a sheepish desire to distance herself from these women—not that she drew such lustful stares when she was on her own.

Titania said, "Luckily, you are still too young to know how gruesome it is. I don't understand women who aren't feminists. Only a cretin would fail to notice the raw deal we get from brain-dead males who assume we're stupid because if we had any brains at all we'd figure out how to have a penis. Unless we rub our tits in their face and then they decide we're brighter than they'd thought. I know women aren't perfect. But compared with what men do to women, the worst things we do to each other don't amount to a hill of beans."

Intent on what she was saying, Titania had stopped walking and, from politeness, so had Martha. Now they had to hurry to catch up, and as they neared the gate, they found the others involved in some sort of fracas at the check-in counter.

"What do you *mean* you put us in the smoking section?" Starling was demanding of a young man with a clipped reddish mustache. "We made reservations *years* ago for nonsmoking seats."

"Smoking and nonsmoking," said the man, "cannot be reserved in advance."

"On what planet is that?" Starling's voice shot up an octave, partly to compete with a broken light buzzing behind a crumbling ceiling panel dribbling crumbs of asbestos. The clerk said, "There is legislation pending that will make all domestic flights nonsmoking. But for now the last eight rows are still reserved for smokers."

"The last eight rows!" Isis paled visibly. "Oh, I get awfully airsick."

Hegwitha said, "Smoking won't be so bad . . . And it's safer, sitting in the back . . ."

Starling regarded Hegwitha first with incomprehension, then horror, then flung one arm around her shoulders and dragged her up to the counter.

"We have sick people with us," Starling said. "This young woman has a critical illness. Several of us have asthma and could have potentially fatal reactions to cigarette smoke."

"Do they have medical clearance to fly?" the young man asked threateningly.

"Of course not!" said Starling. "It's not like that at all!"

"What is that frightful noise?" said Titania.

"Broken light, ma'am," said the clerk. "Sorry. We're working on it."

"Ma'am," Titania mimicked, but the clerk gave no sign of hearing as he counted the women in the group.

"I have ten tickets here," he said. "Are there two more traveling with you?"

"They'll be here any second," said Starling.

"I hope so," he said. "We'll be boarding in about twenty minutes. As soon as you board, tell one of the flight attendants that there's a problem, and whoever has time will try and switch you with a passenger in nonsmoking."

"Thanks a lot," said Joy. "Someone is really going to volunteer to get lung cancer so we can ride together up front."

The young man shrugged. Turning, they followed his transfixed gaze and saw Freya and Sonoma running toward them.

"Blessed be," said Bernie.

"Blessed be," said Diana and Hegwitha.

"What the heck are they *wearing*?" said Joy.

Freya had on a safari suit in a flowing buff-colored silk. Sonoma was decked out in Western boots, a fringed vest, and an Australian bushmen's hat, and was trussed into her white satin miniskirt and gleaming cowboy shirt.

"Check this out," whispered Joy. "Ernest Hemingway and Buffalo Bill."

"Please," said Titania. "Isak Dinesen and Annie Oakley."

"I can't believe it," said Diana. "The whole point of our trip is to study with Native Americans, and Sonoma's done up like some nympho cowgirl. Is she aware that cowpokes were not exactly the Native Americans' best friends?"

"Of course she isn't," said Freya, who by now had reached the group and was fervidly kissing the air near the other women's faces. "Unfortunately my daughter is too old for me to rip the cowboy hat off her head. What is that awful buzzing?"

"Broken light," Martha said.

"Sisters, let's not trash each other for our fashion choices." Isis seemed to have regained some of the presence she'd lost on hearing they might have to ride in the last eight rows.

Sonoma said, "Oh, duh, Mom. How retarded do you think I am? I know what I look like, I know about cowboys and Indians. That's why I put on this stuff—to, like, call attention to it. This whole trip is middle-class white bullshit. You talk about respecting the Native Americans and remembering whose land it was. But *we're* not doing anything to help the

Indians get back their land. We're just paying them to let us hang out with them in some nowhere desert town."

It was the longest, most articulate speech Sonoma had ever given. The women listened in stunned silence, at once humbled and annoyed to be receiving moral instruction from a thirteen-year-old. Martha thought of Jesus preaching to the elders in the temple. It was hard to picture the pre-adolescent Jesus as anything like Sonoma—resentful, un-communicative, impossible to reach. Once, at Isis's beach house, Martha was left alone in a room with Sonoma, who had refused to speak and seemed to enjoy Martha's deepening discomfort.

Bernie said, "Sonoma, that's marvelous. We really had no idea that you were so politically conscious."

Sonoma's rare smile was triumphant. It was daunting to watch her add the weapon of moral argument to her standing arsenal of youthful recklessness and sullen intractability. "We're hitting all the tourist sights, like the Indians are Disney World. We're flying out to see them, they're not flying to see us. Most of them probably couldn't even afford to travel by plane—"

"Maria takes lots of planes," said Isis. "She flies absolutely all over the place to do conferences and workshops. I saw her in Bolinas and the next week in Atlanta. She says her career is the equivalent of the seasonal tribal migrations—"

"I'll bet the unemployed alkies on her reservation aren't traveling so much," said Sonoma.

"Right on, Sonoma," said Joy.

"Unemployed alkies," said Freya. "Sonoma, I love it, where did you learn this?"

"Sonoma really is conscious," said Bernie. "Very good, Sonoma."

"Oh!" said Diana. "Speaking of conscious. Freya and

Sonoma, we forgot to tell you: Joy and I aren't a couple any-more!"

"Cool," Sonoma said.

"Should we say we're sorry?" Freya asked. "Or should we say we're happy for you?"

Just then they heard the voice of the man at the check-in desk, his peevish impatience amplified by the hoarse speaker system. "Due to a slight mechanical malfunction, departing flight 407 will be briefly delayed." He expressed his airline's apologies for any passenger inconvenience.

"Briefly?" said Starling. "What's briefly?"

Titania said, "Fuck that. What's a slight mechanical mal-function?"

With a dizzy lurch of panic, Martha thought: I don't want to die with these people! She longed desperately to find a telephone and call Dennis, then her mother, then Gretta. Or maybe she'd call Gretta first, then her mother, then Dennis.

Dennis and her mother didn't know she was going to Tucson. They would not think to seek her name among the lists of dead and missing. They would believe she was safe at home, or in her cell at *Mode*, when in fact she was ash and bone, sprinkled over the desert. She imagined a news photo of charred luggage scattered for miles, in this case the baggage she'd traveled with in the back of Joy's van. She imagined phoning Dennis . . . and Dennis not taking her call . . .

Isis said, "Let's take a moment to lift ourselves out of the negativity we're into and try to get centered and back in har-mony with our higher Goddess minds."

Only then did Martha notice the other passengers in the waiting area: the elderly couples in matching pastel madras, making their winter escapes with the maximum carry-on lug-gage; a dozen teenage army recruits, whose pinfeather hair made Martha reach up and ruffle her own. A deaf couple argued in sign language; the woman gave the man the finger.

Parents carried young children, sleeping in their arms, as if taking babies on a dangerous plane were a reasonable thing to do.

Just behind Starling was a handsome Latino couple and their two children. At one point the mother looked stricken, and, handing the baby to her husband, scrabbled frantically in her purse and at last came up with the tickets. The father lifted the baby and sailed it through the air, bringing its smooth wide forehead in for a landing against his lips.

Isis herded her group into an empty corner, where they sat in the closest approximation of a circle that the fixed plastic seats would allow. From her Tibetan shoulder bag Isis produced a large pink crystal, which the others passed around.

When it was Titania's turn, she looked into the crystal and said, "This beats a magazine!"

"Blessed be," said the women.

Starling had been delegated to negotiate the seat change, but as soon as the no-smoking light went off, anarchy erupted, with the women gasping and coughing more than was possibly warranted and pounding their stewardess call buttons and squirming in their seats.

"A gag-in," cried Joy. "Excellent!"

The flight attendant dispatched to deal with this volatile situation was the chilly evil twin of the man at the boarding gate. At first he insisted that their problem couldn't be helped, but finally offered to see about it and, after some time, returned. Apparently he had managed to find eight flexible or greedy passengers who, in return for some undisclosed bribe, had agreed to inhale passive smoke for five lung-destroying hours. But nothing could dislodge two last selfish travelers, so that two of the Goddess women had to ride all the way to Tucson in a carcinogenic miasma.

Hegwitha had already produced her crumpled pack of

American Spirit cigarettes when Martha offered to join her. Martha felt compelled to do so, felt that it was expected, because she alone among the women hadn't paid for her ticket. Giddy abandon swept through her as she volunteered, but when her offer was accepted, her eyes filled with self-pitying tears.

The scattershot seating arrangement complicated the meditation that the group had planned to begin as the plane readied for takeoff. Their aim was to pray for the spirits of the other passengers, the crew, the pilot, and the copilot, and from there to let their positive vibrations extend to the plane itself, to the engines and panel controls and sensitive radar equipment, and beyond that to the clouds outside and the earth below. Luckily, Isis had distributed Xeroxed instructions, which each woman, separated from the rest, could follow on her own. Martha tried to beam healing love down to a damaged planet, but was distracted by Hewgitha, breathing loudly beside her.

Isis had promised that the meditation would make them one with the plane and calm whatever normal fears they might have about flying. But Martha's attempts to find inner peace only sharpened her awareness of how high above the ground they were, how fast they were traveling. She yearned for a magazine, for its powers of distraction, its ability to make you think of shampoo instead of fiery death. If she found herself reading pieces for the fact-checking challenges they must have presented, even that would replace her dread with a more manageable set of concerns.

The other problem with Isis's airplane meditation was that Martha didn't know when to stop or how to decide if the earth had soaked up enough positive healing vibrations. Perhaps this would have been clearer had they all been together. Possibly this question was addressed on Isis's Xeroxed instructions. But to find the directions and read them would end Martha's meditation, regardless of whether it was safe yet to do so.

Hegwitha was groping in the sides of her seat cushion, presumably for her cigarettes. Oh, predictable Hegwitha! Silently Martha thanked Hegwitha for releasing her from the airplane meditation, for once again having piloted her through a minor procedural snarl. From the start, Hegwitha had been her guide in the most basic Goddess matters. Guiltily, Martha knew that one reason she could so freely ask Hegwitha's help was that she cared so little about Hegwitha's good opinion.

Martha much preferred the abstract idea of Hegwitha—stolidly facing down the world and even death itself—to the less heroic and more irritating reality of her presence. Martha still felt accountable and implicated, charged with an almost familial responsibility for Hegwitha's well-being, despite her secret suspicion that Hegwitha didn't much like her, though she continued to represent herself as Martha's dearest friend.

Hegwitha took several deep pulls on her cigarette before acknowledging that Martha was watching.

"Listen," she said, "I have to tell you something. It's really heavy duty. So tell me now if you can't handle it."

Martha instinctively inched away, then made herself move back toward Hegwitha. "What is it?"

"I don't know if I can lay this on you."

"I'd be happy to listen," lied Martha.

"Happy?" repeated Hegwitha. "Whatever. All right. I think I'm having a recurrence. I mean, I know I am."

It took Martha an instant to figure out what Hegwitha meant. Then she felt slightly weightless and queasy, as if the plane had suddenly lost altitude.

"Are you sure?" she said.

"I've got a tiny lump in my neck," Hegwitha said. "I don't know what else it could be."

She leaned toward Martha, showing her neck. Did she mean for Martha to touch it? Martha couldn't even look. "Maybe it's a swollen gland. I had this fat cyst once, on my arm—"

"I doubt it," Hegwitha said. "I'm pretty sure it's Hodgkins again. It doesn't necessarily mean I'll die—though I guess it could come to that. But the bottom line is that it guarantees more doctors and chemo and shit."

"That's terrible," said Martha, so sincerely sympathetic that her voice caught in her throat and sounded strained and insincere.

"What I wonder," said Hegwitha, "is if I should tell the group. I mean, their healing energy might help me, plus it would be a major drag for me to pretend that nothing was wrong. On the other hand, I'd feel weird about taking up everyone's time, so that this retreat that's meant to be about learning from Native medicine might get dragged down to being just about my cancer."

Hegwitha was right on all counts. Scientists admitted that no one knew how body and mind were connected. And if Hegwitha even *imagined* the group could help her recover, how could Martha tell her to hide her illness from them? Besides, the sick and dying had the right of way, their wishes were granted first. Meanwhile, Martha's less noble self was recoiling from the prospect of how grim it would be if Hegwitha's health became the focus of the trip.

"Tell people if you want," said Martha. "I mean, if you think there's even a chance that talking about it will help. Look, I'm sure everything's going to be fine—"

"What would you know about it?" Hegwitha snapped.

"Nothing," Martha admitted.

"Sorry," said Hegwitha. "I just don't know if I'm ready to deal with it so openly. Maybe I could use a week of meditation to start to handle it myself . . ."

But how could Hegwitha get through a week before she (121) called her doctors? Would the delay make a difference, and didn't she want to know?

Just then, Joy appeared, lurching down the aisle on the lighter cast she'd gotten from her doctors.

"If either of you wants to switch seats," she offered, "I'd be glad to sit here. That is, for around five minutes tops—my absolute total tolerance for nicotine, benzene, carbon monoxide, and all the other free-circulating poisons."

"No, thanks." Having just heard Hegwitha's confession, Martha could hardly rush off. "It's not so bad," she added, defensively.

"That would be great," said Hegwitha and, to Martha's shock, got up and left.

Joy flopped down with as much abandon as her cast allowed. "Well, here we are at thirty thousand feet in a giant jet-propelled penis. I don't think aeronautics is a female preoccupation. If we ruled the world, time travel might have preceded travel in space. Wouldn't you love to be able to hop a ship and hang with an ancient shaman priestess in a cave with a tribe of hunter-gatherers somewhere in the South of France?"

"The South of France would be great," murmured Martha, in the vague tone of someone making a date she has no intention of keeping.

Joy said, "Wouldn't it have been neat to have lived before we knew the planet was dying? How do people get through the day knowing it's going to happen and not doing something or hating themselves for not doing more? I know ecologic selfishness isn't just a male thing—I *like* my van and my washer-dryer. But I can't understand why only people like us are panicked about it, why everyone else tools along . . ."

Martha said, "You should be the last one to worry about not doing enough. Getting your leg broken by a train carrying nuclear wastes—"

Joy said, "I hate myself every minute I'm not lying down in front of the train. By the way, I think your friend Hegwitha is putting the moves on Diana."

"You're kidding," Martha said. "What makes you think that?" She had never seen Hegwitha as a sexual being and could not imagine her putting the moves on anyone—a gross example of prejudice against those outside the narrow norms of good health and good looks. Maybe Joy was paranoid, jealous, and suspicious, faults Diana had often accused her of in their public fights. Pity the unfortunate lover whom no one believes and who so often turns out to be an oracular source of truth. Martha recalled the quiet rage in the eyes of Dennis's ex-girlfriend, whom they'd visited in the country and on whose couches and living room floor they'd made love whenever their hostess stepped out.

Joy said, "Oh, paranoia. Plus lots of tiny things I've noticed. Like Hegwitha always sticking up for Diana. Nothing you'd pay attention to unless someone was siding with your lover against you."

Hegwitha was so often grouchy and disapproving, Martha hadn't registered her as being on anyone's side. But now, as she considered it, Hegwitha and Diana seemed made for each other. They were both prone to melancholy, chronically aggrieved—at least Hegwitha had good reason. You could picture them fanning each other's smoldering resentments until the heat of passion cooled and they turned their peevishness on each other.

Often, one heard stories about the dying falling in love.

Martha hoped that Hegwitha *was* putting the moves on Diana. She stifled the urge to tell Joy the bad news about Hegwitha's health. But it wasn't gossip to pass on for a dramatic reaction, or to console a nervous lover, or even to lighten the burden of being the only one who knew. It was Hegwitha's secret, hers to confess or conceal.

Joy said, "Watch, just watch Hegwitha go up in front of the cabin and somehow get everyone switched around so she can sit next to Diana. Speaking of switching seats—here's Bernie!"

"Joy!" said Bernie. "What are you doing here? Get back to your seat. Every lungful of this you inhale will keep you in that cast another week."

Joy rose obediently. As Bernie settled into the empty seat, she said, "We all feel awful about you and Hegwitha being stuck back here, so everyone's table-hopping to unload their guilt without having to take the giant step of actually offering to swap." Bernie looked deep into Martha's eyes. "I won't like it, but I'd be willing to trade seats with you."

"No, it's okay," Martha said.

"Oh, I have the most wonderful feelings about this trip!" exulted Bernie. "I've seen journeys like this work therapeutic miracles. I've seen people leave home in shreds and come back whole. So many of us *are* in pieces, sleepwalking through our lives while our victim self drags around all its pain from the past. I love the group meditations, like the one during takeoff, sending energy out into the world. Look—here's Titania!"

Rising, Bernie squeezed Martha's hand. "We'll share more about this later." Wasn't everyone awfully eager to get up and leave, to be rescued and replaced by whoever came down the aisle?

Sitting down, Titania said, "If this were a humane world, they'd bring the drinks cart to the smoking section first, on the theory that these are nervous types who need their alcohol sooner. I know *I* do. In fact, if they don't bring it around pretty quick, I may have to trash this plane. I've just had the most upsetting experience—I'm positively shaken!"

"What happened?" Martha asked. What was going *on* up there in nonsmoking?

"Well!" said Titania. "It was during the group meditation, which I did with my eyes open. I was looking out the window—and suddenly my daughter's face manifested in the clouds. You do know that for six years my daughter's been a follower of the Reverend Sun Myung Moon? I assume everyone knows everything in our little hotbed of Goddess gossip."

"I heard . . ." Martha stammered.

"Of course you have," said Titania. "Probably you have also heard that it was all my fault, the consequence of my neglecting my child while I got my business together. Don't imagine I haven't thought that. What did I do to deserve seeing my child shelling shrimp in a Moonie seafood processing plant? Even if you believe that they come into the world fully formed, or that some force—call it the Goddess—is in charge, even so you know you're to blame. I would disintegrate completely if I let myself remember when she was a baby and we would just stare at each other until the world disappeared."

"Oh!" said Martha. The sound seemed to have been squeezed out of her by a sharp painful memory of staring into Dennis's eyes.

"Anyway," Titania went on, "I was looking out at the sky, and I saw my daughter, telling me that everything was fine, that she was happy and didn't blame me. I know I'm the last person you'd expect to hear this from. I'm not some fruitcake like Diana! I'm a very grounded person. My entire chart is earth signs. And I'm seeing visions above the clouds!"

"That's wonderful," said Martha, longing to call *her*

mother, whose house they might be flying over at this very moment. But the halting conversation she and her mother would have would only leave Martha feeling more alone and unhappy.

"I know it is," said Titania. "I *guess*. But I keep thinking I should be happier. If *you'd* seen something like that, wouldn't *your* mood improve? Isis saw that chariot, and it was so empowering that she built a career around it. Speaking of Isis, here she comes . . ."

For this portion of the trip, Isis had forgone the robes and animal teeth. A thin, self-possessed blonde in a gray silk suit, she turned heads as she strode down the aisle.

"Isis! Come join us!" Titania said, though there were no empty seats. "Sit." Titania rose suddenly. "Ta-ta, ladies! Ciao!"

"I suppose Titania's told you about her vision," Isis began. "This could be a breakthrough. She's been working toward something like this. Not that you'd ever guess. Who would suspect that under that competent-businesswoman Athena head-type exterior is a caring feeling person? There's such a mixture in our group, that's what makes it exciting, like stirring chemicals in a beaker and drinking what comes out. It could be the elixir of wisdom—or it could be poison. Every time we take a journey we see its mythic dimension, Persephone going to Hades before she could return to Demeter. I wonder how deep we'll have to go before we can start resurfacing.

"Of course, with a group the problems multiply exponentially. Everyone is bubbling away in some personal pressure cooker. Joy and Diana breaking up, Freya and Sonoma ready to kill each other, Starling totally stressed out from making travel arrangements, Titania seeing her daughter in the clouds—it could be straight downhill from here."

Isis paused expectantly. Did she want Martha to promise

her that the trip would be fine? But why was she asking someone who'd never traveled with the group?

"And with everyone in crisis," said Isis, "we're heading
miles into the desert, up into the mountains to some funky
Native American outpost that may not even have plumbing,
let alone a pool or a sauna, though I assume there will be a
sweat lodge."

"A sweat lodge?" Of course this had been mentioned, but
Martha had chosen to ignore it. She hated the idea of the heat,
the stifling dark, and the possibility of having to go naked.

"Oh, you'll adore it!" said Isis. "It's the most healing and
·centering experience I've ever had in my life."

Just then the Latina mother whom Martha had noticed
in the airport came wobbling down the aisle, teetering on her
stiltlike heels as her small son pulled her along. The boy looked
troubled, but his mother's face was enviably serene, free from
random anxiety or paralyzing doubt. She knew exactly what
her mission was, what she had to do now, and her child announced it to the whole plane: he had to go to the bathroom.

"I don't get why we're here," said Joy. "This is a private ceremony. These people are grieving for their dead, and we're rubbernecking like it's the changing of the guard at Buckingham fucking Palace."

They were standing on a rise overlooking the desert between the Papago graveyard and the Mission San Xavier del Bac. Far off, the skyline of Tucson winked in the fading afternoon sun. It was All Souls' Eve, and a priest and a small choir of Papago women were chanting the names of those who had died since this time last year. Martha was amazed by how many names there were, and by the voices of the women, keening, otherworldly, as if the dead themselves were singing. A crowd of spectators had gathered, but the priest and the singers were corralled off from the crowd, like a dusty patch of marigolds inside a low picket fence.

"And that mission!" Joy went on. "The so-called white dove of the desert! It's like some Navy destroyer floating off the Persian Gulf."

Two women—German tourists—wheeled around and glared. There were many Germans among the New Age sightseers in attendance.

"Anthropologists!" said Joy. "Their problem is, they can't tell humans from research subjects. Your birthday and your funeral are chapters in their thesis."

Last night, when the Goddess women checked in at the Tucson Siesta Inn, Hegwitha had arranged it so that she would room with Diana. Martha wound up with Joy, who'd become a sort of stand-in Hegwitha: the person Martha walked and talked with when everyone else was taken. But Hegwitha had asked so little of her, as compared to Joy, who made Martha listen to her complaints about Diana and the trip, which so far had consisted of aimless drives past fast-food joints and car lots.

All day they'd been crammed in the suffocating heat in the rented van they'd got from the travel agent—a beefy cowboy named Pete, who met them at the airport. As soon as Pete tossed them the keys and disappeared in his Range Rover, the van stalled briefly, ominously, and began to overheat. While Joy pulled over and waited until the engine cooled, Starling called the travel agency and yelled at Pete's answering machine.

Supposedly familiar with Tucson, Bernie was their tour guide. But the city had changed drastically, and she kept getting them lost and becoming so distraught that they couldn't get angry—or show it.

Somehow they located the art museum, where they spent half an hour inspecting fiber hangings, giant ropy webs like string bikinis for prehistoric creatures (Titania said that was what happened when a male took up weaving), while they waited for Freya to locate a curator she knew. Eventually Freya and a tall boyish man emerged, only to excuse themselves and slip off to lunch at the Cielito Lindo, a name the curator pronounced in such a way as to extinguish all hope for ordinary mortals without advance reservations. The rest of the group dined on rubbery enchiladas and mortarlike refried beans at the picturesque but expensive and touristy Mi Hacienda.

"I don't know," Bernie said despairingly. "This place used to be simple and good and cheap."

"It's fine," said Isis, and the others said, "It's fine, it's fine, it's fine."

"One 'fine' would have been sufficient," said Bernie. "It *isn't* fine, and I know it."

When the conversation resumed, Joy turned to Martha and said, "One thing about women is, they don't get their rocks off humiliating each other in public. A bunch of guys would still be giving Bernie shit for how crappy this place is."

From down the table, Martha heard Sonoma say, "Hooray! I'm so glad Mom's not here! I can eat all the tortilla chips I want."

After lunch they piled back into the searing van. Isis led them in an imaging session, while Joy tried to revive the engine.

Joy said, "That jerk had better give us another van before we head out for Maria's."

The others were straining to picture themselves whizzing down a cool tree-lined highway. They hardly heard the ignition when it finally kicked in. Before long, they were navigating the boiling rapids of Tucson traffic.

They had just gotten lost for the third time on the way to the Arizona-Sonora Desert Museum when Diana finally figured out that the Desert Museum was a zoo.

She said, "I don't *go* to zoos."

Hegwitha said, "I don't either."

"They're barbaric," Diana said. "Totally inhumane. It's like taking the family for a Sunday outing to Alcatraz. This stuff about creating a protected natural habitat for indigenous species makes me want to puke."

"Everything makes her want to puke," explained Joy.

Diana chose to ignore that. "First they steal the land from the Native Americans who lived in harmony with the animals, and then they nearly exterminate *them* and lock up the sur-

vivors behind bars."

"Not bars," protested Bernie. "Moats."

"Don't be naïve," said Freya, who had rejoined the group, energized by her lunch with the curator. "Zoos will be there whether we go to them or not."

"Is there an admission charge?" Titania asked. "I would think that would make a difference—whether or not we're paying to support an animal prison."

"As I remember," Bernie said, "it was quite costly."

"Fabulous," said Starling. "How's the jeep running?"

"Borderline," said Joy.

"This is serious," Isis said. "It seems foolish to begin a retreat by doing something that some of us find morally iffy. Let's take a vote about whether to go to the zoo."

"Goody!" said Hegwitha. "Let's vote."

"It's not a zoo," Bernie said weakly. "It really is a museum. There's a section about mining and the most marvelous film of a volcano—"

"How many for going to the zoo?" Starling interrupted.

Bernie, Freya, and Titania were for the zoo. Diana, Hegwitha, Isis, Starling, and Sonoma voted against it—and finally Martha did, too. Once again she was conscious of acting for the wrong reasons, not from concern for the animals but because she hated the idea of visiting the zoo with a bunch of grumpy Goddess women. Joy abstained from voting. She was concentrating on driving and, like most people having car trouble, was unreachable by normal means. They knew that Joy would have voted for the antizoo position. Perhaps she had abstained to avoid being on the same side as Diana.

The antizoo faction carried the vote. Now what would they

do? The most thrilling thing, Bernie said, was to hike or drive through the Saguaro National Monument. But no one trusted the car to brave the desert in this heat. Otherwise, the major attraction was the Mission San Xavier del Bac. But they were saving that for the evening, when they would go there for the Papago ceremony in honor of All Souls' Eve.

Back at the hotel, the women decided to swim in the pool. Joy asked Martha to help her make a protective sleeve for her cast from a trash bag and duct tape.

After Joy left, Martha reveled in the air conditioner's soothing whir. Muffled voices seeped in from the carpeted hall. She recalled the day when she'd pretended to enjoy being alone on the beach at Fire Island; now she actually treasured her moments of solitude. How could she not be grateful to the Goddess women for having restored her pleasure in her own company?

Martha ventured onto the terrace overlooking the pool, gingerly avoiding the cracks in its concrete floor. Below, the landscaping impersonated a Zen pebble arrangement around a shriveled cactus and two puckered aloe plants. Had she lived in another place, had another job, Martha might have wound up in a hellish Southwestern condo not unlike this hotel. Another job? What other job? At least she would *have* a job. Martha remembered her meeting with Eleanor and went back inside and lay down.

She stretched out on the cool woven spread and played with the remote control, settling on a medical program about valley fever, a chronic lung disease contracted from breathing desert air. Martha took a deep breath, and down in her chest something snagged and burned. She rolled onto her side to study a catkin of hair and dust that clung to the air conditioner. She watched it flutter in the breeze until she dropped off to sleep.

She awoke in time to shower and dress and ride out to the mission, where now the afternoon heat was reversing all the good effects of the shower. Martha eyed the dust devils blowing great swirls of valley fever at her. She concentrated on the ceremony, the priest, the wailing old women, the *cantoras*, who, Diana said, were descended from the Meso-American priestesses.

Finally the singing stopped. The priest inscribed three crosses on the air between himself and the congregation, then hurried, trying not to run, up the path to the mission.

"Look at that jerk," said Joy. "Checking back over his shoulder to see if the Indians are gaining on him."

"That was so powerful," Bernie said. "If we had a ritual like that, I'd be moving more easily through the stages of mourning Stan. The way their dead are still with them—"

"Very much with them," said Diana. "The Papagos believe the dead hang around for three days and three nights. They leave their doors open and set out food and deal them in at card games—"

"And the only ones who come through those open doors are the anthropologists," Joy said.

"Oh, cram it," said Diana. Being able to say that to Joy was a tonic for Diana, who, just since the start of the trip, already seemed less bleary and resentful. Martha hoped that Diana and Hegwitha were becoming an item.

"Let's go to the church!" cried Freya, running up, slightly breathless. "The crucial part of the ceremony is about to begin. The Indians file past the altar, past the wooden statue of their saint, and they try to lift it. They believe that only those without sin will be able to pick up the statue. Only the pure in heart will have the strength to move it, and the others—the sinners—can't budge it with a crowbar—"

"We heard all about that, Mother," said Sonoma. "Diana told us sixty times in the van. What planet were *you* on?"

"Sonoma, dear," interceded Bernie. "I think Diana was talking about that at lunch when your mother wasn't there. So that's why she didn't hear it."

"Yes, that was at lunch," Titania said, and they all fell silent, darkly contemplating the latex tortillas they'd eaten while Freya was savoring her wild-mushroom-and-blue-corn tamales.

"Right," Sonoma said. "Mom was out there hustling her career while we were eating shit. As usual."

"Oh, sin, sin, sin," mused Isis. "What a phallocratic concept. The god with the scales and balances punishing wrongdoers, in this case with the public humiliation of being unable to heft some penile wooden object that babies can probably pick up in one hand."

"How heavy *is* the statue?" asked Sonoma, tipping her head back slightly, braced for whatever fresh idiocy the adult mind had cooked up.

But Freya was already rushing up the hill to the mission, and Sonoma's question went unanswered as the others followed. A group of Papago men in jeans and straw hats paused to watch a parched hot breeze lift Freya's, Titania's, and Isis's filmy skirts.

"They think we're their ancestors' ghosts!" Starling said.

"I doubt it," said Diana.

Inside the mission, the cool air was thick with spicy botanical incense. The walls were painted a checkerboard pattern, red and yellow and blue cubes ascending in dizzying diagonals.

At the main altar a priest was saying mass, assisted by two yawning acolytes and ignored by the crowd milling near the side chapel, the source of a steady drone and buzz of movement and hushed conversation. Babies were crying, mothers genuflecting to spit-wash children's faces, while a long procession inched through their midst toward the side-chapel altar.

There were occasional flashes as rude anthropologists or sightseeing boors took illegal snapshots. As if to compensate for their bad manners, Martha tried to be discreet as she studied the unreadable patient faces awaiting their turn in the chapel. Which were the secret sinners steeling themselves against public exposure, against the statue betraying them, turning to lead in their arms? Martha's own conscience was demoralizingly clear, except for having had evil thoughts about Dennis, Lucinda, Eleanor, and, all right, some of the Goddess women . . .

Could evil thoughts keep you from lifting the statue, or were evil deeds required? What *was* the relation between sin and upper body strength? She didn't think she'd committed a major sin, unless you counted sleeping with Dennis, and anyone would agree that she'd been punished for that already.

It didn't matter, it wasn't her ceremony. She wasn't waiting in line. And really, Joy was probably right—they had no business watching.

As the believers prepared to mount the three shallow steps to the altar, a sudden epileptiform charge energized their limbs. With swift, tense gestures, they crossed themselves, whispered a prayer, then lunged for the statue. They were trembling when they picked it up, but every one of them managed to lift it, and even from far away Martha could feel their terror and their relief.

"Awesome," said Sonoma. "Look at all those people hugging that sick wooden mummy."

The saint was exceedingly mummylike: a walnut-colored wooden corpse lying on its back and wrapped in a satin brocade cloak to which worshippers hurriedly pinned hand-written prayers and notes. The statue so effectively suggested rot and decomposition, it was a miracle in itself that all these people wanted to touch and even kiss it. Everyone in line was either

Papago or Mexican. No Germans, New Agers, or tourists waited to test their clear or guilty consciences.

Martha looked from face to face—and at last gave a stifled gasp of surprise. There—at the end of the line—was Isis.

Isis caught her eye and beckoned, and Martha burrowed into the crowd, using elaborate and, she hoped, unmistakable body language to communicate that she was just visiting and not breaking into the line.

"I have to do it," Isis confided. "I suppose it's yet another ordeal I feel compelled to endure. If we want some major transformation to happen this week, it would be good to know what kind of baggage we're bringing with us. I'm not doing this for myself but for the group. So it may be the group's fault—the weight of our collective sins, I mean—if I can't lift the damn thing. What sins? What am I saying? Oh, it's all so awful! You can take the girl out of Catholic school but you can't . . . oh, well. Waiting on this wretched line is the first stage of the test. Why do we do these things to ourselves?"

"It's pretty brave," Martha said. "I don't know if I'd . . ."

But Isis had already drifted off into the same pacified state of unfocused wariness as the Papagos around her. Martha lingered nearby, but finally moved away when Isis's eyes rolled up in her head and she slipped into some sort of trance.

The bobbing and lifting continued while the worshippers shuffling toward the altar turned further inward, perhaps examining their hearts for one last hidden sin. Even if Isis weren't the only Anglo in line, she would have stood out in her black chiffon caftan with gold ribbons criss-crossed vestal-virgin-style over her bodice. But only the tourists and the Goddess women were paying her any mind. The Indians stared at their relatives, slowly approaching the saint.

Isis drew nearer the altar. The chapel was hot and cloyingly sweet. Once, when Martha was a girl, the scent of night-blooming lilies in her mother's garden had so disturbed her as she tried to sleep that she'd got up and gone outside and pulled them out of the ground. Well, that's who she was, even as a child: the cranky, pleasure-denying puritan Dennis saw in her, the withholding standoffish person who couldn't relax and hug strangers, the prude Hegwitha had spotted, the girl who could take off her gym suit without showing an inch of flesh. If Martha tried to pick up the statue, the saint would know all that, and the stems of those night-blooming lilies would bind it to the altar. But what was her sin exactly? Modesty? Shyness? Pride?

How nervy of Isis to make the attempt when any lifetime contained so much that could weigh the statue down. Isis must truly believe in an accepting Goddess who would love and forgive you—bad thoughts, bad deeds, and all. Whereas Martha still envisioned a punitive old man with a special problem regarding disobedience in the garden. Martha counted the people between Isis and the statue: four. Then three. Two more.

Isis took a deep breath, crossed herself, then put her hands together, fingers pointed down, and mounted the steps to the altar. Martha saw Isis as she must once have been: a tense girl at her First Communion. Isis knelt, took the saint in her arms, and yanked at it, mumbling and straining.

At last something gave. Isis lifted the saint's shoulders a few inches off the altar. She hesitated, then continued, apparently unsatisfied with the slight upward lift which had sufficed for the Indians. She seemed to be trying to pull the statue all the way up to her breast.

The effort threw her off balance and, as if in slow motion, she tripped—first gracefully, then less so—backward down the steps. The statue fell and thumped the altar with a resounding hollow thunk that boomed throughout the entire church and brought everything to a standstill.

For a long time no one moved or spoke. Mercifully, the statue hadn't fallen to the ground, but the saint's feet hung off his resting place at an awkward angle. His robe was rucked up, revealing a naked brown wooden leg. Several of the messages pinned to his cloak fluttered to the church floor.

Crouching, Isis duck-walked around, gathering up the fallen notes and frantically refastening them to the saint's garment, lest prayers go unanswered because of her. But this left unsolved the problem of the crooked statue, which was still sticking out from the altar as everyone stood around staring.

Helping Isis this time was more problematic than saving her from drowning. For one thing, her life wasn't in danger. Nor would an expanse of ocean screen Martha's rescue efforts from the curious eyes of the crowd.

This time it was Sonoma who rushed to Isis's aid. She pushed and straightened the statue with swift nurselike competence, tucked the saint's robe under him so that everything was as before, and even gave him a tender pat, as if to make sure he was comfy. Only now did a collective shudder pass through the onlookers: Sonoma was wearing her cowboy hat and satin miniskirt. At last the priest and the altar boys ran over, their faces frozen in the dutiful grimaces of football players jogging onto the field, or of firemen hustling into a burning house.

The procession had started moving again; the devotees lifted and kissed the statue. Relieved, the priest and the acolytes stayed for a moment, then retreated.

With her arm around Sonoma's shoulders, Isis fled the church, and the other Goddess women flocked anxiously behind them. Martha didn't catch up till they were halfway down the dusty road to the graveyard.

From afar, Martha saw clearly the familiar configuration: Isis talking and talking, the others hanging on every word.

Drawing nearer, she heard Isis say, "It was a life-and-death struggle I felt in every cell, as if every ounce of patriarchal power was concentrated in that statue. It was struggling to withhold the tiniest smidgin of female empowerment, battling (138) my whole childhood, my entire previous life, every minute of Catholic school and its power for evil—and I faltered underneath that weight, I became a statue myself . . . Oh, thank you, Sonoma, bless you for getting me out of that mess . . ."

Once more Martha wondered if Freya and Starling might have been right about Isis attaching herself to her latest savior. But it would be too humiliating to be jealous of Sonoma!

Martha noticed everyone staring at a spot beyond her, and she turned to see the red fireball of sun slipping under the horizon, bouncing twice on the desert before it disappeared. The sky above the brushy hills blazed a nuclear orange. The cactus turned black, and its backlit spines took on atomic white auras.

"Oh, thank Goddess!" cried Starling. "Am I ever grateful to blow that dump of a town!"

"Whew!" said Joy. "I didn't want to mention it till we were on our way, but several Tucson streetcorners are Number One on the EPA list for having the highest concentration of pollutants, a carcinogenic cocktail for the *Guinness Book of Toxic World Records.*"

"And in this *heat!*" said Freya. "Everything's so much worse. My friend Michael—the curator—said he has never experienced an October anywhere near this broiling."

"We *know* he's the curator, Mother," Sonoma said. "Why do you have to keep bringing him up?"

"I still think it's a lovely city," said Bernie. "Though the urban sprawl is appalling."

They felt light-headed with that particular pleasure—one of the joys of travel—the special delight of leaving a place where you haven't been happy, and of realizing that you *can* leave, because your life is somewhere else. How superior, how successful they felt for being smart enough not to live there!

Beneath this cheer was the disaffection, the negative side

of unhappy travel, the fear that their failure to enjoy the place had been their own fault. Last night, Bernie had made yet another mistake, telling the hotel desk clerk that they'd just returned from the mission. The pretty blond clerk turned out to be a graduate student in cultural anthropology, writing her thesis on Papago kinship patterns. She said the best part of the All Souls' Eve celebration came after the mass, in the graveyard, when the Papagos lit candles and decorated their loved ones' tombs with wooden crosses and paper flowers, had family picnics on the graves, and sang all night long to their dead.

"What graveyard?" demanded Bernie. "I hate to think we left the mission too early!"

"The graveyard," said Sonoma. "It was right below that little hill where that asshole priest and those weird old ladies were singing."

"Sonoma!" said Freya. "Your language!"

"Oh, the observational powers of the young," Isis said. "How much we lose as we age! I myself didn't see the grave-yard, though I must have been staring right at it. But you, Sonoma, with your unclouded eyes, picked up on it right away, just as you noticed the trouble I was having with that beastly statue—"

"*I* saw the cemetery," Hegwitha announced.

"Of course you did, Hegwitha," said Isis. It was obvious why Hegwitha might register graveyards, though none of them—except Martha—suspected the new urgency it signified now.

Hegwitha had been quiet through much of the trip. She'd hardly spoken during lunch and their frustrating drives around Tucson. When she did talk, she whispered to Diana, to whom she'd attached herself with the gluey persistence with which she'd once stuck to Martha. Martha missed Hegwitha's com-

pany, though she'd never exactly liked it. The loss of Hegwitha's constant presence, irritating as it was, left Martha
feeling strangely bereft, insecure, and friendless.

She twisted around to see Hegwitha, who didn't look at
all well. Her eyes had a mucid, syrupy glaze, and she sat at a
funny angle, as if at any instant she might slide off onto the
floor.

"Hegwitha," Martha said softly, "are you okay?" She
knew it wasn't a good time to ask, but she couldn't help it.

Scowling, Hegwitha didn't reply.

"What *isn't* okay," Joy said, "is this fucked-up vehicle. I
cannot believe that creep couldn't get us another one. We
should have known from the beginning—we should have been
smarter than to agree to even get *in* a vehicle called a Ram."

Then they all fell silent, recalling the scene this morning
with Pete, the travel agent, who had driven the van away last
night, presumably out of their lives forever, and reappeared
this morning in the exact same defective van. Pete claimed
that his mechanic had checked the engine and replaced several
vital parts. No one pretended to listen to his list of auto
hardware.

One by one, like tag-team wrestlers, the women waded
into the fray. First Starling, then Joy, then Titania, then Freya,
then Isis took up arguing with Pete, who just turned his big
palms up and smiled a silly grin—his friendly male amusement
deflecting their viragoish female hysteria.

Finally Titania said, "I guess that's it, girls. Once again,
female disempowerment in the face of male entitlement, em-
bodied here in this glorified cowboy schmo." Befogged with
soupy dread and defeat, they'd filed back into the van.

"If we break down in this heat on this road," said Joy,
"we're vulture delicatessen."

But Joy's concern seemed alarmist—they were still on the

highway amid a stream of traffic and drivers quite ready to assist a vanload of stranded Goddess worshippers. Or maybe Joy was simply expressing the disquiet all of them felt: the sense that bad luck had its own momentum, and once small things began to go wrong . . .

"Delphi!" exclaimed Isis. "What a superb name for a town!"

"Delphi," echoed Bernie. "Why couldn't we be stopping *here*?"

"Because there's no *here* here," Titania said. "Where is the town, exactly? This convenience store?"

"Oh, relax," said Starling. "From what I've heard, Maria's place makes Delphi look like Times Square."

Isis said, "Maria told me that where she lives, there is nothing around but desert, and the loudest sound you hear at night is the howling of the coyotes."

"Happy day!" said Diana.

"Coyotes?" Martha said.

"Delphi?" Freya was saying, first dreamily, then louder. "Delphi, Arizona? Christ! I can't believe it!"

"I can't either," Diana said. "What amazing synchronicity! That the place we're going is named for the temple where the Oracle spoke with women's intuitive power to see the future—"

"Maria isn't *in* Delphi, exactly," said Starling. "Her place is somewhere near it."

"Synchronicity?" shrieked Freya. "I'd say synchronicity. Delphi, Arizona, is where my ex-husband, Sonoma's father, has bought a ranch with a whole bunch of other middle-aged failed artists living out their cowboy fantasies with a slew of twenty-year-old middle-aged-failed-artist groupies."

"My dad?" said Sonoma. "You knew we were going to pass by my dad's house and you didn't tell me?"

"I didn't make the connection," Freya said. "I have more important things on my mind. And since when, I want to know, since when has this man—this bastard who hasn't written or sent either of us a penny in years—since when has he become *my dad?*"

Isis leaned forward and rested her hand on Sonoma's shoulder. Starling put aside the road map and picked up the page of handwritten directions.

Joy slowed at the entrance to a secondary road. The jeep stalled before it turned into the desert.

"Check the numbers on these mile posts," Starling said. "We're searching for a road that starts at mile post forty-four."

"A smaller road than this?" said Sonoma.

In the distance, mountains rose in hostile, abrasive crags. Predatory beings disguised as harmless cacti waved their arms to distract them from counting the markers along the road.

"One," said the women in unison and, a long time later, "two."

Isis said, "This could be a marvelous centering exercise, counting slowly together. Feel the concentration . . ."

"Yes, it is," Martha murmured, but Isis didn't respond.

At last they counted forty-four. The jeep rolled to a stop.

"This is a joke," said Titania. "This is not serious. This is a dirt road."

"That's what it says," said Starling, and read aloud, " 'Mile post forty-four. Left turn onto dirt road.' "

Joy swung the wheel around and left the pavement. From underneath the chassis came ominous bumps and scrapes. They pitched against one another as Joy crept forward. A boulder struck the undercarriage.

"How many miles of this?" asked Freya.

"I can't tell," Starling said.

"Five? Ten? Twenty?" asked Titania.

"Medicine women don't live in the suburbs," said Starling. "Or in convenient urban centers. Shamans don't hang out at luxe fat farms, at least the real ones don't. The whole point of medicine-women lore is its connection with nature."

"Nature!" said Titania. "I've had it with nature, and we're hardly out in it yet. Personally, I'd settle for the fat farm. I'd trade the medicine woman sight unseen for a good masseuse."

In the silence they heard Sonoma ask Freya, "Do you think we could visit my dad on the way back to Tucson?"

"Absolutely not," said Freya.

The jeep coughed several times and died.

"This is suicide," said Titania. "We're like a bunch of Goddess-worshipping lemmings heading over a cliff."

Joy switched the ignition off and, centimeter by centimeter, turned the key to the right.

"Oh, dear Goddess," Joy prayed for them all, "help us get this piece of shit moving." The motor sputtered encouragingly and after a moment started up.

"We can still turn back," said Titania. "Instead of heading further into hostile terrain in this gas-guzzling death trap."

"And do what?" demanded Diana. "Go back to Tucson and soak in the hot tub? Miss our chance to learn from a wise woman who might change our entire lives?"

"Right," said Hegwitha. "And just because some prick ripped us off on the vehicle?"

"I'm just the driver," Joy said. "You tell me what to do."

"Keep going," Isis ordered, and even the van complied.

Starling pored over the directions as if she might have misread how many miles they had to go, and another reading would reveal a more agreeable number. The road dipped into a canyon. Rubbly hummocks rose on both sides, so that now rocks also pelted down at them instead of just jumping up from beneath.

Joy said, "I'm only asking, but are we in one of those killer arroyos you hear about—the ones that go from bone dry to flash flood in about five seconds?"

"I don't think so," said Starling.

(145)

"How do you know?" said Diana. "You just made that up. Starling's been riding shotgun for half a day and already she's caught a terminal case of male-answer syndrome."

Only Bernie laughed, and not for long; her tense chuckle stopped when the van collided with a rock.

At intervals, Titania pointed out, "We could walk faster." But eventually even Titania slipped into a heat-bludgeoned daze and let herself be thrown about by Joy's swerves around potholes.

Once Isis said, "Isn't this an extraordinary meditative state we're in? What's amazing me about this trip is how the simple work of getting from place to place keeps putting us in previously unexplored states of consciousness."

It was too hot for anyone to reply. Martha put her feet up. Joy hung one arm out the window, steering with the other.

"Sure," said Sonoma. "Driving through the desert in a Rent-a-Wreck jeep is the fabulous new high."

When had the focus of Sonoma's scorn shifted to include Isis? Isis said nothing and sighed deeply. A shiver ran through the group.

"All right!" Joy pumped her fist in the air.

"Yess!" Sonoma hissed.

By now the other women had sunk into tortoiselike states of remove out of which they gradually hauled themselves, blinking their gritty eyelids. They stared unseeingly at a sign-post poking out of the desert and a handmade sign, elegantly calligraphed in Gothic script:

Four Feathers Institute
Be Welcome
Go in Peace
Trespassers Will Be Prosecuted

"Talk about mixed messages," said Joy.

"Would you *stop* it?" said Diana.

A feathered arrow pointed toward a driveway that they followed over the sand and around a hill, until it stopped in front of a sort of derelict motel, a circle of pitted adobe cabins, prefab shacks, and campers. In the center was a mammoth cream-colored RV, pinstriped, painted with lightning bolts and kachina figures, and armored with extra bumpers and a shiny chrome ladder to nowhere. Near its door a pack of skinny feral dogs, mottled with patches of pink and silvery blue, arched and convulsed in the dust.

"What the hell?" said Titania.

"Awesome pups," said Sonoma.

As the van pulled up, the dogs began to bark, then ran out and surrounded it, growling deep in their throats.

"Oh, dear," said Bernie. "Perhaps we should lock the doors and windows."

Martha regarded the ugly dogs, sliming the windows with drool as they sprang up, scratching the van.

Joy said, "Hey, fuck this. I'm out of here."

"Relax," said Starling. "It's not our vehicle. Serves the bastards right."

Just then they heard several loud pops.

"Firecrackers?" said Freya.

"Yeah, right, Mom," said Sonoma. "Champagne corks."

"Gunshots, I believe," said Starling.

"Golly," Bernie said.

The dogs had heard the shots, too, and crawled back to the trailer.

All this so unnerved the women that only now did they notice the short barrel-shaped person who had emerged from the RV: an Indian woman with long braids, an orange beaded headband, faded jeans, and a black T-shirt that said *Harley-Davidson Club of Tucson*. She was carrying a rifle pointed up in the air.

"Righteous firepower," said Sonoma.

"Is that Maria?" said Diana.

"Certainly not," said Isis. "Maria's thin and gorgeous."

Joy and Starling jumped from the van, then waited for Isis to take the lead. Trailed closely by the others, Isis approached the woman.

"I'm Isis Moonwagon? We're looking for Maria Aquilo?"

"Maria's not here," the woman said. "She had to go teach at a conference in Santa Fe."

"What conference?" Isis said.

The woman thought a moment. "Earth Sisters Week."

"Earth Sisters Week?" said Isis. "They must be holding that early this year. Usually it's in April, I hadn't heard . . . I mean, I've *done* Earth Sisters Week for the past four years . . . I can't imagine why I wasn't . . ."

"Oh *that* one," said Freya. "Didn't I do that one in 1988?"

"I wouldn't know, Mother," said Sonoma.

The woman said, "Maria left last night. She'll be in Santa Fe all week. For the conference."

"I *know* the conference lasts a week," snapped Isis. "We'll be gone before she gets back. We're supposed to be studying with her. I met—I taught with—Maria in Bolinas. I'm Isis Moonwagon."

"Right," said the woman. "Maria asked me to fill in for her. I am Rita Ochoa. I am a medicine woman and storyteller. I was expecting you tomorrow. Got my signals wrong, I guess. The Grandfathers used to send messages with clairvoyance and ESP. But the white man jammed our frequencies with his telephones and telegraphs, and now part of the Native peoples' struggle is to reclaim our old ways of communication."

"Are you from Maria's tribe?" Bernie asked.

"We are from different tribes but we are all the same people," Rita replied.

"Oh, I *know* that," said Bernie. "But I meant—"

"I am Yaqui," Rita said. "Maria is half Papago and half Mescalero Apache. But I have studied the lore and legends of all our indigenous peoples, and I travel often, telling our stories and legends. I did the August Powwow in Seneca, New York. I did the Oklahoma State Fair. Just now I did a purification sweat lodge at the Rebirth Center in Boulder, Colorado."

"I've been to Boulder," said Isis.

"I've been to the Rebirth Center," Hegwitha said. "They have superfabulous hot springs."

"Yes," said Rita. "Our people hold such springs sacred to Mother Earth and Changing Woman."

"Changing Woman!" said Diana. "Changing Woman's a Navajo goddess. I thought you said you were Yaqui."

Patiently, Rita repeated herself. "I have studied the lore and legends of all our Native peoples."

"Of course," said Isis. "Well! Excuse us a moment. We need to get some things from our car."

"Need help?" offered Rita.

"Oh, it's nothing," said Starling.

"We travel light," said Isis.

"Good," said Rita. "Ancient hunter-gatherer people always traveled light."

"Hunter-gatherers!" Isis brightened. "I think about them all the time."

Rita watched the Goddess women till they disappeared around the side of the van, where they huddled, out of sight.

"I don't get it," said Isis. "Maria had my phone number. It is just *so* unprofessional . . ."

"What saddens me," said Bernie, "is that this is a woman doing this to other women, making promises and not keeping them because she's gotten a better offer—"

"I don't know about *better offer*," said Isis. "Earth Sisters Week is a ton of work for hardly any money. I can't *fathom* why they didn't call me. I helped *found* that goddamn conference."

"All right," said Starling. "The question is: What now? Not only did we get the wrong vehicle, we got the wrong medicine woman. There must be some recourse, something we can do, even if it means lawyers and suing the ass off these shitheads."

"Outstanding!" said Sonoma.

"Can't you see it on *People's Court?*" said Joy. "Today we hear the case of the Goddess priestesses versus Canyon Country Travel and two Native American healers."

"Who says Rita's a healer?" said Freya. "It's not clear that she has any bona fide credentials whatever. Anyone can hang out a shingle and call herself a medicine woman."

"She taught at the Rebirth Center," said Hegwitha.

"So she claims," said Starling.

"Ladies," said Isis. "Concentrate. We have a crisis to resolve."

"Gee, it's hot," said Bernie.

"Let's get out of here," said Freya.

"I agree," said Titania. "We've got a stand-in medicine woman—and this place is a dump. I didn't pay hundreds of dollars to vacation in a camper in Death Valley. Do we know if there's air conditioning? We'll fry in those little tin cans."

Sonoma said, "We'll cook like microwave popcorn."

"What we have to remember," said Isis, "is that this is not about whether Four Feathers or Tucson has the softest beds."

"That's not what I meant," said Titania. "I'm not *that* shallow, Isis."

"I realize that," said Isis. "We have to address the fact that some of us want to leave and others want to stay, and what I think I'm hearing is a big undecided middle. Are we going to write this off as a dead loss—another case of white liberals being ripped off by people of color who can hardly be blamed for wanting to repay us for centuries of oppression? I mean: Maria's no-show seems minor compared to Little Big Horn. Let's call it a teaching lesson about politics and history—"

"Herstory," corrected Starling.

"Whatever," Isis said. "Or are we going to trust the journey itself and see why the Goddess has sent Rita instead of Maria."

"The Goddess?" said Titania. "For all we know, Maria got some cousin to put on a headband and come here and play shaman."

Bernie said, "Are we sure we'll get anything to eat?"

"I'm starved," said Sonoma.

"Dear," said Freya. "You ate an entire bag of cookies in the van."

"You had cookies and didn't share?" Joy said. "Oh, Sonoma, you creep!"

Isis said, "I don't know. I keep thinking about all those stories in which the Buddha comes to the door dressed as a beggar. How do we know if the real teacher is Maria—or Rita?"

"The Buddha was a man," Joy said. "That was a really male trip: sending some psycho to your door and then saying you're not going to find enlightenment because you didn't invite him in. What sane woman *would* invite him in?"

Diana said, "Who needs Rita? We could just be here in the desert. It's fine with me if Rita splits and leaves us alone for five days."

"Five days!" Titania groaned.

"That's a lifetime," said Martha despairingly.

"Seriously," said Bernie. "Nourishment is central. Is there food here or not? It's miles back to the 7–11. Is there even a phone?"

"I see phone lines," observed Sonoma, for which Isis rewarded her with a sweetly approving smile.

"Isis is right," said Diana. "This is all about trusting the Goddess. It's wrong to privilege one medicine woman or one tribe over another."

"That's right," said Hegwitha. "Just because Maria is the superstar medicine woman and Rita is the warm-up act. Goddess religion is not supposed to be a hierarchy of main attractions versus openers. It's about the wisdom of all women, and if Rita says she's a teacher and healer . . . I'm sure she has something to teach us because of who she is and where she lives."

"Where *does* she live?" said Freya. "Do we know? Her ancestral tribal home may be a . . . trailer park in Muskogee."

"As opposed to what, Freya?" said Starling. "A mansion in Palm Beach?"

"Mom's real problem is that Rita's fat," said Sonoma. "Mom can't imagine learning from someone who isn't rich and skinny."

"Overweight is a major health issue for Native Americans," said Bernie. "Genetically, they were never meant to subsist on the white man's lousy beer-and-balloon-bread diet."

"Trailer parks can be sacred spaces," Hegwitha pointed out.

"Hegwitha's right," Isis said uncertainly.

"If she lives in a trailer park," said Joy, "it's because the white man's put her there."

"Perhaps," said Titania. "But I'm not sure the solution is moving into the trailer park *with* her."

"Oh, look, here's Rita!" cried Martha, who had just spotted Rita advancing like a ship gliding into port.

"Dinnertime!" trilled Rita, trying to sound hospitable, despite the chill, paranoid twinkle glinting in her eyes. "You ladies must be starving. I bet you could eat a buffalo. But first we have to kill it." She gave a fierce little bark of a laugh, and the women smiled unhappily.

Motioning for them to follow, Rita headed back to the trailer.

"Well, Bernie, it looks like there's food," said Titania. "You were so upset about that."

"Wait a minute," said Joy. "I wish we knew how literally she meant that about killing the buffalo. C'mon, ladies, you've read those books where someone goes to live with Native healers and the first thing they're asked to do is help butcher a bison."

"Fabulous," said Titania. "I can just see myself filleting buffalo steaks."

"I don't know," said Isis. "That could be a lesson."

"Taking a life?" said Diana. "And eating it?"

Isis said, "That's how Native people lived. Why privilege vegetarians?"

"When I was a girl," said Freya, "I often helped my mother and sisters kill chickens and even pigs."

"Totally gross," said Sonoma. "No wonder you're so fucked up about food."

"Sonoma, please," said Freya. "I've begged you not to talk that way."

"Why not?" said Sonoma. "Everyone else does."

"You're a child," said Freya.

"Oh yeah, really, Mom," said Sonoma.

Hesitantly they followed Rita around the trailer to a sandy patio under a trellis made from wood slats that cast pretty patterned shadows on the picnic table and benches. The air smelled appetizingly of charcoal and salty fried food.

"The ramada," Rita said.

"The ramada," Bernie repeated.

The table was set with Mexican earthenware bowls, from which a mahogany-colored stew sent up wisps of steam. On the ground, over a fire, oil bubbled in an iron caldron that Rita bent over, poking at a defenseless round fritter.

"Her Indian name," Titania whispered, "is Eats High Cholesterol Diet."

The tiny shed in which the dogs had been shut seemed to be howling and rocking, like the witch in Russian fairy tales disguised as a walking hut.

"Inhumane," said Diana.

"Tomorrow's dinner," said Joy.

"Shut up," Diana said.

"Navajo fry bread and chili," Rita explained. "I hope you ladies eat meat. The life of our Native people was very much about hunting and thanking the spirits of the four-legged ones who give of themselves so freely so that two-leggeds can live."

"Right," said Joy. "Thanks a bundle, dead animal friends."

"Oh," Isis said. "It must be thrilling to live so close to the ancient hunter-gatherer ways."

"Those are our Grandfather ways," Rita said proprietarily.

"And Grand*mother* ways," said Diana.

Suddenly Rita dipped her head and put her fists over her ears. "Thank you, Great Spirit, for our food. Thank you, Earth, our Mother. Thank you, spirit of Brother Deer, for giving so freely of your self so that we may live. Amen."

"Blessed be," said the women.

"That's what we say in Goddess religion," said Starling. "We say 'Blessed be.' "

"Eat!" Rita tore off a section of fry bread and used it to throttle a thick chunk of stew.

Several women did the same, though more gingerly and with less gusto. Martha tasted a cube of meat and some gravy-soaked fry bread—delicious!

Half the group were vegetarians, but one by one they started eating the fry bread and chili. Isis, Joy, Hegwitha, and Diana were the last to surrender, and they compromised, mopping up sauce and avoiding the meat with surgical precision.

"What kind of meat is this?" said Starling.

"Venison," said Rita.

"Bambi," said Diana. But even she kept taking dainty nibbles of bread and gravy.

"Ha ha, Bambi," Rita said.

"Did one of your hunters shoot it?" said Bernie.

"It's roadkill," explained Rita. "We found it on the road."

Everything stopped. The women looked at her.
Rita wasn't joking.

"Roadkill!" said Joy. "Are you telling us that we're fucking eating roadkill?"

"This is a sacred space," Rita reminded her. "We do not use white man's filthy sex talk here."

"You're joking," Isis said. "About the roadkill, I mean. We agree about the language. Sorry."

"I'm not joking," Rita said. "It is very important in our Native culture not to waste the earth's bounty. White people think they can kill for pleasure or sport, but Native Americans believe there is only one kind of killing. It's an insult to let our animal teachers waste their lives for nothing. There is good and bad roadkill. We have learned to tell how—and when— a creature's spirit left its body. We will not take anything that's been dead longer than a chicken goes unrefrigerated on the way to your supermarket."

Had Rita imagined that she could get ten women from the Upper West Side cheerfully eating roadkill? Martha considered Rita's point—did it matter how animals died? Hunger made it easier to see things Rita's way. The stew glistened invitingly, a lacquery reddish brown. Bambi's spirit could have left its body after the gentlest fender-tap, and its corpse could have rolled to the side of the road, pristine and not run over. But why had Rita told the truth? Admitted it was roadkill? She couldn't have thought she was making their meal more attractive to eat. Maybe Rita was seeing how far they would go: testing the limits of their fear, obedience, and politeness.

"Actually," Joy said, "this may be ecologically far-out. I heard a story on NPR about a food bank in Montana that feeds thousands of homeless daily on what they scrape off the road."

"Get away!" said Sonoma. "No way I'm going to eat this shit. It's like so racist to expect us to eat this crap just because she's Native American and we have to be polite."

"Sonoma," said Bernie, "Rita's our host. You can't be rude to her just because her culture differs from ours."

"Bullshit," said Sonoma.

In the ensuing silence Freya announced, "At least Sonoma's found something she won't eat."

Isis said, "Freya! She's a child!"

Sonoma said, "You're a real bitch, Mom. You know that?"

Everyone put down their forks. Now they could stop eating and pretend that it was not from squeamishness about roadkill, but because they'd been robbed of their appetites by a mother-daughter squabble. Martha saw Isis smiling beatifically at Sonoma.

"Eat up, ladies," said Rita. "Soon we will have fasting."

"I take it back," whispered Titania. "It looks like there *isn't* food."

"How soon?" said Diana.

Rita ignored the question. "Before we go on our vision quest, we will fast to purify our bodies and rid ourselves of toxic impurities to make our spirit helpers welcome."

"A vision quest?" Diana pushed her plate away. "Great!"

"Shit," said Joy. "I thought we'd settled this."

Isis said, "Maria didn't mention a vision quest."

"Yes," Rita insisted. "Maria does vision quest. She does sweat lodge. She does dream work and Talking Stick and drumming and spirit dance intensive."

"Sweat lodge," said Titania. "Marvelous. I could go for a sauna right now."

"The planet's a sauna right now," said Joy. "Where we're sitting is a sauna. I thought part of the sweat-lodge thing was an icy stream or cool air outside."

"At night," said Rita, "we will have sweat lodge. Then the desert will be plenty chilly."

"Brr," said Bernie.

"Desert ways are tricky," Rita said. "Like Coyote. Always giving with one hand and taking back with the other. But Mother Earth is different. Giving and giving and giving. Native lore is about the difference between Coyote and Mother Earth."

"Like the difference between Demeter and the male sky god," suggested Hegwitha.

"Okay," Rita said. "Now we go to our rooms. Then we come back out when it's cooler for Native storytelling and dancing."

Rita directed them toward the cabins and retreated to her trailer. Each woman dived for her luggage and scrambled for a cabin, although there were ten women and five identical cabins. The haste, the edge of panic reminded Martha of grade-school fire drills when screaming teachers and clanging bells whipped them into a frenzy in which they each had to pick a partner and walk, don't run, to the nearest exit. How unlike the orderly grace with which the Goddess women once moved as a group, dividing into smaller units and separating from the larger crowd of women on the beach that first weekend on Fire Island.

Martha tried to pretend that she didn't see Joy hurrying toward her. Titania caught Martha's eye and said, "Go for it," and they headed for one of the cabins.

Martha and Titania surveyed the room in dismay. Rorschach blots of furry black mildew blossomed on the cracked walls.

"Oh, thank heaven," Titania said. "Indoor plumbing. I can handle anything, even a dump like this, if I have my own bathroom and can take a shower and lock the door and read on the toilet. Do you care which bed you get?"

Martha shook her head no.

"Good," said Titania. "Then, if you don't mind, I'll take the one by the bathroom. Among the negatives of cronehood is getting up to pee all night. God, why don't I feel like someone who's just had a life-changing vision on a 747 over the Midwest?"

Martha put her suitcase on the bed by the window and went into the bathroom to wash her face. The hot water tap leaked a few brackish drops, then sputtered and ran dry. Martha spun the faucet, increasingly enraged. When she flushed the toilet, the water sucked from the bowl, and no fresh water replaced it.

"Great," she said.

"Did you say something?" Titania called in.

"Nothing, no," Martha said.

Martha didn't want to be around for Titania's first encounter with the plumbing. Leaving the bathroom, she made many patting motions that Titania might, if she wished, interpret as Martha drying her face.

"I'm going for a walk," she said.

"Watch it," said Titania. "It's a hundred and ten out there. Major rattlesnake population."

Cautiously Martha opened the door and checked for the nest of vipers. The desert was peaceful and benign, pricklier but more open than a forest or a field. Its colors were harmonious, subtle, and mild—the silvery green of the cactus, the clear green of the paloverde. Which was the jumping cactus that shot you full of spines? Best to pretend they all were and be careful where you walked. There was a faint chirp of crickets, the smell of sage, something smoky. The wind felt hot and clean on her face: skin damage disguised as pleasure. No doubt the desert would scare her more if she knew what lethal surprises it concealed.

Martha climbed the hill above Four Feathers and was soon covered with sweat. She flapped her arms to help the wind dry her underarms and chest. The world dropped away before her—she might have been flying over the desert, Roadrunner walking out on thin air until he notices and falls. The white sky unfurled before her like a roll of gauze.

Suddenly Martha's knees sagged, unhinged by fear of getting lost or dying of thirst or snakebite. She grabbed onto a reddish rock, lowered herself, and sat down. She clung to the stone beneath her as she gazed at Rita's trailer and the dogs writhing and thumping the dust with their chewed, stumpy tails.

The wind was saying something, or at least translating the

rumbling, hostile mutter of a deep male voice. She'd thought there were no men for miles around except for the serial killers streaming over the desert to shoot fish in this barrel of females, whose posthumous Indian names would all be Sitting Duck. Martha was just scaring herself. The voice was coming from Rita's RV.

Then she heard a woman's voice—Rita's—higher but as angry. Falsely, no doubt, this reassured her; the man was someone Rita knew. She wondered how the others would respond to a man in their midst: probably the way chickens react to a fox in the henhouse. Could they hear him through their cabin walls, or had a trick of wind and geology carried the sound to Martha alone, to be her unwanted secret, like the truth about Hegwitha's health?

Where were the Goddess women? The cabins looked abandoned. Most likely Rita and the man had butchered all the others while Martha was out walking and were waiting to finish her off when she returned. A racist fantasy, of course: the Indian massacre. But couldn't you be on the Native Americans' side and still not like or trust Rita?

Curiosity and unease drew Martha down the mountain. Crossing in front of the cabins, she found Hegwitha standing outside, smoking. She ground her cigarette in the sand, a gesture that telescoped Martha back through the past few months and planted her like a cigarette butt on the beach at Fire Island.

Hegwitha said, "I always think that before we consider starting an affair we should get notarized affidavits from the person's previous lovers. Everything Joy used to complain about—all of it was true. Diana saw my cigarettes and gave me a two-hour lecture on smoking. We've only been together two days—this was not a long marriage. Now I can't tell her about my recurrence because she'll make me feel it's my fault."

"Is that . . . thing on your neck still there?" There was no point even imagining that Hegwitha might say no.

"*In* my neck," said Hegwitha.

"Have you decided if you're going to tell the group?"

Hegwitha shrugged. "I'm leaning toward it. I keep wondering if it would be healing and who exactly would heal me. I'm not so sure about Rita. So I wonder what we'd be missing if we focused more on my illness and less on learning from Rita. Or maybe we could heal *ourselves* by getting into this magical landscape."

"Maybe you *should* tell them. Let them help you with it." Martha hoped she had Hegwitha's best interests at heart and wasn't merely seeking a clever way to sidetrack the vision quest and the sweat lodge.

"Great Goddess, it's hot," said Hegwitha. "Almost sunset and it's brutal."

"Sunset," Martha said absently. "Sunset would be nice."

They watched the trailer door open. Dressed in a beaded headband, a modified feather bonnet, layers of butter-colored chamois fringe and squash-blossom turquoise jewelry, Rita stepped outside.

"My God," Martha said. "She looks like a Ralph Lauren armchair."

Hegwitha said, "That's very unfair of you, Martha, very prejudicial to people of size, a group that absolutely everybody feels perfectly free to dump on and that I happen to belong to. Rita must be expiring from heat."

But Rita seemed quite comfortable as she went around gathering firewood for the fire pit by the ramada. Then she walked out into the desert and picked up a large stone that she lugged back and arranged with more rocks in a ring.

"Look at her," whispered Hegwitha. "She's making a sacred circle. And positioning the holy fire along the sacred path."

Once more Hegwitha was Martha's guide, a storehouse of ritual knowledge; her awed tone made Martha feel dejected and annoyed. Hadn't Hegwitha just said she wasn't so sure about Rita? How could she be so easily swayed by a circle of rocks?

Rita adjusted a stone or two, then surveyed her work and seemed satisfied with the circle and the wood. She sat down by the picnic table and lit a cigarette.

Hegwitha said, "If only I could learn to use tobacco like Rita does, as a ceremonial helper. I'd be able to give up smoking!"

The deepening light turned the sky a paisley orange-and-black. Rita rose from the bench and doused the wood with lighter fluid. Flames shot up in the air. She struck the crusty greenish bell hanging from the ramada, and the cabin doors swung open, like doors on a cuckoo clock.

The women converged on the ramada. None looked rested or washed, but they had all changed clothes. Most were in jeans or running suits. Sonoma had put on her cowboy outfit and Isis her red robe.

Martha and Hegwitha reached the ramada at the same time as the others, some of whom were glancing covertly at Rita's outfit, like dinner guests discovering that they've underdressed. Rita greeted them individually, clasping their hands between her palms. Several of the women closed their eyes and inhaled as if trying to suck Rita's Native wisdom up through their arms.

Martha joined a group of women conferring in a corner.

Bernie said, "I still think it's hostile, serving roadkill to your guests."

"I don't know," said Isis. "Best to treat everything as a lesson until there's evidence to the contrary."

"Oh, Isis," said Starling affectionately. "You're so tolerant and open."

Hegwitha said, "Anyway, it's not uncommon. I've read a

lot of books about women who go to study with medicine people and wind up eating roadkill. It takes some getting used to, but they all test you in some way—"

Rita motioned for them to sit at the picnic table. Then she went and stood where the fire cast spooky shadows on her face. She flipped a switch that activated a spotlight, which shone down on her—then punched a button on a large boom box. They heard men's voices chanting.

Rita swiveled her head from side to side, widening her eyes and listening, as if she were a hunter or, alternately, prey. Lifting her knees like a huge squat elk, she paced to the edge of the ramada and put the side of her hand to her forehead.

It looked, Martha thought, like a grade school version of an Indian dance or like the stagy gestures of Victorian poetry recitation. How depressing this New Age snake-oil show was: an act that should have been retired along with Buffalo Bill. But you couldn't blame Rita for trashing her own culture. After all, the white man had done such a job on the Indians that one of the few options left was Native American show biz.

"Welcome, Earth sisters," Rita chanted. "Welcome Ancestors, welcome Mother Earth. Say welcome with me, sisters."

The women said, "Welcome."

Rita picked up a black feather and a bundle of sage that she held in the fire till it smoked.

"Great smudge," whispered Hegwitha.

Rita closed her eyes and said, "I am Rita Ochoa of the Two Deer Clan. I have been a healer and a woman of vision among my people since I was small. No one chooses to be a healer. Something chooses you.

"I was seeing visions before I was three. Luckily, Native people have a vision tradition. Still, I knew how hard it was for girl children the spirits choose, and I did everything possible to keep my visions from coming."

"Isn't that wacky?" said Bernie. "Most of us would give our eyeteeth to have visions and Rita was trying *not* to have them."

"You will have visions," Rita said.

"Promise?" said Diana coyly.

Rita frowned and continued. "When I was six, I died and left my body three times. Once I ate rat poison; once I was burned in a fire; once a flash flood carried me down the arroyo, and the men in my village found me twenty miles away."

"Flash floods," said Titania. "Crikey."

Bernie laughed. "Your mom must have had her hands full."

"See, Mother," said Sonoma. "Rita's mom had it worse than you."

"I suppose," said Freya.

"Child neglect," Titania whispered to Martha. "I wonder what a team of competent social workers would do to the world child-visionary population."

"I heard that," said Joy. "That's racist."

"My visions continued," said Rita. "I tried to escape my calling. I asked a great medicine woman, Grandmother Talking Raven, to help me silence the voices in my head."

"Grandmother Talking Raven!" said Isis. "I spent two weeks with her at Mount Shasta."

Rita said, "Grandmother Talking Raven warned me there was nothing I could do. The sacred path had chosen me and I had to follow. And at last I had a teaching vision that resigned me to my calling."

Rita seemed about to describe her vision but, perhaps in the interests of brevity, thought better of it. "On behalf of Native people everywhere, I welcome you to the Storytelling Path. For our people, stories have always been pathways to knowledge that the white man is only now beginning to walk—"

"And the white woman," corrected Bernie.

A spasm of impatience tweaked one corner of Rita's mouth. "And our white sisters," she said. "For generations our stories have healed Native people. Now we must heal the white man with the power of our stories before he wipes out our animal teachers and Mother Earth herself."

"Amen," said Titania.

"A-women!" Joy called out.

"Stories can do many things," Rita said. "They help Native healers cure disease. They are strong tools to help us find the sacred way. Tonight I will tell stories about the emotions, which our ancients knew better than all the white men's psychiatrists."

"That's not saying much," said Joy.

"I beg your pardon?" said Bernie. "Quite a number of us here have therapy backgrounds."

"I'll say," said Hegwitha. "Sometimes I can't believe it. Everybody here's a famous therapist or writer or Goddess person or artist."

"Hardly *everybody*," said Titania. "I'm just a businesswoman and you are a health worker and Martha works at a magazine and Diana's an academic—"

"An academic dropout," said Joy.

"Martha *worked* at a magazine," said Martha, but no one seemed to hear.

"Right," said Starling. "Some of us are the CEO's of ecologically correct megabuck cosmetics firms."

"Yes, well," said Titania. "That's not precisely my job description. And some of us are glorified handmaidens for high-profile celebrity priestesses."

"Ladies!" said Isis. "I'm horrified!" In fact, she seemed pleased, perhaps by the reference to her as a high-profile celebrity priestess: reassuring, after not being invited to wherever Maria was teaching.

"Rita," said Isis. "Did I hear you say something about Talking Stick?"

"I do Talking Stick," said Rita. "I do storytelling. I do sweat lodge. I do drumming."

"Maybe we should do Talking Stick now," Isis suggested. "Maybe it would help us get where we're trying to go."

"Tonight we do storytelling," said Rita. "Later we do Talking Stick."

"Of course," agreed Isis.

"Okay," Rita said. "The first story I want to tell you is a story about fear."

"You've found the right crowd for that one," Hegwitha said. Martha turned, but Hegwitha was in the dark, beyond the spotlight and the fire.

Rita began pacing. "Once upon a time"—her voice was stentorian—"the Earth, our Mother, was taking a nap, and the world was more dangerous even than now."

"Hard to imagine," Freya said, but no one paid any mind because they were all gaping at a young man approaching with a smoking smudge pot in his outstretched arms. He too was dressed in fringed leather, turquoise, and beads. He was slight, with a ferretlike triangular face, thin curly hair, a wispy beard, and ice-blue eyes jittering in their sockets.

"*El Diablo!*" said Titania.

"Who in the Sam Hill is that?" said Starling.

"Ladies, meet Scotty Red Deer," said Rita. "Like me, he is a healer, chosen against his will to walk the healer's path. Scotty was in Vietnam and came home to another battle, this one against post-traumatic stress disorder and substance abuse—"

"It was a bitch, man," said Scotty.

"Hold on, buddy," Joy said. "I think we should counsel.

Some of us may have negative feelings about a man being around."

"Scotty's kind of cute," whispered Titania. "He can beam me up any time."

Rita's eyes narrowed. "Scotty is my partner on the sacred path. Scotty is my teacher, just as I am his. He has learned the teaching stories and the secret ways that the ancients used to shoot stories like arrows into our hearts."

"Oh, great," said Starling. "The neo-Native-American Charlie Manson."

Earlier, when Martha heard Rita arguing with a man in her trailer, she'd assumed, from the sound of his voice, that he meant to harm them. Had her time with the Goddess women so estranged her from men that anything deeper than a countertenor made her anticipate damage? Dennis had a beautiful actor's voice that Martha loved to hear, even his vocal exercises, embarrassing gurgles and growls.

"For my story," said Rita, " 'The Girl Who Was Not Afraid,' Scotty will be Fire Man, tending the fire and smudge."

" 'The Girl Who Was Not Afraid?' " said Hegwitha.

"Cool," Sonoma said.

"Wait a minute," said Starling. "Some of us have feelings about women-only rituals. A special thing seems to happen when it's pure female Goddess energy—"

"Some of us just hate men," said Joy.

"*Not!*" Sonoma said.

"The teaching of the sacred way," Rita said, "is that it's wrong to hate."

"We're getting off the subject," said Starling. "Which is having this guy at our healing retreat."

"I can't stand it," said Diana. "The minute we try to do anything, to reclaim our spiritual power, a man appears out of nowhere to tell us how to do it."

"My sense," said Isis, "is that Scotty won't be doing much of the actual telling."

"Scotty helps with the storytelling," Rita said. "Little details—"

"*Little!*" Scotty said. "Try it without me, Rita babe. Go ahead. I dare you. Try it."

"This is bullshit!" said Diana.

"Please," said Isis. "My impression is that Scotty is at most a sort of stagehand—"

"More bullshit," said Joy. "One minute a guy claims he's just a delivery boy humping incense to the Goddess temple, and the next minute he's the Pope, outlawing birth control and abortion."

"Right," said Hegwitha. "One minute a guy's watching the Dionysian priestesses perform the ancient mysteries—"

"I didn't think there *were* male observers at the ancient rites," said Freya. "Wasn't there some danger of getting torn limb from limb?"

"Not at all!" said Isis.

"That's male propaganda," said Diana.

Scotty had put down the smudge pot and turned off the tape recorder. His lower lip had a sullen Elvis droop: sexy and moronic.

"Poor Scotty," said Bernie. "The poor guy, hearing us talk about him like that."

"Don't feel sorry for Scotty," said Hegwitha. "Women get that shit all the time. Western civilization is based on rituals excluding women."

"Then if we know how it feels," said Bernie, "why would *we* do it to Scotty? Isn't that falling into the trap of the exclusionary male-power trip?"

Isis said, "Well, I don't see how this young man's presence can stop us from listening to Rita's stories. If we're so easily distracted, maybe *that*'s telling us to work on our concentration. Anyway, I'm sure we can compromise. I don't imagine Scotty will be around when the heavy stuff begins.

"Rita . . . ?" Isis's tone was at once coercive and wheedling. "We're not going to have Scotty with us for the sweat lodge, **(169)** are we? I think some of us might have a problem wearing nothing or just a bathing suit—"

"Oh, no!" Rita said. "Scotty won't be at the sweat lodge."

"Too bad!" said Scotty. No one returned his menacing leer, though he looked around expectantly.

"Excellent," said Isis. "Perhaps we should agree that Scotty is welcome for the storytelling. Then he has to go away when we do our rituals and ceremonies."

"All right," said Rita. "We can do that." She checked with Scotty, who nodded.

Rita walked to the edge of the circle and glared over the women's heads. "Once upon a time, there was a girl who was not afraid. A rich woman in her village died. Someone had to care for her house. And only the girl was willing to do it, because the house was haunted."

Scotty crossed behind Rita and threw some powder on the fire. Blue flames shot up.

"Oooh," chorused the women.

"Awesome," said Sonoma. "What is that shit, do you think?"

"So the girl," continued Rita, "went to live in the dead woman's house. The first night she heard voices. 'Help! I'm falling! I'm falling!' The girl wasn't scared. She said, 'Go ahead. Fall.' And"—Rita paused—"a skeleton dropped in her lap!"

"Yikes!" Diana said.

"Then," said Rita, "the girl slept—in the dead woman's bed. Suddenly she opened her eyes and saw the dead having a party."

Scotty turned up the boom box, and the chanting got

louder. Rita shouted over the noise. "Everywhere skeletons were dancing and drinking rum and smoking cigarettes!"

"Yum," Hegwitha said.

"The little girl joined in, drinking and smoking. She saw a man with no eyes, a woman with no head, but she wasn't afraid. Finally she was partied out and fell asleep.

"The next morning a woman rode up to the house—an ugly woman dressed in black on a black horse."

" 'Are you the brave girl who spent the night in my house?' " This was Scotty talking in a spooky, quavering falsetto.

Rita went on: "The little girl said yes she was. And the woman said"—Rita waited a minute till Scotty picked up his cue—" 'Brave little girl, you may have my house and land and animals and clothes. I must go back to the graveyard now. Everything is yours.' "

"So," Rita said, "the girl put on the dead woman's clothes and rode into town, and the people saw her wearing the clothes and riding the dead woman's horse. They got scared and ran away. And she was left alone in the town—the town belonged to her."

It took the women a while to realize that the story was over. There was a smattering of applause.

"Isn't that wonderful!" Diana said. "You never hear stories about brave girls—only brave boys. It just goes to show how much respect the Native people had for the feminine."

The others looked disappointed. Perhaps they'd expected a story about how the girl came to be fearless, full of improving pointers on how courage could be attained. But what could be learned from Rita's tale about spending the night with the dead? Clearly it was about the practical advantages of bravery, but what good did it do the girl at the end—living alone in a town she owned because everyone else had vanished?

"Second story," said Rita. "A young man was traveling in the desert. He was not a hunter. He liked powwows and fiestas. The only weapon he carried was a heavy club."

Rita paused as Scotty walked around the circle with a studded club, a cross between a baseball bat and a medieval weapon. He showed it to the women like evidence at a trial. One by one, the women averted their eyes with distaste, or in some cases with a light shudder, reflexively flirtatious.

"Oh, dear," moaned Bernie. "I can't believe she lets him run around loose with that thing!"

"As he traveled over the desert," Rita said, "a rattlesnake crossed his path. He hit it once in the middle, and the snake slid into the brush. At last the man came to a village he'd never seen before—and right away he began to feel strange. Just then a man came out and invited him to meet the chief.

"In the chief's house, a young girl with a bandage around her waist sat against the wall. The chief said, 'Young man, why did you beat this girl this morning?'

"And the man said—"

Scotty sounded disconcertingly convincing in the role of the young man: " 'Hey, what girl you mean, man? I never beat no chick.' "

"You'd almost think he'd said it before," Titania whispered.

Rita cleared her throat. "The chief said, 'Woman, is this the man who beat you?' And the girl said, 'Yes, with that very stick.' And the young man said—"

Scotty said, " 'I mean it, man. I never saw this girl. I never hit a woman in my life.' "

Rita said, "Since it was the young man's first offense, the chief agreed to let him go. When the young man got back to his own village, he told the medicine woman what had happened."

Scotty turned up the boom box louder in preparation for the finale and threw more powder on the fire.

"The medicine woman," said Rita, "told him that every animal has its own soul, its own laws. She said, 'When you injured the snake in the desert, the chief of the snake people called his council to deal with the snake's complaint. They took human form to punish you—but you were lucky this time. Never again hurt an animal that is not doing you any harm.' "

This time the applause was heartier.

"I love it," said Isis. "A story about woman's rights *and* animal rights, together."

"Isn't that always the way?" Bernie said. "Everything is connected."

"Last story," Rita said. " 'The Funeral of the Squashes.' "

Scotty changed the tape, and they heard a keening dirge like that of the women calling the dead at the mission in Tucson.

"Once upon a time," Rita said, "a woman planted a garden. She harvested squashes, what our people call *calabazas*. She filled her house with gourds—orange, yellow, and green —and that very evening the woman took sick and died."

"Yes." Bernie nodded. "*Calabazas* means squash."

"Soon," Rita said, "the woman found that she was at her own funeral. There were lots of people, but she didn't recognize any. What was even stranger was that the mourners were singing a song, '*Calabazas, calabazas, calabazas*' and eating squash. At dawn the mourners left, the woman awoke. She discovered that she wasn't dead. But all her squashes were gone."

Once more there was an awkward pause. The storytelling was over. Now the women applauded wildly. Rita and Scotty bowed.

"What do you think that one was about?" Titania asked Martha. "Vegetable rights?"

"Maybe about not wasting food," Martha said. "Maybe something like that."

"Lordy," said Joy. "My *mother* was into *that* one."

"Any questions?" said Rita.

No one asked what the stories meant. No one said a word. Several of the women were glaring pointedly at Scotty.

"Cheers, ladies," said Scotty. "I can tell when I'm not wanted." He took his vial of magic powders and left.

Only then did Hegwitha raise her hand. "Excuse me," she said. "But I was wondering . . . You said before that Native people use stories to heal disease . . ."

You could feel the women's desire to tell Rita that Hegwitha was really sick, sense their dread that Rita might sound flip or dismissive. But Rita probably knew that; probably many who came to her were ill.

"Stories are for teaching," Rita said. "Little Sister Herbs and Plants are for healing. Later we'll talk about Little Sister Herbs and Plants. Indigenous peoples knew herb magic that could cure any disease."

"Oh, goody," said Hegwitha.

"When will we have our sweat lodge?" said Starling, always the schedule checker.

"Later we have sweat lodge," Rita said. "Now we have spirit drumming."

Rita went to the trailer and returned with Scotty, lugging a heavy conga under each arm. It took him several trips to bring out all the drums. Then he wrapped his knees around a conga and played a long aggressive solo before slinking back to his lair.

Rita spoke about the importance of drums in indigenous cultures. She described how drumming attuned us to the Great Spirit, how it quieted our chattering brains and opened our ears to our animal teachers, the thumping of Brother Beaver and Little Sister Rabbit. She began whacking at a large fur-covered drum, accompanying herself with guttural cries. Between drumbeats, she brandished her drumstick, encouraging the others to join in.

(174) "Find that special drum partner that is you," Rita said. "Among all those drums, one is calling your name."

Isis chose the biggest drum, Freya the next largest. The others prayed for guidance, then chose their drum partners from a heap of nearly identical tom-toms. By the time it was Martha's turn, all the drums were gone. Two large rattles lay on the ground. She bent and picked them up.

It was not clear that shaking rattles could put you in touch with the Great Spirit. Perhaps that was why she felt like the one sober guest at a drunken party, or as if she were playing the triangle in her grade school band, watching the others with their gleaming flutes and soulful clarinets, while she made the pathetic clinks grudgingly scored by composers to preserve the fragile self-esteem of unmusical children.

At first the women watched Rita for direction, but soon forgot themselves and relaxed. As Rita's drumming grew more frantic, the Goddess women flailed at their animal hides. Their jaws drooped and their eyelids clenched with effort. They rocked their shoulders and shook their heads. From time to time one of the women would break into a manic solo.

Watching the firelight play on their faces, Martha was alternately annoyed at them and furious at herself. She was the Goddess archetype that the women liked least: the Athena type, the rationalist, always thinking, always judging. But what was wrong with thinking? That's what she wanted to know. What seemed wrong to her was *what* she thought, how cramped and unpleasant it was. How could she look down on these poor souls who needed this so badly, who had been so damaged and were being given a great gift: a half hour—surely no longer, she hoped—of forgetting their pain and problems.

Martha caught Rita looking at her and smiled weakly and shook her rattles.

Martha noticed that Sonoma had thrown away her drumstick and was pounding her drum with her fists. Her eyes were shut, her mouth open; a thin trail of drool slicked her chin. As she gripped the tom-tom between her plump spread knees, unattractive pink wedges of thigh pouched out around the rim.

Sonoma was such a difficult girl, selfish, stubborn, spoiled, permitted complaints and cruelties no adult could get away with. But Martha was an adult and was shocked at her own harshness, her lack of feeling for this sad child briefly escaping the prison she shared with a mother whose parameters ranged from boasting about her career to nagging Sonoma about her weight. The shameful part was that Martha secretly suspected that her dislike for Sonoma was really about Isis, who, ever since the incident with the statue at the mission, had fixed on the girl with the absorption she'd once reserved for Martha.

The women were drumming so feverishly that Rita had to go around and grab each one by the shoulders, like clock pendulums she had to stop by hand. The women looked sleepy but rested, and Martha crankily observed the blurry gazes of postcoital gratitude they bestowed on Rita.

Then Rita announced that it was time for spirit dancing. "Our dance is a way of thanking the Earth, our Mother, whom we dance on with our feet to call our spirit helper. That is one thing I hope you will all do this week—find your spirit helper, or let your spirit helper find you. It may be a sacred animal or symbol, a power that keeps you from danger—"

"Some of us already have that," Freya interrupted competitively. "We call her Goddess."

Rita said, "Your spirit guide can be a creepy crawler, a creature from any part of the world. One of mine is an African and another a slant-eyed Chinese who likes to stand on his head."

Joy edged closer to Martha and said, "That's the grossest, most racist thing I've ever heard in my life." But Joy snapped to attention when Rita said, "When you have a spirit guide, you don't need a radar detector. You can do ninety, and your spirit helper will tell you when a cop's hiding behind the billboard."

"Far-out," said Joy. "That's my kind of spirit guide."

Rita slipped another tape into the boom box and turned up the volume. Dervish drumming and shrill Middle Eastern flutes Dopplered off the mountains—most likely some New Age men's group reinterpreting Native American chants to express their resentments toward their absent fathers.

"Close your eyes," Rita ordered. "Dance your connection to Mother Earth, touch her veins and her roots, reach for healing—"

Though Martha should have known better by now, she was still amazed that these women she'd known for months—women who drove and cooked and held important jobs and were writers and therapists with money, fame, and success—were capable of throwing back their heads, lifting their arms, and spinning like born-again evangelicals or locked-ward schizophrenics. She felt at once mildly contemptuous—and horribly alone. It was bad enough shaking rattles when everyone else was beating drums; not dancing along with the others was something else altogether.

Suddenly Martha heard a scream.

Isis sank to the ground.

Rita shut off the music. The women clustered round Isis.

Starling said, "Goddamn it! Of all the goddamn places in the world to have a medical emergency."

"Don't move her," someone said.

But Bernie was already cradling Isis's head in her lap, and within seconds Isis opened her eyes and smiled and wriggled her shoulders. She looked around, disoriented, then burst into sobs.

Through her tears, Isis said, "First it prowled around me—this . . . giant friendly jaguar. I was scared. It started to pounce. But then it reached out its paw, and I knew it wanted to help me. A sinking sensation came over me—that's when I screamed and blacked out."

"Your spirit helper," Rita pronounced. "You have found your spirit helper."

How like Isis to meet her spirit helper before anyone else! Martha wondered if the others minded. Isis had already *had* her vision of the moon goddess. Or maybe that was how it worked, as with multiple childbirths: each vision made it easier to have the next and the next.

"You were a member of the jaguar clan. Perhaps in some other lifetime." Rita sounded extremely relieved: Isis's vision had done wonders for her credibility. Rita must have been nervous about a week with these high-powered New York women who didn't appreciate getting stuck with her instead of Maria. For the first time Martha felt real sympathy for Rita—a feeling that should have come earlier, say, the first time she saw Scotty.

But straight on the heels of this new compassion came great swells of irritation. Because now they were really in Rita's power, and Isis had put them there. It no longer seemed likely that they would leave early and spend the extra days around the pool in Tucson. They were in for the desert walk, the sweat lodge, the fasting, and the vision quest.

"Tomorrow," Rita said, "we will greet Dawn Spirit Rising with drumming. We will meet here at five-thirty and drum Father Sun up over the horizon."

Martha reached beneath the covers and, languorous and ecstatic, scratched the lumpy flea bites encircling her legs like anklets. The bright air streaming in through the screen brought with it the fresh turkey-stuffing scent of sage. For a few blissful seconds she imagined she might be happy, until a less benign breeze blew in a ragged flurry of drumbeats.

Martha couldn't imagine joining the other women. Instead, she picked the bites on her ankles till they erupted in bright dots of blood, and wallowed in a deep trough of isolation and sorrow, which she deepened, experimentally, with painful thoughts of Dennis: the muscles rippling in his back as he got out of bed in the morning. Once more Martha was alone, a shivering spectator at a rink crowded with happy skaters: normal people falling in love, getting married, having children, gathering to drum in the dawn and worship a kindly beneficent Goddess.

The other bedsprings squealed, and Martha stiffened with anxiety until she heard Titania say, "Mother of God. What's the racket?"

"They're drumming the dawn in," Martha said.

"Horseshit," said Titania.

So Martha wasn't the only one not taking part in the drumming! The fact of Titania's presence—or really, that Martha wasn't alone—filled Martha with an irrational glow of optimism and well-being.

By the time Martha and Titania went outside, the drumming session had ended. They found the women in the ramada, settling in for another of Rita's lectures.

"Today on our medicine walk," Rita said, "we will learn desert ways."

"Excuse me? Did we miss breakfast?" Titania asked.

Joy said, "No. Get this. We're fasting. In preparation for the vision quest tomorrow. I could personally go for two eggs over and hash browns and take a miss on the visit from Little Sister Bunny Rabbit."

"Maybe it's better this way," said Bernie. "I don't know how many more roadkill meals I could handle."

"Two more, I think," said Diana. "We get lunch today and then nothing, fasting till tomorrow evening. Then a feast so we can stuff ourselves before we go into the desert, to make sure we have enough protein and don't faint and sue them, even though for the Native people the solo vision quest was *about* fasting—"

"Would you quit it, Diana?" said Joy. "You're enjoying this, aren't you? You'd love to turn every one of us into a world-class anorexic."

"Not eating should be a choice," Bernie said. "We should honor Diana's decision but be free to make our own—"

"Are you ladies finished?" asked Rita.

"Sorry," Diana mumbled.

Joy said, "Can you believe this?"

Rita said, "Going into the desert is like going to see our

family. Because we are related to everything—the prairie dogs, the rattlesnakes, the little creepy crawlers."

"My," said Titania, "she's pathologically obsessed with little creepy crawlers."

Isis sat near Rita, gazing at her adoringly. Well, there was no telling how hallucinating a giant friendly jaguar might alter one's point of view. Wasn't Isis's life a testament to the transformative power of vision?

Starling, Bernie, Freya, and Hegwitha still hoped to meet their jaguars and so were willing to give Rita the benefit of the doubt. They sat up front with Isis and mirrored her worshipful look. Joy, Diana, Titania, Sonoma, and Martha sat slightly farther back. But when Rita said, "Don't be strangers, sisters," the holdouts moved forward and the acolytes made room.

"This morning," Rita continued, "we go for a two-hour walk in our church. Ours is not the white man's church: a building with a roof and a cross. The Earth our Mother is our church, and every time you walk the earth you enter our temple. Our Asian brothers and sisters remove their shoes to go into their temples, but when we enter our desert church, Native people put on heavy boots—if they know what's good for them." Rita lifted one columnar blue-jeaned leg to display a cracked, dusty work boot. "Everybody got strong shoes?"

"Yes," said Bernie, and the women raised their booted feet.

Rita put her hands on her thighs and pressed herself out of her chair. The others picked up knapsacks, canteens, and walking sticks. Weren't they somewhat overprepared for a two-hour hike? Maybe this was just their way of dealing with the unknown. Martha had brought a small water jug that had come with the bike she'd had in the city; she'd kept it as a memento after the bike was stolen. The canteen fit in her purse, which she'd taken when she left her cabin. She knew it was an uptight, distrustful New York thing to do, but something about Scotty made her want her cash and credit cards with her.

Bowing her head, Rita asked our Mother the Earth to share her medicine with her New York sisters. Then she set off toward the same trail that Martha had taken yesterday afternoon.

The desert was less lovely with other people blocking the view, but the compensation was that Rita strode confidently past the point at which Martha had panicked and quit. Rita paused for impromptu botany lessons about various cacti and other plants.

Holding up a branch, Rita asked, "What is this, ladies?"

"What *ih-iz* a branch?" Sonoma said.

"Wrong," Rita said. "When Native people look at this, they see a part of a tree. You know the difference between a branch and part of a tree? We see everything as connected to everything else in creation, and it all teaches us secrets about medicine and health. Native people were the first to extract aspirin from a branch like this one."

"That one?" asked Hegwitha.

"*Like* this one," Rita said.

Martha kept catching up and then falling behind and growing more sullen, just as she had on nature walks with her grade school classes. Anyone might think that children would be glad to get out in the air, but Martha recalled feeling put-upon and insulted when teachers bullied them into inspecting the dirt and trees. The only thing the children had cared about was who was walking with whom; the boys and girls were like baby bats, operating on sonar, not looking but acutely aware of where the other sex was. Those nature walks had simmered with repressed sexual tension. If the teacher had known to study that, she might have learned about nature, too.

Rita kept pointing out especially large or oddly shaped

giant saguaro cacti. She said, "Native people believe saguaros are magic creatures. Some say they are our ancestors—or visitors from outer space. If you stand between the arms of a saguaro cactus—not the kind that grow straight up, but the ones that put their arms out and circle them around you—you will hear strange noises. And we say that the cactus arms are talking to each other."

Giggling uneasily, the women took turns standing between the arms of a huge two-pronged cactus and closing their eyes and listening. Some gave it longer than others, their faces contorted with effort, but even the most suggestible women wore silly smiles of bewildered relief as they scurried away and gave the next woman a turn. No one was saying whether or not she'd heard the cactus speak, or what she'd overheard.

Sonoma spent a surprisingly long time between the cactus arms, with her eyes scrunched shut and her cheeks puffed out, as if blowing up a balloon. Finally, she shook her head and sneered in disbelief.

By the time it was Martha's turn, the others had all moved on, thus saving her the embarrassment of public ritual eavesdropping on cactus conversation.

Now Rita was talking about harvesting plants in accordance with time-honored ritual, and how living green things would save you if you got lost—provided you respected their spirits. She showed them water-bearing stems, plants with edible buds, poisonous plants identical to ones that were nourishing and delicious.

It was dawning on Martha that she might really be expected to spend two days alone in the desert. Yesterday she'd got frightened hiking up not even this far. She would have to find a way to avoid the vision quest without losing face completely.

Rita was talking about how many of her neighbors' lives were saved by their knowledge of roots and herbs. How strange that so many people should have got lost and had to subsist on prickly pears! If Martha was pressured into going alone, she would stay in sight of the cabins and hide and pretend that she'd gone farther.

The desert shimmered so prettily in the silvery light that it was hard to imagine Brother Rattlesnake sleeping fitfully under a rock. But Rita could hardly get out a sentence without mentioning Brother Scorpion, Sister Black Widow Spider, and other members of their extended creepy-crawler family. Was Rita just a worrier, or was she trying to make her world seem like a minefield that they needed her to guide them through? Rita said that many tribes believed in the spiritual benefits of fear; your journey would go faster if you started it in terror.

The morning was cool, the air fragrant and pleasant. Martha began enjoying the hike. The women goggled admiringly as Rita named the desert plants, some of which cured diseases like dropping sickness and centipede fever, so now they knew what tea to brew if that was their diagnosis. Rita showed them a hive of honeybees living in a rock, guarding the entrance to their cave like a battalion of fuzzy helicopters, and listed twenty different kinds of honey that her people knew how to make.

"Gosh," said Bernie. But what impressed Martha was that Rita had found this hive in the vast expanse of desert, which did seem to indicate that she knew where she was going.

The hike proceeded without incident, except for one bad moment when Rita unwrapped a stick of gum and tossed the wrapper onto the ground. Appalled, the women watched the wadded-up silver foil and green paper tumble like sagebrush over the sand.

Otherwise, the walk went so pleasurably and quickly that they were shocked to discover that Rita had brought them full circle back to the camp. They laughed when they came over the hill and saw the trailer and the cabins.

Hurrying ahead, Rita disappeared into the trailer, from

which she emerged with a pail of ice and individual bottles of Gatorade. Rita held up a jar of purple liquid and said, "Native healers have understood for centuries what white doctors know only now about replacing fluid electrolytes."

The women's brief resistance was less about the drink's toxic color than about their disappointment at not being offered some organic bark infusion. But they overcame their reluctance and fell on the Gatorade, which Martha had never tasted, and which hardly had a taste: cold liquefied grape candy.

As the women sat at the picnic table, swigging their fluid electrolytes, Rita asked how they'd enjoyed the walk.

"It was so beautiful," Isis said, and the others nodded.

Diana said, "I feel I got centered just from that practice hike. I can't wait till it's time to go out on our solos."

Rita rolled her eyes. "Later we will talk about vision quest. Now we are talking about desert walk." She asked if any of the women had questions from the walk. "But don't expect me to answer. Folks are always disappointed when they think I have answers. But it's good to say our questions out loud and counsel together about them."

Hegwitha timidly raised her hand. "I'm interested in healing? And in what you said about herbs? Do indigenous people know ways of curing . . . the life-threatening illnesses that more and more people seem to be getting these days?"

"For every disease," said Rita, "there is an herb that will cure it."

"Cancer?" Hegwitha asked.

"Naturally," Rita said.

"Then if the Native people know it," said Hegwitha, "why aren't they sharing that knowledge with—"

Rita cut her off. "Because no cure is as simple as the right herb and the right dosage. There are reasons we get ill, things we think and say and do, ways we get out of alignment with the Earth, our Mother."

Everyone watched anxiously to see how Isis would deal with the fact that Rita was contradicting what she always said: Hegwitha hadn't caused her illness. Isis stared at Rita, oblivious to the others' stares.

Finally Joy said, "I have a question about something that happened on our walk. I'm sorry to bring this up, but as a group we're pretty conscious . . . No matter where we go, we try not to impact on our surroundings. But we saw you throw out that gum wrapper, and I can't help wondering how that fits in with respecting the Earth, our Mother."

Rita looked at Joy as if at a creepy crawler—put off but grimly determined to honor its repulsive tiny spirit. She said, "The Earth Mother will heal herself. She is woman, giver of life. She isn't finished with us yet. She will make her changes, do her shifting. Oh, yes. She will heal herself."

"In a rat's ass," mumbled Joy.

"Rita's insane," whispered Titania.

"And now," Rita said, "we will talk about the sweat lodge. Tonight we will counsel with the Great Spirit and the powers of the four directions. We will gather rocks for our altar and willow for our fire, and strip naked to rid ourselves of the white man's negativity. We will enter our sweat lodge and ask the Great Spirit for healing visions and guidance."

Rita smiled regretfully and after a moment cleared her throat. "This is a difficult subject that has caused many problems for my white sisters. But there are rules from the time of the ancients that Native people respect. One is that we ask our sisters who are having their time of month not to come and sweat with us because it is not the Great Spirit way."

"And *why* not, may I ask?" said Joy.

"Because," Rita explained, "we believe that at a woman's moon time, the Great Spirit is helping her eliminate poisons and negativity, and she should be off by herself for a personal ceremony alone with Mother Earth."

"Hear, hear!" cried Diana.

Sonoma gave her a withering look.

From the beginning, Martha had hated the prospect of being shut in with the others, naked. Her hesitance was partly from modesty and partly from fear that her body would cave in at a heat that hardly bothered anyone else. While they were merrily chanting and seeing lions and jaguars, she would be off, unnoticed, suffocating and dying.

Rita said, "I'd like the sisters who are having their moon time to please raise their hands."

Rita was providing the perfect excuse, the ready-made escape. Martha could pretend to be having her period and not have to strip and subject herself to the heart-stopping heat. And yet she couldn't raise her hand. She was sure she would be found out, and besides, it seemed unlucky, like getting out of something by pretending you were sick. It was irritating after all these years to still have to fake your period, just as you did in high school to be excused from gym or swimming, on those rare days when your hair looked good and you didn't want to ruin it.

None of the women lifted a hand. Martha was surprised. Even if Titania and Bernie were past menopause, the rest of the women were still menstruating, and the odds were that one was now.

Rita said, "Are we sure? There are no secrets in the sweat. Nothing can be hidden. Not even a tampon string!"

"Ugh, gross," said Sonoma.

"Rita," said Diana. "I'm glad you brought this up. Because our little sister Sonoma has recently come into her moon time, and I know that there are traditional rites that Native women do to mark this passage."

"Yes, there are," said Rita, warming to the subject and to the fact that Diana seemed to be on her side. She must have encountered plenty of menstruating women who resented missing ceremonies they'd paid good money to take part in.

"In some tribes a girl goes off to a special house called the moon lodge. She puts a deerskin over her head and asks the spirit of the sun to help her be reborn. After ten days the other women join her and sing ancient songs. The girl prays to be purified and promises that all her life, until her moon time stops, she will spend ten days a month renewing herself in the moon lodge."

"Ten days a month!" said Bernie. "Most Anglo women are still fighting for maternity leave."

"It's *like* maternity leave," Rita said. "Necessary for health. Many cases of female sickness, tumors, and infertility result from women skipping their moon-time ceremony."

"Hear that?" Diana asked Sonoma.

"Stop it, please," said Freya. "Diana, I'm tired of you telling my daughter to go out in the desert! You do it if you want to—but leave Sonoma alone! It's sick, your pressuring a child into getting lost or killed."

"Well!" Titania said. "The maternal instinct asserting itself! Who would have suspected, Freya?"

"What do you mean?" Freya turned on her. "Just because you drove your daughter into the arms of the Moonies . . ."

"Oh, dear," said Isis, laughing. "What is this? The feminist Goddess-worshipping *Lord of the Flies*?"

"All right," said Rita, "if there are no more questions, we'll break for lunch."

Lunch was baked beans from an institutional-sized can, heated lukewarm over the fire, and a stew of slimy okra and gummy cornbread pillows. Rita called it pozole: an ancient recipe from her Aztec brothers and sisters.

Martha chewed the yellowish squares that wadded up in her mouth. Tucking a soggy mass into the pocket of her cheek, she brooded on the gnocchi dinner that marked the end of her romance with Dennis. She'd felt that everyone in the restaurant knew what Dennis was saying, that the insinuating young waiters were enjoying every minute and left the accusing plate of gnocchi before her long after it was obvious that she wouldn't be able to eat it.

"After lunch," Rita said, "you may take time to meditate or walk and get in touch with the Earth Spirit. But, please, ladies, no more food till tomorrow night. We are fasting for our sweat."

More food? Where would they find it? Did Rita mean prickly pears?

"At five," said Rita, "we will regroup to find stones for our sacred fire."

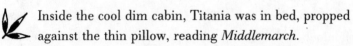 Inside the cool dim cabin, Titania was in bed, propped against the thin pillow, reading *Middlemarch*.

"My idea of heaven," she said. "Forget the happy hunting ground. This is like a cruise or mountain vacation or being sick as a kid. There's nowhere I can go, nowhere I have to be, no way anyone can reach me, nothing to do besides stay in this room and read this terrific novel."

Martha was shocked to realize that she hadn't brought a book. There were times when she'd traveled with a library for fear of having nothing to read. Had *Mode* destroyed her pleasure in the written word, turned each sentence into a slippery eel that had to be chased down and dissected? A stab of covetousness for Titania's copy of *Middlemarch* made her long to grab it and escape to that verdant English village.

"Isn't it wonderful," Titania said, "not to have a telephone?"

"It sure is," Martha said. But whom would she have telephoned, and whose calls was she avoiding? Such thoughts led down a murky well of self-pity and sorrow, the black hole of her jobless, loveless situation. She *was* the Little Match Girl. All right, the Little Match Woman.

Titania sat up and sighed. "I can't believe we're not getting dinner. I just have to *think* I'm missing a meal and it feels like the end of the world. Oh, listen. Attention! There's Rita's dreary bell."

Once more Martha came late, and Freya and Starling turned to watch her arrive with barely concealed vexation. Rita was explaining how to hear the voices of those stones volunteering to be part of the sacred fire circle.

She said, "The ten lost tribes of Israel knew how to listen to the stones. That's why the pyramids have lasted to this day."

"Amazing," said Isis.

"Amazing," Starling agreed.

"I believe it," said Titania. "First they listened to the giant boulders and then they schlepped them hundreds of miles with some Egyptian slave master whipping them along."

"Each rock is alive," Rita said, "and has energy at its center. That is why we cannot recycle rocks that have already taken part in our sweats. They have given their lives for us, their vibrations have entered us. Some rocks must be avoided; they don't want to work with humans, and they try to harm us by exploding in the sweat lodge." Rita held up an example of one such lazy, hostile rock, and the women passed around the reddish stone, holding it at arm's length. How dangerous it suddenly seemed to send out amateurs who might, through inexperience, bring back murderous hunks of granite.

"These rocks are our allies," Rita said, passing around more stones. As soon as they left Martha's hands she forgot what they looked like and only hoped the others were paying closer attention. "Whenever we get a rock for our fire pit, we apologize to the rock family for moving it from its home and to any bug people we might be disturbing. If the rock's too heavy—it means it didn't want us. Now let us go out with the help of our spirit guides and find the stones that want us!"

"Yo," cried the women and got to their feet for a round of slapping each other high fives. They managed to gaze into each other's eyes and at the same time unfocus their own, so as not to confront the tensions and slights of the last few days. Martha tried to relax so she could hug and be hugged. But no one touched her, not even Hegwitha.

Though she knew she was being paranoid, she wondered if they'd planned this. Yet she couldn't imagine any one of them suggesting the group freeze her out. They were basically good-hearted; she had done nothing wrong. This was not the eighth grade, where girls treated each other like that, exiling and embracing on a whim, calibrating their powers.

No one smiled or slapped her hand as she went out to find a suitable stone, neither ostentatious nor pathetic. What should have been deep communion between herself and the earth had instead become a rock beauty contest in which shape, size, and color counted.

The other women laughed and joked as they headed up the trail. Martha hurried to catch up to Joy.

Joy said, "Can you believe that shit about the ancient Hebrews listening to rocks? I can just imagine the pharaohs letting them do that." But she didn't wait for Martha's reply and rushed ahead to walk with Freya.

Isis was at the head of the line, a few steps in front of Sonoma, whom she grabbed for each time Sonoma's slick-soled cowboy boots fishtailed on the gravel.

Martha let the others go ahead, then ducked behind a boulder where she could pretend to search for that special rock. Her dread of the sweat lodge was so intense that gathering the rocks inspired morbid thoughts of massacre victims forced to dig their own graves. A sauna was not mass murder! Even Martha knew that. People *paid* to take steam baths at intimidating health clubs.

Luckily, the first rock Martha saw had a fossil imbedded inside it, a creepy crawler fully preserved in all its segmented beauty. Martha felt a surge of happiness or at least consolation. Maybe Rita's spiritual boot camp wasn't so bad if it had made her notice this minor miracle she might otherwise have missed.

Martha scraped around the rock with her fingernails, then, using her wrists as fulcrums, tried to pry it out of the ground. She kept on scrabbling and had nearly given up, when the stone shifted slightly and, a few minutes later, rolled over.

She gasped as a head poked out of the sand, followed by a wriggling insect that looked like a large yellow banana-pepper with two fat rubbery antennae. The bug snapped its lips and shuddered, probing the dirt for a way back to its hiding place. How could Martha replace the stone without crushing the bug? Nothing could have induced her to touch that rock again, nor did she have any intention of engaging this hideous creepy crawler as her spiritual teacher. This was not her rock, after all. That's what Rita would have said.

At last she found a sandstone volleyball, almost entirely round. Perhaps its perfect shape might compensate for its perfect dullness. It rolled out of its niche in the sand, declaring itself her rock, and she and her rock joined the phalanx of women lugging stones down the mountain.

How long had they been up there? And how, in that short time, could Rita have built a whole structure, a sturdy igloo with a frame made of branches covered with hairy brown blankets and a blue plastic shower curtain? Scotty was picking up animal hides and handing them to Rita, who passed each one through the sage smoke before layering it onto the sweat lodge. The women's faces brightened when they caught sight of the hut, but darkened an instant later when they noticed Scotty.

Scotty said, "You can dump them rocks here." The women did as they were told. Rita hefted the rocks and took them, one by one, into the sweat lodge.

"Look, no hands!" Scotty laughed and held up his hands, palms out, high over the rocks. "The slightest contact with my nasty male vibrations could blow the entire operation. That's what Rita tells me. And I'm sure you girls agree."

Diana said, "It's crummy we don't get to watch Rita build the sacred fire pit inside the hut."

Scotty said, "It gets pretty jammed in there with everyone moving around that tiny space. Especially with Rita carrying enough rock to crush someone's foot. Shit happens."

Rita was praying over a stone, thanking it for coming. Each woman watched her own rock, as each child at a birthday party focuses on her gift to see how the birthday girl receives it. Rita seemed satisfied with each stone, and Martha was relieved when her rock vanished inside the sweat lodge.

When all the rocks were gone, Rita said, "Now we will gather kindling to heat our stones and bring water to pour on our sacred fire pit, so the power of the Great Spirit will cleanse our bodies of toxins and negativity. The sweat lodge entrance is narrow and low, and when we enter and leave, it is like being reabsorbed and born again through the birth canal."

"Wow," said Bernie and Diana.

"Oh, sick," Sonoma said.

Martha knew absolutely: she wouldn't be able to do it. She would panic and not be able to strip and crawl up the birth canal. Once, in high school, she and her friends had gone to a water park at which you climbed a high rickety ladder and corkscrewed into a shallow puddle. It was rumored that a girl from a nearby town had broken her spine on the water slide and wound up quadriplegic. Martha's friends seemed nervous, but Martha was so sick with fear that at the last possible minute she bolted and ran and bought cotton candy. She waved as her friends hurtled past, and later, when they said it was fun, she was sure they despised her no matter how neutral they sounded. But the moment she'd stepped out of line was worth all their contempt. How erotic and swooning it was, succumbing to her fear.

Now she affected a distracted look, as if listening to distant voices. Then she cried out, "Oh, no!" and hurried off to her cabin.

She could simply have sat on the bed for a plausible length of time but instead went through the charade of going into the bathroom and taking down her jeans. Who did she think was watching? Was her gesture pure self-consciousness, propitiatory magic, or her version of how the faithful experienced the omniscient nearness of God? She hoped no Higher Being was present as she sat on the toilet, so weak with superstitious dread that she fully expected blood: abnormal bleeding, instant punishment for having lied about her body.

She had no faith in a Higher Being but believed only in retribution and in an ironic destiny, mischievous and malicious. She was playing at Goddess worship, but she had her own religion; the church of fear without comfort, of nemesis without God.

On her way back to the ramada, she passed the women heading back up the hill to gather kindling. No one said hello or asked why she was going the opposite way. Rita stood near the sweat lodge, engaged in an animated but one-sided conversation with Scotty, who gazed morosely out at the desert.

Martha said, "Rita, can we talk?" Humiliation zoomed her back to being fifteen and buying tampons; the boy at the cash register (it was always a boy) was always around her age.

Rita said, "Yeah. What?"

"In private?" Martha said.

Scotty curled his lip and shrugged. "Shit, man, I'm out of here."

When he was gone, Martha said, "Rita, the most awful thing happened. I just got my period. It's like . . . five days early. I'm so sorry. I'm so disappointed. I'm really really upset."

Should Martha have said "moon time"? She couldn't have spoken the word. Finally Rita seemed to catch on, raised one eyebrow, and smiled wryly. Either she knew that Martha was lying or, worse yet, believed her and was about to assign her a solitary ritual involving sand and menstrual blood.

Martha always assumed that one should act as if menstruation made no difference: deal with small or large amounts of blood and get right back to work. She recalled Rita's warning about women ignoring their moon time, and tried not to dwell on the dire fates Rita had described. What a burden to put on women, to threaten disaster unless they underwent a monthly period of enforced isolation, while protecting the male population from their filthy female bodily fluids. And yet this seemed to be a law that women were enforcing, and what was wrong with a week every month to contemplate the eternal? But shouldn't you—not your ovaries—schedule your vacation?

But Rita wasn't thinking up a designer menstrual ritual. Overseeing two ceremonies—Martha's and the sweat lodge— would have been a lot to take on. Besides, it wasn't necessary. Rita had sized up the group and surmised: Martha wasn't a major player. Martha could be safely ignored, which was what Martha wanted. Rita smirked at Martha. She knew that Martha wasn't sorry about having to miss the sweat lodge. In fact, she knew Martha was faking and wanted Martha to know that she knew.

Rita said, "Tonight you must be very careful. Because when we are in the sweat lodge all kinds of energies and bad spirits are set free. Do not leave your cabin. If you do, you must come to me before sweat lodge begins and get a sacred power object."

"A power object?" Martha repeated.

"Something to protect you," Rita said, "to keep the bad

spirits expelled in the sweat lodge from entering your body."

Her tone reminded Martha of threatening chain letters that attempt to blackmail their recipients into compliance with news of the sudden, violent deaths of those poor fools who broke the chain.

By late afternoon everyone had heard that Martha would not take part in the sweat lodge. Rita must have told them; Martha's paranoia deepened. The women gave her consoling pats and promised she'd get another chance. But they seemed eager to get away from her, and were clearly relieved when, near sunset, Martha went to her cabin.

Now, just after twilight, Martha lay dressed on her bed. Who cared how many creepy crawlers wriggled into the sheets. Stuffing the pillow over her face she thought, I'm Othello *and* Desdemona. Then she recalled the rehearsal at which she'd guessed about Lucinda: how she'd hated Dennis for enacting Othello's jealous pain and being so oblivious to Martha's. Later, Martha had said, "Don't you think Lucinda's a little shrill?" And Dennis said, "She's got that high-strung female quality lots of guys find sexy." So much for the power of art to make you a better person!

Drumming and chanting blew in on the warm night air. Then the music stopped. After some time Martha heard a muffled thrum—from inside the sweat lodge, she guessed.

What a blessing to be spared the suffocating heat, the

claustrophobic darkness, the headache-inducing drums. The idea of it made Martha want to rush out and get some air, though normally she would have preferred to stay, safe and comfortable, in her room. Another reason she wanted to leave was that Rita had told her not to go out unless she got a power object—which, of course, she hadn't. Was Martha trying to prove that there were no dangerous spirits abroad, that the sweat lodge was nothing more than a fuzzy homemade sauna?

Martha stood in the doorway. Somewhere in the distance a dog barked, furiously but without hope. The half-light turned the cactus and hills into flat black silhouettes. Just then the moon rose, so large that Martha could see its goofy encouraging wink. She took a deep breath and ventured outside, a friendly overture to which the moon responded by growing smaller and more distant.

Martha sat at the picnic table and gazed across the ramada toward the hut. Light shone through the blankets and skins not covered by the shower curtain, dimming and then brightening when the fire inside flared up. Smoke ascended from the hole in the top: a white pillar in the moonlight. In silhouette the sweat lodge looked menacing and organic, like a large dozing bison it would be smarter not to wake.

Suppose they were all asphyxiated? The drumming and chanting went on. Martha had to trust that Rita knew what she was doing, in which case Martha shouldn't be outside without a power object.

After some time a bulky figure stumbled out of the sweat lodge. Martha assumed it was Rita, come to fetch water or wood, and tried to make herself invisible so Rita wouldn't see her.

But it wasn't Rita. Someone else lingered near the entrance, performing the clumsy balletic steps of dressing in the dark . . .

"Sonoma!" Martha called out.

Sonoma froze.

"Don't be scared," Martha called. "It's me. Martha."

Even from a distance, Martha could see the postures of (199) anomie and contempt slithering in to fill the gaps left by the fear draining out of Sonoma.

Sonoma finished dressing, sauntered over, and sat on the bench. "God, it was gaggy in there. No wonder they didn't let us eat, everyone would be heaving chunks. Everybody sweaty and naked. Yuck. Cellulite and drippy underarm hair. I was in better shape than anyone, and I have a disgusting body."

"You certainly do not have a disgusting body," Martha heard herself say.

"Yeah," said Sonoma. "Nothing thirty pounds of liposuction wouldn't fix."

"Come on," said Martha. "It's part of being the age you are—everyone goes through thinking they're ugly and fat. Everybody feels that way—even boys."

Had Sonoma never heard these platitudes about adolescence? Were they what anyone needed to hear, and were they even true? Martha wished she could say, "You'll grow out of it," and promise that there would come a time when confidence and experience would make Sonoma feel pretty. But Martha was afraid of sounding unconvincing—or unconvinced.

"Save it," said Sonoma. "Everyone thinks they have to tell me how great I look because my mom is always giving me shit about my weight."

"I'm not talking just about you," Martha said. "I'm talking about how everyone feels at your age."

"Really?" said Sonoma, skeptical but curious, like a child hearing a fairy tale from an unreliable adult. Did the witch really give Snow White the poisoned apple? Did Rapunzel really let down her hair for the prince to climb up? "This boy in my class calls me Elephant Girl. I know I'm totally bloated. I think I look a little better from not eating dinner."

"Everyone your age feels ugly," repeated Martha, searching for an exemplary anecdote from her own adolescence. All sorts of relevant wounding ordeals came cooperatively to mind, but what kept her from mentioning them was that she couldn't remember how she had gotten through them.

"I ought to kill myself, really," Sonoma said. "Or at least run away for a while. Then my mom would be sorry. Or maybe she wouldn't notice, and the joke would be on me."

Poor Sonoma! Flooded with pure sympathy, for once unalloyed with annoyance, Martha reached out to hug her but wisely pulled away, sparing them both an awkward exchange that would only have estranged them.

Whooping cries rose from the sweat lodge.

"Jesus," said Sonoma, "I did not get out of that pit one minute too soon. When I got up to leave, Rita told me I should get a power object from her. I think it's so disgusting, what we've done to the Native Americans to turn them into morons like Rita. Rita said I was leaving myself open to the bad spirits of the night, but I think she just wanted me to come over so she could grope me or something."

Martha had forgotten the evil nocturnal spirits. This was the closest she had ever come to a conversation with Sonoma and, as far as she knew, the only sustained conversation Sonoma had ever had with another human being. How could that be evil?

"God," Sonoma was saying, "I had no idea my dad lived around here. I'd really like to go see him and maybe get some answers."

"Answers?" This struck Martha as the very definition of a mission doomed to failure. Martha was thinking of the kindest way to tell Sonoma to forget it, when they saw someone creep out of the sweat lodge and shake herself like a wet dog. Obviously in no hurry to dress, she stood naked in the moonlight, then rose on her toes, tipped back her head, and flapped her arms at the moon.

Martha and Sonoma watched Isis's moon-worship rite, which involved a great deal of genuflecting and swaying and flailing her arms. At last Isis wrapped herself in a blanket, then turned toward the ramada, and called very softly, "Sonoma?"

"Goddamnit," said Sonoma. "If it's not my mom, it's her."

Isis kept calling Sonoma's name in a voice that soon lost its low vibrato and grew so vexingly insistent that Martha hissed, "Answer her, Sonoma!"

"Huh?" Sonoma's reply was more of a grunt than a question.

"Oh, thank the Goddess," cried Isis, running over. "I was so worried. Your mother shouldn't have said those awful things when we were all sitting there nude and defenseless. The sweat lodge is a place to leave behind our negative feelings, not somewhere we go so our moms can reinforce them."

"Forget it," said Sonoma.

"Oh, hello, Martha," said Isis.

"Hello," Martha said.

"Sonoma, dear," said Isis. "Are you coming back to the sweat lodge or not?" Isis knew that impatience wasn't helping her case, which only made her more desperate to have things settled at once. Martha understood the impulse. She'd had a bad habit with men: when she felt they were ceasing to love her, she began asking questions that were veiled requests to get her feelings hurt. Near the end, she'd asked Dennis if something was wrong with her laugh, and Dennis had looked at her strangely and said, Well, it was sort of tight.

But Isis wasn't in love with Sonoma. She just wanted Sonoma to admire her, to think that she was cool. That was the power youth conferred: it *meant* something if a child liked you. Did only women feel that way? Only women without their own children? Freya didn't seem to care if Sonoma was fond of her or not. It was shocking to Martha: how much she wanted Sonoma's approval. The conversation they'd just had pleased her beyond all measure.

"Christ, no," said Sonoma. "I wouldn't go back in that torture chamber for a zillion bucks."

"Please," said Isis. The word hung in the air. She didn't care—she hardly knew—that Martha was present, listening. "I've seen purification sweats do miracles, bringing people together. It would be so good for you and your mom—"

"I doubt it," Sonoma said.

"People have visions," said Isis. "Experiences that change them. Something from another world that's shown to you alone to help you live your life." How like Isis to see a vision as personal attention, like a livery driver sent to get you at the airport or a waitress conversant with your dietary restrictions. Sonoma must have been used to it. Freya talked like that, too.

"Right," said Sonoma. "Uncontrollable hallucinations are really going to help me make it through eighth grade."

"The only gift I wish for you is faith that your life will get better and plenty of those rare moments when everything seems marvelous just as it is." Isis's tone was valedictory. She was bequeathing Sonoma a testament, if Sonoma would only take it.

"Sorry," said Sonoma. "Forget it. Would you get off my back? You're as bad as Diana nagging me to go get lost in the desert."

Isis laughed her throaty laugh. "Well, then, good night, ladies. See you in the morning. Wish me luck!"

"Good luck," Martha called after her as she headed back to the sweat lodge.

After a moment Isis called, "Thank you. Blessed be."

"Blessed be," mimicked Sonoma. "Give me a fucking **(203)** break."

It was dawn before Titania got back to the cabin. Martha's fury at being awakened was compounded by the special ire of being roused by someone returning from a party she hadn't attended.

Titania fell asleep at once, and soon the rhythm of her breathing was grating on Martha's frayed nerves. Now she understood why insomniacs suddenly turned on beloved snoring spouses and smothered them with pillows. This retreat was doing nothing for her spiritual development. Martha counted the hours till she could leave—two days in which to find a way to avoid the solo vision quest. But what was her hurry? Staying here kept her from having to face reality, a word, she'd noticed, always used to mean something unpleasant.

She couldn't have imagined that her mood could sink any lower until she went outside and recalled that there wouldn't be breakfast. The clearing was empty. The women must have been sleeping off their night of life-changing visions. An occasional wisp of smoke puffed up from the sweat lodge, as from the smoldering ruins of a city charred and razed in battle. In the morning light the hut looked less furry and unfriendly, less like a slumbering dangerous beast than like the burrow beneath which the beast is peacefully sleeping.

Only then did Martha notice Isis sitting on the ground with her knees drawn up and her back against the sweat lodge. Isis had her eyes shut but must have sensed Martha's presence. She looked up and beckoned her over.

"Have a seat," she said.

Once Martha would have been flattered by the invitation. But last night Isis had talked to Sonoma as if Martha weren't there, and Martha had realized how superfluous she was to Isis, little more than an orange-haired speck bobbing past the edge of her vision. A stronger person might refuse to chat and pretend to be going off to commune with the desert, and Isis would respect that person's need for personal space. A weakling like Martha, however, sank obediently onto the sand.

Isis said, "I'm so zapped with energy I'll never sleep again. I can't describe what happened in the lodge last night, the flood of knowledge and healing that descended on us all. Rita was magic, guiding us through levels and waiting while we visited every avatar of the divine, from the growling dogs guarding hell to the highest Athena mind. Sometimes the hut was so crowded with entities it was like a rush-hour subway. Lights were whipping through the air: the special effects were amazing."

Isis paused long enough for Martha to mumble, "That sounds terrific. Was everyone having visions?"

"Not everyone," said Isis. "Freya claims she saw fireworks, serpents from Norse mythology—and a jaguar of her own. But she's so competitive with me, it's hard to know what's real. Bernie said she felt warm blankets falling on us, wrapping us up together. Isn't that pure Bernie, loving and smothering at once?

"But the most mind-blowing moment came when Rita

summoned us from our visions and led us in a group chant. Time stopped. I don't know how long we chanted, but when we finished, a cloud of pure love had settled around us. Joy

went and hugged Diana. And guess what? They're a couple again!"

"What about Hegwitha?" asked Martha.

"Hegwitha?" repeated Isis. "What a dear precious warrior!"

By now the others were appearing from their cabins and filling their lungs with desert air and grinning dazedly up at the clouds. Converging, they embraced one another and shook their heads in wonder, as if their shared experience had obviated the need for words. They hardly seemed to touch the ground as they floated over to Martha, who felt obliged to stand up and ask them how the sweat lodge had been.

Unbelievable, the women said. Unbelievable. Unbelievable. Who knew you could get so high without alcohol or drugs? Though they all echoed some version of this, Martha sensed a difference between the women who'd had visions and the ones who hadn't.

Rita skipped the small talk and pleasantries and shifted straight into high gear: "The sweat lodge is the hamburger of the Native people's spiritual life. But we say that the vision quest is the filet mignon."

"Is filet mignon a Native American cut?" Titania whispered to Martha. Titania wasn't one of those who had met their spirit helpers, and Martha felt faintly guilty for having so resented her snoring.

Joy and Diana stood with their arms entwined while the others came up to congratulate them on their rapprochement. Martha was shocked by how easy it was to hug them and say, "I'm so glad for you." But some lingering shred of integrity made her ask, "Where's Hegwitha?"

"She's sleeping," Diana said, apparently without a trace of remorse for having toyed with Hegwitha's heart. "She had a fabulous sweat. We joined hands and made a circle around her and worked up all this great healing energy, praying for her to stay in remission."

"To *stay* in remission?" Martha repeated.

"Yep," Diana said. "All she needs is three more years to be considered cured."

Martha had to muscle down an almost overpowering impulse to inform them that they'd squandered all that great healing energy praying for a lie. But if Hegwitha hadn't told them, certainly Martha shouldn't, and, anyway, she could hardly imagine a less appropriate moment to do so.

"Hush," said Diana, because now Hegwitha had come out of her cabin and was squinting in the morning light. Martha was struck by her pallor. Hegwitha lit a cigarette, took a few puffs, and came over. Diana gave her a friendly hug, as did Joy and Martha.

Joy said, "That was an amazing sweat. My mind was totally blown. Hegwitha, there's no *way* you could get sick again after something like that."

Hegwitha evaded Martha's glance. Martha walked away.

Much of the day was spent preparing for the vision quest. The morning was devoted to locating your power spot, finding the patch of desert where your spirit guide could find you. Rita talked about her first parents and the generations of ancients, all very genealogical, like the begats in the Bible. As a child, Martha had read the Bible for sexual information. The affairs of the patriarchs and kings hinted at adult secrets, and even those lists of begettings made her feel strangely aroused. Perhaps that too was evidence of an inner spiritual life.

As Rita talked about the ancestors' bones singing under the desert, Martha scanned the hills above them for some likely-looking hollow in which she could spend her vision quest hiding unobserved. Her idea of a power spot was one from which she could look down and make sure that Rita's RV was still there.

In the break that followed the power-spot discussion, Martha went over to Hegwitha and asked, "How do you feel?"

Hegwitha still couldn't look at her. Neither knew how to talk about Hegwitha's lying to the group: a lie of omission, maybe, but a serious one nonetheless, allowing the women to keep praying for what was already lost.

"Like shit, pretty much," said Hegwitha.

"Physically or emotionally?" asked Martha.

Hegwitha said, "Really, Martha, I can't believe you've been into the Goddess since August and it hasn't occurred to you that the two things are connected." Starting with that eventful day on the beach at Fire Island, Hegwitha had been her first teacher in this new religion, and now even Hegwitha was giving up on educating Martha.

In contrast, Rita's pedagogical energy was apparently limitless. Already she was reconvening the group for a talk on spirit helpers—the available options in visitors from the other world. Brother Beaver, Sister Spider, Cousin Coyote, Uncle Black Bear—each relative came with a story, stories which blurred in Martha's mind and made her feel cranky, like a child at a toy store, weepy from the pressure of too many choices.

Rita ended the afternoon session with a sobering lesson on orienteering and first aid. She advised them to let Father Sun guide them in his journey west, or else wait for night and head toward the Great Bear constellation. Brother Scorpion and Sister Rattlesnake didn't want to mess with humans, but if they did, the women should get back to camp a.s.a.p. They might want to bring bandannas to use as emergency tourniquets and clean penknives for making cuts so they could suck out the venom.

"And speaking of poison," said Rita, "our spirit feast is tonight at seven."

Almost twenty-four hours had passed since they'd eaten. Martha had expected wakefulness and hunger pangs but instead got deep depression and a depleting afternoon nap, without the sense of achievement she'd gotten when she'd starved for a day to get thinner so some man would like her, or like her a little more.

The room was warm and shadowy; outside it was growing dark. The smell of roasting meat cheered Martha until she remembered the upcoming feast.

Titania must have gone out. Martha was alone. Her hair was so greasy her scalp ached; her skin was sticky with oil. The lack of running water was starting to take its toll. If she'd gone into work at *Mode* like this, her coworkers would have assumed she was having a nervous breakdown. Did that mean they noticed her, cared more than the Goddess women, or just had narrower standards for grooming and dress? Now Martha wouldn't be going to *Mode* looking any way at all. There was nothing like getting fired to make you appreciate your job, nothing like getting left by a man to make you love him more. And if she did fall out of favor with the Goddess women, Martha knew she would come to feel that they were the sanest, kindest, most fascinating people the world had ever known . . .

She opened the door and stepped into a cloud of barbecue smoke. A whole cow was roasting over the fire on a spit attached to a crank that Scotty turned until the animal's hooves pointed straight down, at which point Scotty let go and the cow rolled over with a sudden thunk that startled Martha and that Scotty found extremely amusing.

"Big cow," Martha said.

"Sure is," Scotty replied. "Native people used to stuff themselves with meat before their vision quests. They would pump up that layer of fat till they had enough to burn for weeks, or, in cases like Rita's, enough to burn for a good while longer."

Martha was slow to understand and then she could only

stare. Was she meant to join Scotty in a fat joke at Rita's expense?

No wonder Freya nagged Sonoma: she was just passing on the damage. Even Scotty had the male knack for making women feel ugly. Dennis was a genius at it—Martha saw that now. Why would anyone choose to be with someone who pretended to think you were pretty but later made you believe you were committing a crime by leaving the house without a trash bag over your head? (211)

Poor Rita! Martha was having one of those moments when the curtain suddenly parted, showing you someone else's life for the tragedy it was. It was not unlike the flash of sympathy she'd felt last night for Sonoma. The trouble with those revelations was how quickly the curtains closed, how soon you forgot whatever you'd seen and your heart hardened again.

Scotty said, "I guess there's some big eaters in your group." Were they still on that? Was he complimenting their appetite for life or calling them fatties like Rita?

"Some," Martha said.

Scotty said, "I should have been one of those guys who guess your weight on a midway. I like big girls, in Rita's league. Most guys secretly do. No one likes bones but a dog."

And now was Scotty informing Martha that she wasn't his—or most guys'—type? Was he suggesting, for health and aesthetic reasons, that she put on extra weight? What *was* this male compulsion to give you beauty advice? The first time Dennis said she'd look better if she got some sun should have been a tip-off: his concern was for this summer's tan, not next year's melanoma. And whose advice were you meant to take if men told you opposite things? Dennis's considered opinion was that Martha should be ten pounds thinner.

"What do you weigh?" asked Scotty. "Hundred nine? Hundred ten?"

Asshole, Martha thought. But she had to give him credit. He had guessed exactly. Though that was what she'd weighed at home. She probably weighed less now.

"How big is the cow?" asked Martha.

"Before or after cooking?" asked Scotty. "Pounds and pounds of suet have already dripped into the fire. Native people would save it and use it to make candles. It's another sign of how the white man's fucked up our culture that I'm standing here watching it soak in the ground."

But Scotty was a white man. Was he pretending to be an Indian? Or had some Native American genes been driven into hiding by Scotty's blondness?

Just then, Rita hurried over and pried Scotty's hand loose from the barbecue crank.

"What crazy stuff has Scotty been telling you? Scotty, baby?" Her voice turned cajoling. The Goddess women would have died before they talked like that to a man. "Scotty, honey, go stir the dinner?"

Scotty grinned and gave Rita a pat on her blue-jeaned behind. Then he trudged over to the fire and lifted the lids off the pots. He stirred as if he knew his way around a vat of chili.

He said, "Jesus, there's enough shit here to feed an entire troop deployment—"

"Gee," said Bernie, who had wandered over. "I hope Scotty isn't comparing our vision quest with a war. Though we are a sort of army, I guess—"

Martha said, "I hope he isn't comparing our food with shit."

Joking with Bernie at Scotty's expense provided a brief spell of comradely warmth. Rita couldn't have heard them, but still she glared at Bernie and Martha, then went back to watching adoringly as Scotty prepared the meal.

While the other women studied Rita for spiritual direction, Martha observed the power dynamics between Rita and Scotty.

It was Scotty who carved the cow, carried the meat and chili to the table; Scotty who fetched the tub of coleslaw from the trailer, where, Martha hoped, it had been refrigerated; Scotty who filled his plate first and sat down and began to eat. But it was Rita who rang the bell and called, "Okay, chow down, ladies."

Joy hopped over to Rita and set down her crutches so as to form a barricade between Rita and the food.

"Just a darn minute," said Joy. "No one said anything about having a man at the spirit feast. I thought we decided he could be around for the storytelling and then he'd be gone. We've been more than patient, no one's said a word. But some of us have real objections to male energy interfering while we nourish our bodies for our vision quests."

"Right on!" said Diana. "Let's be up-front about this. If he eats here, we don't."

"I'm sure we could compromise," Bernie said. "Maybe we could wait until Scotty's through, and then eat."

"Fuck you," said Scotty. "I ain't leaving. I'm a human being, I'm not your fucking butler who serves you and sits at the fucking servant's table."

"Well, fuck you, too," said Joy.

"I'm not at all sure that Scotty's butler material," said Titania.

"Get used to it, Scotty," Diana said. "Third World women do the equivalent daily and they don't get special treatment. They don't even get to complain—"

"Third World women?" Scotty repeated. "Third World women? Are you listening to this white-man shit, Rita?"

"What we're saying, Scotty," Starling explained, "is that this is not exactly free sharing of knowledge on Rita's part. We've paid a pretty penny to come out here and study with Rita. Actually, with Maria—"

"Maria!" Isis cried mournfully.

Everyone got very quiet.

"We're getting *paid* for this?" Scotty said. "Goddamn it, Rita, why didn't you tell me?" He flashed them a loopy grin, then went back to eating his dinner.

"He's out of here." Joy glared at Rita.

"Joy!" said Isis. "Ladies, please. Rita and Scotty are sharing their food and love with us, and the most positive thing for our vision quest is to shut up and be grateful and eat it."

This earned Isis many doubting looks. But eventually, with loud resigned sighs, the other women gave in. They picked up their paper plates and plastic Sporks and filed reverently past the barbecued beef, pots of chili, and tubs of coleslaw. Even the vegetarians helped themselves to the meat, except for Diana, whose plate stayed bare but for a few shreds of cabbage.

It was dismaying and comforting to have seen the rotating cow: sad that a living creature had died for their dinner, but reassuring to know that their food hadn't been tenderized on the road. Martha forked a slab of beef onto her plate, then added dollops of coleslaw and beans. She sat down at the table near Hegwitha and as far as possible from Scotty.

Hegwitha said, "It's lousy that we have to eat with him. It's like being kids again and having to placate Dad, the whole family waiting to see what kind of mood he's in and terrified of saying something to accidentally piss him off."

Hegwitha's plate looked like an artist's palette—discrete, tiny dabs of dinner. Martha dug in as if to show her how but then stopped eating, too. She was starving, but the food was inedible and repulsive. The greasy meat separated along every slippery muscle striation, lumpy islands of beans emerged from a lake of eggy mayonnaise.

The others were packing it away.

"Sonoma," Martha heard Freya say. "Look how you loaded your plate!"

Bernie said, "I had a client whose Sunday dinner, every week of her childhood, was spent waiting for the dad to get steamed at the mom and throw his plate of food on the floor."

By now Isis had sat down. "Are we still going on about **(215)** Scotty? How amazing that we can come all this way, go through what we've gone through—the sweat lodge, the fasting, the visions, the healing, to say nothing of the years spent serving the Goddess—and still the only thing we can talk about is—men!"

Titania said, "I guess when you get down to it, it's still the only subject."

"Speak for yourself!" said Starling.

"Yeah," said Hegwitha, in unison with Joy and Diana.

Joy said, "Damnit, Titania, why can't you get real? You didn't come to the desert looking for your spirit guide. You came out to Tucson looking for a fuckable cowboy."

"Me?" said Titania.

Everyone found something to focus on so as not to have to look at Scotty. Martha noticed that Sonoma's face had turned a marbleized red and white, mottled with embarrassment on behalf of the adult world.

"Let Titania be," Freya said. "I am so sick of your . . . antiheterosexual prejudice, Joy, making those of us who like men feel like traitors to the Goddess."

Sonoma said, "Of course you would stick up for men, Mother. They're the ones who give out museum shows."

Freya said, "I have never been discriminated against on account of being a woman."

Bernie said, "I thought the Goddess was about accepting what we are, regardless of whom we sleep with—"

Titania said, "And regardless of our age. Whatever happened to cronehood?"

Joy said, "I realize it's a problem, privileging gayness. But lesbians are still back where African-Americans were in the early days of Black Power—"

Starling said, "I can't believe you're comparing two-income lesbian couples with oppressed people of color—"

Joy said, "Would you listen to Ms. Political Correctness. Ms. Starling White-Ruling-Class Background."

"Would you *stop* it?" said Sonoma. "This really sucks."

"Sonoma!" said Freya.

"Sonoma's right!" said Diana. "I'm sick of all of you dragging everything into the mud, turning every spiritual conversation into some nasty catfight or political discussion—"

Freya said, "Better that than trying to make everybody stop eating and pressuring children into getting lost in the desert."

"I'm not a child," said Sonoma.

"Don't talk to Diana like that," Joy told Freya. "We're sick of your ego and your stupid art career. And we're sick of watching you treat your daughter like dogshit."

Sonoma pumped her fist in the air. "Woo woo woo," she said.

"While we're on the subject of ego," said Hegwitha. "Sometimes I think this group is a lot more ego-involved than Goddess worshippers should be. Everybody fighting to be at the head of the pecking order and meanwhile claiming that Goddess religion doesn't *have* a pecking order—"

"Cluck cluck cluck," said Scotty. Laughing, he got up from the table, tossed his paper plate into a plastic trash bag, and went off to the trailer.

"Got rid of *him*, I guess," said Titania.

"Oh, thank the Goddess!" cried Isis. "Thank the Goddess for saving us from negative vibrations. Blessed be."

"Blessed be," said several of the women.

"Let's center ourselves," Isis said. "Then clear our plates

and go on. I'm hearing some buried hostility here that needs to be brought out in the open instead of our sniping at each other and not saying what we mean. Maybe we could work with the Talking Stick and share our feelings before starting our vision quests. Let's chant."

As the women's eyes shut, Martha looked around just long enough to observe Rita's surprise at Isis having somehow managed to reclaim her leadership position. But eventually Rita closed her eyes and joined in the chanting.

Isis sent Starling back to their cabin to fetch the Talking Stick. When Starling returned, she was smiling at the stick, as if at a long-lost friend.

Isis winked at Rita. "Talking Stick," she said.

Rita said, "Yes. Talking Stick."

Isis took the Talking Stick and thanked the Goddess for Her love and protection even here in the middle of nowhere, and then thanked the Great Spirit and (with a nod at Rita) our Mother, the Earth. She asked the Talking Stick to help her sisters weave their stories and share them with their sister-priestesses.

Isis said, "I feel very lucky to have come to this place and learned all the great things that Rita has to teach us."

"Blessed be," Bernie said.

Isis passed the Talking Stick to Joy, who said, "Talk about lucky! I'm blown away with happiness that Diana and I are back together. I thank the Goddess for making us go the distance—geographically and spiritually—we had to go in order to see how much caring was still there."

The women applauded Joy and Diana's showy hug. In mid-embrace Diana took the stick from Joy, waved it like a trophy, then passed it on to Freya.

Freya pushed the bangs out of her eyes. "Most of you already know about the jaguar I saw last night in the sweat lodge. But now I want to say what I haven't shared, and tell you what I think it means."

Rita said, "When our animal guides come to us in the sweat, we *think* we know what it means, but lots of times it takes years till we know what it really means."

"Rita, dear," said Isis. "I'm sure that your people have their own way of using the Talking Stick. But in our group, only the person holding the stick gets to talk. The rest of us keep quiet and try not to interrupt."

Rita gave Isis a hateful look. Then she shrugged, thrust out her lower lip, and gazed off into the distance.

Freya said, "The jaguar was a female, devouring her cub. And I knew the jaguar was my ego, ripping into Sonoma." Freya rubbed her eyes. "All today I kept thinking about when Sonoma was tiny and we'd have these battles and she'd cry herself to sleep. Later I'd go watch her sleep—she was so beautiful and helpless—and then go back to bed and stay awake all night thinking about how I'd failed her, how I'd hurt her with my selfish impatience and the cruel things I'd said.

"Now, ten years later, it's gotten worse. Sonoma is almost grown up and gone, and soon I will have lost my chance to make things up. She's the only daughter I'll ever have, and I will have failed completely. I want to tell Sonoma that I'm sorry for what's happened, and I want her to help me be better from now on. To be a better mother, a better person in general."

Several women had tears in their eyes.

"Tell her!" Bernie ordered.

Freya looked at Sonoma. "I'm so sorry, Sonoma," she said.

"Give Sonoma the Talking Stick!" Starling said.

Sonoma took the Talking Stick.

"Sure, Mom. Fine," she said.

Freya hugged Sonoma, who went rigid but allowed it. "Great, Mom. The time you loved me most was when I was asleep." She passed the stick to Titania, who handed it on to Bernie.

Bernie said, "I think I'll pass, too. I just want to add my hopes for a terrific vision quest."

There was another round of applause, and the stick went to Starling. Starling rarely said much when she had the Talking Stick, except to express discontent with herself, pale resolves for the future, her wish to live in the present and not worry about details. The other women protested: they needed Starling to worry. They'd be lost unless she made the practical arrangements. Now Starling scrunched her eyes and seemed to be delving inward, seeking something deeper than the desire for self-improvement.

Starling said, "Since we've been here, a childhood memory has surfaced. It's been running around my brain like a rat in a maze."

"Great image," Isis said.

"Childhood memories are always telling us something," Bernie said. "Oops! I don't have the stick!"

"I know they are," said Starling. "And I think I know what this one is saying. The memory is from when my dad was stationed in Thailand. There was a Thai who worked at the base. He said he'd been a dancer and could teach the American girls classical Thai ballet. His name was Mister Toon. After a while he said we were good enough to put on a performance. He had a beautiful wife, who was going to make us costumes. She came to our houses and measured us and our moms paid her to buy the silk. My costume was red with gold brocade, a tucked-up sarong and a tight jacket with epaulettes like angel wings, a pointy helmet, fake fingernails, tons of makeup—I felt gorgeous."

Martha tried to picture Starling swathed in red brocade, her buttony eyes, ringed with kohl, tracking from side to side.

Starling said, "Maybe the moms should have suspected something when Mrs. Toon said it was Thai bad luck for us to take home our costumes before the performance. Well, there was no performance. The night of the recital came and the Toons didn't show up. It turned out that she'd shown every girl the same costume. They took our money and left Bangkok." Starling smiled. "It's funny now, but it wasn't then."

"What's it saying to you?" Bernie asked. "How does it connect with the present?"

Starling said, "This part is tough. I guess because it has to do with my feelings about the group. What I thought in the sweat last night is how there's a part of me that's always expecting the Toons not to show up, afraid I won't get to wear my beautiful Thai costume. Part of me is always holding out, not letting go, not trusting. In the past it's come between me and the group and made for some negative feelings. But now I know those feelings were all inside my own head, and it's up to me to change them."

Starling reddened and burst out crying. Bernie and Isis rushed over to sandwich her tightly between them.

Martha was next in the circle. As if the stick were glowing hot, Martha tossed it from hand to hand, thinking she'd hold it a second, mumble, and pass it on. But something stopped her and she said, "I've also been having a memory . . ."

"Share," said Bernie, and the others said, "Oh, yes, do, yes, do," welcoming this chance to gather Martha back into the fold and offer her the healing she'd missed by sitting out the sweat lodge.

"It's about my old boyfriend. Dennis."

Joy said, "Oh, no, not *him* again!"

"Joy!" said Isis. "Martha has the stick. One awful thing

about psychic suffering is how often it lasts beyond the point at which our friends hate hearing about it. Martha, please, go on."

Martha gave Isis a grateful smile. "I keep thinking about (221) the time Dennis was playing Othello—"

Bernie said, "Was your boyfriend black? I don't think I knew that."

"No," said Martha. "He was white. *Is* white."

"Didn't they have a black person in the class?" Diana said.

"I don't know," said Martha.

"*Othello!*" said Joy. "Another great Dead White Male classic about battering and killing women."

Martha gripped the Talking Stick. "All during rehearsals, Dennis seemed to be getting sadder. Until one night we were eating at an Italian restaurant and I finally got the nerve to ask him what was wrong. He said Othello was depressing him. He said it made him jealous, playing a guy who loved his woman so much that he would kill her rather than lose her. It made him realize he had never felt anything *near* that passion for me."

Titania whistled through her teeth.

"Thank your lucky stars he didn't," Starling said. "You could have wound up like Desdemona."

Joy said, "Didn't anybody ever tell this guy that *Othello* is a play about two closeted gay men?"

"Really," said Diana. "Didn't anyone ever point out that it's not about a guy who loves his woman so much he kills her, but about repressed homoerotic—"

Isis said, "You're lucky to be rid of that sadist."

"Definitely!" said Titania.

"Wait a sec," said Bernie. "Let me ask you something, Martha. Dennis said he never felt like that about you . . . but did you feel that way about *him*? Did you feel, for one moment, that you wanted to kill . . . the woman . . . What was her name?"

"Lucinda," Martha said miserably.

"That's brilliant and helpful, Bernie," Isis said. And the other women chorused: Brilliant, brilliant and helpful.

Martha didn't think it was brilliant at all. It was just therapy talk. She hadn't wanted to kill Lucinda. She had just wanted to die.

"I guess you're right," said Martha, and thrust the Talking Stick at Hegwitha.

She knew what she wanted to happen now. She wanted Hegwitha to tell the truth, to say that she was sick again and had let them pray for a lie. That would make them think twice about their self-righteous self-satisfaction, their cheap little therapeutic insights. How small of Martha to want to use Hegwitha's illness as if this were some kind of trial, Martha vs. the Goddess women . . . And what was her case against them? What had these women done? Taken her in, treated her well, brought her to Arizona. Did she feel they were losing interest in her and so was preemptively turning against them?

Hegwitha took the stick and said, "I don't have much to share. I'm so grateful for the healing energy I got last night in the sweat lodge. I feel really positive that I'm going to stay in remission . . . And like I've already taken tons of everyone's time."

How could Hegwitha lie about something so important? Martha was appalled and yet unwilling to blame Hegwitha for wanting to be part of the group and not wanting to upset them. It was like those stories one hears about polite guests nearly choking at dinner parties, reluctant to make any trouble.

If Martha had any courage, she would have made Hegwitha tell the truth. That would show Isis and the rest what their religion was about. All their talk about loving and sharing and recovering their spiritual natures, and one of them was dying and didn't trust them enough to confess. All that talk about getting in touch with Brother Rabbit and Sister Mouse, and some part of them was completely walled off from Brother and Sister Human. But what would that accomplish? It would humiliate Hegwitha and shock the Goddess women without inspiring them to change, or reconsider. And who was Martha to tell them that they should be different or better—Martha, who was willing to sacrifice a sick woman's privacy to teach these harmless women a lesson, to punish them for having tired of Martha's judgmental Athena mind?

Hegwitha passed the stick to Rita. The women held their breath as if they shared a single respiratory system; no one exhaled until Rita grabbed it with both hands. Rita's chin sank to her chest as she closed her eyes and emitted a low hum.

Finally she said, "My dad used to drink a lot. Then he'd come home and beat my mom. I was the youngest of nine, so it had gone on a long time. Then one night—I was three years old—he started wailing on my mom, and I started singing a song, I don't know where it came from. I sang my song over and over. Dad backed off and got quiet. Later Mom brought me to the elders and made me sing my song, and they said it was a sacred peacemaking song of the ancient ones.

"After that, whenever my dad started in, I used my medicine, I'd sing and put my hand on Dad, and he would fall asleep. Any time a guy on the reservation started beating on his family, someone would come and get me and I would use my medicine."

"That's wild," said Diana. "That people would use this three-year-old . . . baby to take on a village of drunken batterers."

Rita smiled proudly. "This is how my people discovered what strong medicine I have."

"They should record that song of yours," said Titania. "The uses for it would be legion."

Rita looked insulted. "My medicine song wouldn't work unless I was there to sing it."

"Ignore Titania," said Starling. "Always the business-woman."

For a moment Martha wondered if Rita's story was true. It was troubling that this woman had begun life in terror and grief and impossible responsibility. But it was just as unpleasant to think she'd invented the perfect story, the legend that these women most longed and needed to hear, a story about female magic pacifying male violence. Martha's anger at them subsided, leaving her hollow and drained.

Isis took Rita's hands between hers.

"That's beautiful," she said thickly.

How long had Martha been sleeping? The back of her neck was soaked. She'd awakened in that weightless free-fall she sometimes slipped into falling asleep. She'd been dreaming that she was about to trip down the steps of her childhood house. Young and smiling and healthy, her father was running to catch her. Waking, she realized that he was dead and she had to stop from crying out.

In the other bed Titania tossed and moaned in her sleep.

Martha turned on the lamp and checked her watch. Ten after four in the morning. Her temples throbbed, her sinuses ached. Valley fever, no doubt.

Someone was knocking on the door.

"Titania!" said Martha. "Wake up!" Titania groaned and rolled over.

"Who is it?" Martha called out evenly, as if it were perfectly normal, a visit at 4:00 a.m.

No one answered. There was a louder knock.

Martha thought of Scotty—and now she got really scared. Had she said anything he could have misread as flirtation or encouragement? Had a faint smile crossed her lips when he told his fat joke about Rita? Maybe Scotty had fixed her up with a biker-rapist blind date or the entire membership of the Tucson Hell's Angels.

"Who is it?" she repeated.

A voice said, "It's me, Freya!"

Freya stood in the doorway. She said, "Have you seen Sonoma?"

"Since when?" Martha said. "Is she missing?"

Freya just stared at her.

"Obviously," said Martha. "Sorry."

She was stalling for time to remember their conversation outside the sweat lodge. Had Martha said something stupid? Driven Sonoma away? Should she have been more discouraging about her plans to visit her father?

"What the fuck?" Titania mumbled from her bed.

"Sonoma didn't come back tonight," Freya said. "She wasn't in the cabin when I got back from the feast. I must have dozed off. When I woke up, she still wasn't there."

"I talked to her last night after she left the sweat lodge," Martha said tentatively. "She was saying something about wanting to go find her dad."

"Oh, Jesus," Freya said.

"Freya," said Titania. "Get a grip on yourself. When did *you* see her last?"

"I don't know!" Freya cried. "That's the awful part—I don't know when I last saw my daughter."

"She was there when we did Talking Stick," said Titania.

"I know that, I saw her," said Freya. "But not after that."

"Where *is* her father, exactly?" said Martha.

"Oh, who knows?" said Freya. "I thought it was Delphi, that town we passed through. Maybe it's Delphi, Colorado. Is there a Delphi, Colorado? Could she have gone into town? Looking for her father? How could she have done this after what we said tonight with the Talking Stick? I thought some kind of healing was starting to happen between us. For her to run away after that . . . But why should I be surprised? I was the one who dozed off without knowing where my daughter was. What kind of mother am I? My first thought was that she'd sneaked off to flirt with Rita's boyfriend. What was I thinking? Sonoma hardly knows boys exist. I went to Rita's trailer and stood outside. I heard these rhythmic thumps, like someone being beaten or having S-M sex. Rita answered the door in her bathrobe. Sonoma wasn't there."

"*We* haven't seen her," Martha said. "Titania, have you seen Sonoma?"

"No," replied Titania.

"Jesus," Freya said. "All right, I'm going to look for her. See you. Goodbye. Sorry. Go back to sleep."

"Is she nuts?" Titania said. "Telling us to go back to sleep when Sonoma's missing?"

Martha pulled on her jeans and shirt. Only after she'd tied her shoes did she remember Rita's warning about always checking to make sure that Little Sister Scorpion wasn't sleeping in their boots. Well, let the scorpion bite her, she wasn't going to take off her shoes and check. Martha grabbed a sweatshirt and hurried outside.

Sonoma wasn't anywhere. That much had been determined by the time Martha reached the ramada, where the others were gathered, warming their hands over the fire.

Bernie told Martha, "She left a note. It said: 'I'm out of here. Love, Sonoma.' "

"She's run away," pronounced Isis, a conclusion so self-evident that only Sonoma could have appreciated its full, glorious banality. Martha shivered as a chill of pure fear raised the hairs on the back of her neck, amazing her with the intensity of her concern for Sonoma.

"That's the best-case scenario," explained Bernie. "As a therapist, I feel I have to say . . . Well, given the teenage suicide rate, we can't not consider that."

Freya groaned.

"Don't worry," Bernie said. "Factoring in Sonoma's personality and the tone of the note, suicide seems unlikely. It's more like Sonoma to run away than do anything drastic. Plus, teenage suicides tend to talk about it first, and as far as we know—"

Martha said, "Last night she was telling me about wanting to find her father."

With a sickening lurch of dread, she remembered: Sonoma *had* talked about killing herself. But before Martha could decide how to mention this without making everyone hysterical, Scotty said, "Let's get this straight. When was the girl seen last?"

Excuse me? thought Martha. What was happening here? Scotty was playing detective, not the none-too-bright cop that one might expect but the efficient sergeant—cool, competent, and thorough. What was far more unexpected was that the women were allowing this, turning phototropically to the only man present at the scene of a crisis. Joy, Starling, Diana, Isis—with their contempt for male intelligence, their belief that men were only good for making war and donor sperm—were reverting back to some learned response, some primitive form of wiring that, when lightning hit, conveyed the charge to the nearest male. As soon as her daughter disappeared, Freya had stopped praying to the Goddess and instead kept muttering, "Jesus Christ. Oh, Jesus."

"Did she have a flashlight?" Scotty asked Freya. "Could she have gotten a flashlight?"

Freya said, "I don't know what she has! I have no idea where she'd go. This isn't like her. I don't get it." As she grew more frantic and distraught, Freya aged before their eyes; the furrow between her eyebrows deepened, a wattle flapped under her chin.

Scotty said, "Come on, you're her mom—and you don't know where she is in the middle of the night, or where she might go?"

Who was Scotty to lecture Freya on the duties of motherhood? Why weren't the others defending her against this stranger, this . . . male wielding his privileged male authority to destroy a woman's self-worth? Martha sensed a faint stir of satisfaction rippling through the group as Scotty confirmed their opinion of Freya's maternal capabilities.

Tears left dusty trails down Freya's face, but her voice was clipped and controlled. "This is no time to evaluate my competence as a mother."

"Well, excuse *me*," said Scotty. "It's not my kid who split."

Isis said, "Isn't it odd that even feminists fall into this trap—when something goes wrong with a child, even feminists blame the mother?"

"Thank you," Freya said.

Isis went over and put her arm around Freya. "Sonoma's not an easy kid," she said. "Anyone could see that. She has lots of issues to work through. When she comes back, it's going to be hard, and naturally it will take time and a great deal of help from the Goddess."

Freya said, "It makes me feel better to hear you assuming she *is* coming back."

Then Freya shrugged off Isis's arm, blew her nose, and turned on Diana. "You're the one always telling her to go get lost in the desert, as if it weren't suicide for a thirteen-year-old New York kid to go be rattlesnake bait. The stupidity, the wickedness of putting that kind of pressure—"

"Leave Diana alone," Joy muttered.

"You think Sonoma would listen to me anyway?" Diana was almost shrieking. "You've done such a job on that kid that her whole life is overeating and fucking with your head!"

"Oh, I can't stand it," Isis said. "Something always happens! Something always sabotages whatever we try to do—"

"Oh, Isis," said Starling. "That's not true!"

"It *is* true," insisted Isis. "Someone's always trying to set me on fire or drown me. Those women who burned the corn witches at the beach on Labor Day weekend—"

Bernie said, "I always wished I knew Sonoma better. But she wasn't the kind of girl who would ever let you in. Still, from what little I do know, Freya, I think she just ran away, and we can't blame Diana."

Why was Bernie referring to Sonoma in the past tense? Hot tears welled up in Martha's eyes, and she felt nearly faint with anxiety. Probably Sonoma was safe, and they would find her before too long. But why did Martha think that they wouldn't—that Sonoma was dead or about to be dead, fallen prey to exposure, the victim of a four-legged or a two-legged creature, or of a snake with no legs at all? Perhaps only Martha thought that, the lone doubter among these women with their unwavering faith in a Goddess who was, as they spoke, watching over Sonoma.

Hegwitha spoke up. "Who cares why she left? We'd better get off our tails and find her. It's cold and dangerous out there—"

"Hegwitha's right," said Martha.

"Ladies," said Rita, "the desert critters know when you mean no harm, and they will never hurt you. Sonoma will be okay. The Earth, our Mother, will protect her. Native people have legends about folks who get lost in the desert, and the Grandmothers find them and escort them back."

Joy said, "And we're supposed to sit here until the Grandmothers find her? What if they don't find her?"

Starling said, "I thought Native people never got lost. I thought you said that yesterday, Rita!"

"Not at all," said Diana. "Rita was very clear about lots of Native people getting lost and surviving because of their memories of ancient hunter-gatherer ways. Gosh, I hope Sonoma was listening." **(231)**

Hegwitha said, "Is there a telephone? Can we drive into town and call? Where does this father of hers live? Shouldn't we call over there? Should we notify the state troopers?"

Scotty said, "Hey, no, man. No way. Not the troopers—not those oinkers. I don't think *that*'s a good idea."

"Why not?" Martha said.

Scotty said, "Get serious. There's two hundred years of bad blood between our Native people and those sonofabitches. The minute you invite the law onto our land you get a situation like Wounded Knee."

"We're not exactly activists out here," said Joy. "Not by a long shot, I'd say. They have no reason to want to get us. A child is missing. We need help."

"Sure," said Scotty. "Next, it's in all the papers how we're a bunch of godless satanic Indian savages practicing ritual child sacrifice. We can handle this ourselves. I'll call my friends, we're desert rats, we'll find her faster than a bunch of crackers jerking off in helicopters. I was in Vietnam with those choppers, man. I know what bad magic they are."

Martha would have liked the entire 82nd Airborne out searching for Sonoma. Why wouldn't Scotty and Rita call in all the help they could get? Could Scotty have hurt Sonoma? That was too frightening to consider.

Scotty said, "Okay, I'll level with you. I've got an acre of weed growing out here. Top-grade sinsemilla. The law would not appreciate that."

"Scotty!" said Rita.

"Thank you for informing us," said Starling curtly.

Scotty said, "They'd probably lock us all up until they sorted things out, by which point you can write off the kid. If you ever find her, she'll be put straight into foster care."

"Please," said Titania. "Don't threaten us. We have access to excellent lawyers."

It no longer seemed such a wise idea to call the police right away. Maybe Scotty was right, maybe he and his friends knew the desert better than a posse of overweight cowpokes in four-wheel-drive patrol cars.

Scotty said, "I got a CB in my truck. Let me call my buddies. We'll go looking for her as soon as the light comes up."

"We can't wait till the light comes up!" Freya shrieked. "We have to go out now."

"It'll be dawn in an hour," Scotty said. "Let's get our priorities straight. We'll do better thinking it through and coming up with a plan than rushing out into the darkness with our heads up our butts."

The image Martha saw was out of Hieronymus Bosch: Scotty's buddies scurrying through the night in that odd anatomical position. She didn't like picturing Scotty's friends in any position at all. But now the same women who'd thrown a fit about having Scotty around weren't hesitating to call in the Hell's Angels. In fact, they seemed quite grateful for any help at all.

"That's a wonderful idea," Isis said. "Especially waiting for dawn. There's no overestimating the power of light, of seeing things in a new light. Wait. I have a thought. Let's do a healing circle before we go look for Sonoma. Ask the Goddess and the Great Spirit for help in finding their child, and ours."

Would they really waste precious time on mumbo jumbo when they could be stumbling around, calling Sonoma's name? Martha thought of how she'd met these women, how she'd jumped in and saved Isis from drowning. What was wrong with them, what had happened to leave them so paralyzed and passive that they could stand and witness horrific crises without being able to act? Wasn't anyone objecting? What was there to object to? Perhaps they should wait till dawn rather than go out now and get lost themselves.

Martha still thought they should call the troopers, but Scotty might be right. Finding Scotty's pot plantation might interfere with the search for Sonoma. Sonoma would have had something to say about a healing circle now. She would have crooked her finger into her mouth and pretended to gag.

"All right, Isis, babe! A healing circle!" Scotty stuck up his thumb.

Freya accepted the group decision and didn't insist they start searching at once—though that was surely what Martha would have done, had Sonoma been her child. But she'd never had a child, so how could she possibly know? Was it all right to wait the hour, to let Sonoma get farther away? Would the benefits of daylight outweigh the likelihood of Sonoma wandering that much farther from the camp?

The women shambled about in the vague way that preceded forming a circle. And even Joy, who'd been most vehement about doing something at once, gave in to the always seductive chance to put something off for a while.

Martha knew she couldn't join in—she would not be able to do it.

Hegwitha came over to Martha and said, "This is total bullshit. We can't just wait for an hour. We should blow this place right now and go out and find her."

"Let's go," Martha told her. That was how long it took to decide. Then they stood and stared at each other. What would they do now?

Hegwitha said, "Should we take the van? Shouldn't we

ask someone? If this is really a nonhierarchical situation, it's our van as much as anyone else's. I think we should just take it."

"Can you drive it?" Martha was leery of standard shift, and cars with special needs and quirks.

"No worse than Joy," Hegwitha said. "And I know where Joy keeps the keys."

Martha didn't want to ask how Hegwitha knew. It might have led to Hegwitha saying more about Diana than Martha wanted to hear right then. "How are you feeling?" she said.

"Not great," said Hegwitha. "But not so bad I can't drive."

Hegwitha went to her cabin and came out waving the car keys. She climbed into the driver's seat. Martha got in beside her. Would the women come after them when they heard the van start up?

The women bowed their heads and joined hands. From the van, Martha could hear their tremulous mewing. What a sad minor tune it was, how frail and tender they seemed, with their yearning to believe that their pain and loss were part of some higher design.

Hegwitha turned the key in the ignition. The engine started up. Miraculous! The second miracle was that no one turned to watch them go.

"It's a sign," said Martha.

"Bingo," said Hegwitha.

Hegwitha switched on the headlights. A cactus jumped into the light. She swung the van around and found the driveway.

"All right!" Martha said.

"Yess! Yess!" hissed Hegwitha. She sounded like Sonoma. "We'll find her, I know she's out there. We've just got to tune into her vibes."

Beyond the range of the van's high beams, the desert was silent and unforthcoming.

They bounced along, the needle wavering between five and ten miles per hour. Martha scanned the dark landscape. Oh, where was Sonoma? She concentrated as if Sonoma were a noise she could listen for and hear. She wished she were one of those psychics whom desperate police departments employ to find missing persons, though—she reflected with horror—clairvoyants often had better luck locating the dead.

"She could walk faster than this," said Hegwitha. "If she came this way she might have reached the main road and maybe, Goddess help us, hitchhiked out."

At the end of the driveway, the sky above them opened. The first rays of dawn gave the desert the silvery gleam of mica. An empty two-lane road rolled out toward the distant mountains. Sonoma was nowhere in sight.

Hegwitha shifted into neutral, and, with the engine running, they waited beside the road. It was time for them to decide where to go and what to do, and to admit that they didn't have a plan, or any idea how to find Sonoma.

"Should we aim for Tucson?" Martha asked.

"I don't know. I guess," said Hegwitha. "I keep hoping we'll find her walking by the side of the road."

"That's what I keep hoping," Martha said. "If it were me out alone here, I'd stick pretty close to the pavement."

After a silence, Hegwitha said, "I knew you'd come through. I knew you'd want to do something . . . Because it was you that day on the beach who pulled Isis out of the water."

"Gee," said Martha. "Thanks." How surprising to discover that Hegwitha respected her, when she'd always believed that Hegwitha thought she was a fool and had just latched onto her for entree into the Goddess inner circle. When, in fact, it was Martha who'd wanted into that privileged coterie . . . It was also surprising that Hegwitha would defy the Goddess women, though perhaps her not being able to say that she was sick had changed her feelings about the group.

As if she'd read Martha's mind, Hegwitha said, "A woman's gotta do what a woman's gotta do. I just hope they're not too mad at us when they find the van's missing. Though maybe they'll forgive us when we come back with Sonoma."

The van coughed weakly. The motor sputtered—and cut out. Hegwitha turned the ignition. The key clicked in the lock.

"Oh, Jesus Christ. Oh, Goddess," Hegwitha said. "This was not what I had in mind."

Somehow Hegwitha found the button that popped open the hood of the van. She got out and looked beneath it with a purposeful expression, though it was hard to tell if she knew what she was seeing. Martha felt obliged to peek over Hegwitha's shoulder and demonstrate her helpful intentions.

A funereal black ribbon of smoke curled up from the charred belts and wiring. Hegwitha frowned at Martha, who imagined her suggesting they pray to the Goddess for emergency auto repair.

"The way I see it," Hegwitha said, "we've got two options. One, give up and tuck our tails between our legs and go back to camp and tell everyone we fucked up. Or two, we stay put and hope that an angel comes along, an angel who can fix this heap of shit or find someone who can."

But there was not an angel anywhere for miles around. Not a single vehicle, not a plane in the sky. They heard a howl in the distance.

Hegwitha said, "I don't like this. This really gives me the willies. I keep wondering which is worse: nobody coming along to help and having to walk back to camp—or somebody coming along and, given the high percentage of men involved in recreational murder, getting raped and strangled and left for dead in a drainage ditch."

Martha said, "I always think one of the worst things about being female is knowing that the next guy who drives by could hack you up to bits and leave trash bags full of your body parts in a dozen different dumpsters."

"Right on," said Hegwitha. Then she said, "Cut it out, Martha, okay?"

All at once they felt a subterranean rumbling that in Martha's upside-down state she mistook for a plane overhead. And now they saw a pair of headlights skimming over the road.

Hegwitha said, "Why am I worried? It would probably be more merciful to get sodomized and stabbed than die a painful, boring death in some shithole hospital in Manhattan."

"*You* cut it out," said Martha.

Hegwitha flashed the van blinkers. Across the road, a three-armed saguaro lit up and went black and lit up.

The truck got closer. It was huge—and white.

"Moby Dick," said Martha.

"It's a refrigerator truck!" said Hegwitha. "A meat truck!"

"Perfect," Martha said. "Once I saw a movie about a farmer who kidnapped drivers off the road and ground them into sausage."

"*Motel Hell*," said Hegwitha. "What a great film! The stupid fucker can't decide if he's going to stop or not."

The truck did seem to be going through some crisis of indecision, slowing and speeding up again, its lights brightening and dimming.

Martha said, "Maybe he's trying to decide if we're killers planning to hijack all that prime rib. Wouldn't that be a good sign—I mean, that he wasn't a killer himself?"

"Not necessarily," said Hegwitha. "The fact that he expects violence may mean that he's capable of it."

The truck gave off a porcine squeal but kept inching forward until the driver peered out his window and made sure that Martha and Hegwitha were harmless. On the side of the truck the company name was lettered in black.

"Arizona Meats," Hegwitha read. "This is unbelievable. Instant karma for eating roadkill at Rita's."

The cab door swung open and a tall young man climbed down. It was immediately obvious to both Martha and Hegwitha that this was not the maniac who would leave them dead in a ditch. He was thin, with a tense wiry body, a pale, appealing freckled face, and yellow hair that stood up in a brush. He was probably about Martha's age—biologically speaking. Culturally he was in some time warp, a throwback to greaser prehistory in a black T-shirt and jeans and stubby biker boots with buckles.

He said, "Good morning, ladies. Sorry it took me so long to slow down. We're all pretty careful these days. Hell, you could be Thelma and Louise."

"I hated that movie," said Martha.

"Glad to hear it," the trucker said.

"I loved it," Hegwitha said.

The trucker shook their hands, solemnly. "My name's T-Bone," he said.

"A meat-truck driver named T-Bone?" Hegwitha said. "Totally surreal."

"I'm Martha," Martha said quickly. "And this is Hegwitha."

"Good to meet you," said T-Bone. Then he pulled himself together like a busy doctor who has done the bedside-manner part and now wants to get on with your case.

"What's the problem?" he inquired, intuiting that Hegwitha was the one to ask.

"I honestly couldn't tell you." Hegwitha inhaled, expanding her chest, quasi-military and assault-proof.

T-Bone went over to the van and peered under the hood. What a pleasure, what a relief to have a man take on your car trouble!

"Christ," he said. "What did your gauges say?"

"I don't know, it just conked out." Hegwitha sounded vaguely aggrieved, as if it were T-Bone's fault.

"Well," said T-Bone. "You want me to try and start it?" **(239)**

"We'd appreciate that," Hegwitha said.

In the time elapsed since Hegwitha last tried to start the motor, the click of the key seemed to have grown tinnier and more unpromising. They both flinched at the sound as they leaned in the van windows, watching T-Bone.

"Dead as a duck," he said. "I don't know what to tell you. Where are you girls coming from?"

"Girls?" said Hegwitha.

"Women," T-Bone said.

"We've been staying down the road," Martha said.

"At the Four Feathers Institute," Hegwitha added.

Martha hoped he didn't know what it was. She didn't want him assuming she was some New Age geek. But how self-involved to imagine that he was thinking about her—or about anything except how to start their van. As T-Bone got out and again looked under the hood, Martha watched his strong back under his bomber jacket.

He said, "Your best shot is if I give you a ride to the nearest garage and they send a tow truck to pick up the van. Hey, this thing has rental plates! You can call the agency, though you know the bastards won't come across with a nickel. I hope you girls have plastic. These garage guys will skin you alive." Hegwitha looked alarmed. "I mean, they'll overcharge you."

"We'll take the ride. Thanks." Hegwitha sighed.

"Come on, it could be worse," T-Bone said. "I've got a thermos of coffee and the new k. d. lang tape."

"I love k. d. lang," said Hegwitha.

"I bet you do." T-Bone reached up and opened the passenger door for them.

Without a word it was decided that Martha would sit next to T-Bone and Hegwitha would get the door. That was what they both wanted, though Hegwitha may not have known it.

Let her think that Martha was martyring herself, sitting next to a man.

The interior of the cab was unexpectedly exotic. Cranberry-colored pompons bobbled around the edge of the window. On the dashboard was a tiny magnetized vase of plastic flowers, a silvery miniature mosque, a painting of a white pony with glittery blankets and bridles, and several snapshots in frames.

In the few seconds before T-Bone got in, Hegwitha said, "I'm amazed. I would have thought this guy was strictly *Penthouse* Pet of the Month and Waylon Jennings."

"Do you mind if I smoke?" Hegwitha said.

"Be my guest," said T-Bone.

"What's that?" Hegwitha pointed her lit cigarette at the mosque.

"Mecca," he said. "My partners are two Syrian brothers who drive out of Phoenix. Most drivers get to ride around with naked pictures of Madonna. I get the Ayatollah. Though don't you think that Madonna's sort of like the Ayatollah?"

"Are you high on something?" Hegwitha asked.

"I wish," T-Bone said.

Martha inspected the dashboard more closely. Beaming out of one picture frame was a woman with dark eyes and long brown hair. In the crook of each arm she held a girl whose delicate face mirrored her mother's tidy features and trusting, straight-ahead gaze.

"My wife and kids," T-Bone said. "By the way, where were you girls going at the crack of dawn?"

"Women." Hegwitha would keep correcting him for however long it took.

T-Bone grinned at Martha, and, traitorously, she smiled back.

Hegwitha said, "My friend's daughter ran away. We were looking for her."

T-Bone's grin faded. "Jesus, I'm sorry. That's awful. How old is your daughter?" he asked Martha.

Martha said, "She's thirteen."

Pressed against Hegwitha, Martha felt her tense and relax, and knew Hegwitha had meant for him to assume the child was Martha's. Perhaps it would be easier if they could maintain that fiction without actually having to lie. T-Bone would be more sympathetic, eager to help; it would take less explaining. If Martha said, A friend's daughter, T-Bone might ask, What friend? and Hegwitha would soon be lecturing him on how male sky-god religion had stamped out Goddess worship.

Already Martha was embarrassed by her time with the Goddess women. She knew that true believers were never ashamed of their faith. And religion would be such a help now—a promise that they'd find Sonoma. She felt her lack of faith so acutely she had to remember she'd never had any, and that this was not the searing pain of recent deprivation but the dull pins and needles amputees feel long after the loss of a limb.

Martha said, "It's scary. She never ran away before."

T-Bone gave a low sympathetic whistle and slowly shook his head. Martha was glad that he didn't instantly convert his pity into a long list of practical steps that he would advise—no, tell—her to take. You could live with a man like this, a man who wasn't on a personal mission to improve you or demolish you if you were sluggish about improving. Martha envied T-Bone's wife, though she knew this was a mistake. There were always hidden negatives that one wouldn't want and shouldn't envy. The drawbacks in this case were plain:

here he was out on the road, while she was stuck at home with the children.

In the pinkish gathering light, anyone could tell that T-Bone was imagining how he would feel if *his* daughter ran away. Martha wanted to say: It's all right, your children are home with their mom. But it wasn't all right, nothing was, because Sonoma was missing.

T-Bone grasped Martha's elbow. Pure comfort streamed along her arm down to the bones of her fingers. There was nothing seductive in his touch, however much Martha would have liked it. It seemed unfair that, after all that had happened, the touch of a man—an attractive man—could steady her so profoundly.

"She'll come back." T-Bone hesitated a moment, then said, "My partners would kill me if they knew how many girl hitchhikers I pick up, even though I know it's a lousy idea— legally, insurancewise. Any one of them could be a time bomb who'll go nuts and yell rape and get me sent away for life, or fake whiplash and sue the company for a zillion bucks. But I know they're safer with me than with some psycho. The risk I'm taking is a lot better than their hitching rides with Ted Bundy."

"The Ted Bundys are out there, all right." It was the first thing Hegwitha had said in a while.

T-Bone said, "You know it, I know it. But these kids don't know it. They get in the cab all attitude, like they're doing me a favor. They're not going to talk to me, no sir, not some dumb asshole trucker. And it takes them about two seconds to start telling me their whole life story. Half the time I pick them up they're running away from home. And half the time they've given up and are on their way home again."

Martha said, "I hope we find her and don't have to wait for her to give up and come back."

"If you don't mind my asking," T-Bone said, "how do you plan on finding her?"

Martha looked at Hegwitha. What *was* their plan, exactly? Conveniently, the van had died just as they'd had to decide.

"I don't know," Martha told T-Bone, and was as shocked as T-Bone and Hegwitha when she burst into tears.

T-Bone must have meant to pat her on the shoulder, but missed and wound up pawing her neck, clumsy and endearing.

"Raising kids!" He shook his head. "What an impossible job! In our house the worst thing is the bicker bicker. They'd fight over a dead snake if that's all there was to fight about. But that's not really the worst thing. The worst thing is wanting to protect them and never knowing if you can keep them safe or even what makes them happy."

Martha couldn't believe it. She and Hegwitha had driven into the desert and broken down and flashed their lights and managed to conjure up the totally reconstructed male, an evolved being come to rescue them—in his meat truck, no less. Was T-Bone the guardian angel Hegwitha had asked the Goddess to send? Maybe they could bring him back and show him around the camp, this freak whose every gesture defied the women's low expectations of male behavior. T-Bone loving his daughters wouldn't bring back the women burned as witches nor make up for the men who'd hurt and abused the women in the group. Still, Martha longed to take him to New York as a sort of traveling exhibit, to show the world (including Dennis) what was possible, even for a man, in terms of human kindness and grace. Not that Dennis would know what she meant. Dennis wouldn't get it.

Martha's father would have understood. He'd known what it was like to want to keep your loved ones safe, against impossible odds. He'd spent his working life convincing others and himself that safety could be purchased with convenient low monthly payments. Suddenly Martha felt her father's presence in the cab of the truck, squeezing into the tiny gaps between her and T-Bone and Hegwitha. And for a moment the hum of the diesel engine sounded like his riding mower grazing in the sparkling grass on those sweet summer evenings . . .

T-Bone was saying, "Another tough thing is putting yourself on a kid's wavelength. That's because they inhabit a whole different time and space. Rennie is my wife Sally's kid from her first marriage. She was four when I met her. What did I know about kids? The kid used to ask me what should she draw. I'd say, 'Draw a clown or a horse or a cowboy,' and she'd look at me, totally bored and trying not to show it.

"Then her mom would say, 'Draw a cowboy getting shot by a clown and falling off his horse.' And she'd go off happy and draw a really great picture. Sally told me, 'You have to understand. Things are in motion for her.' That's when I asked Sally to marry me. I was so impressed."

Imagine, that a man would be attracted to a woman because of some insight about a little girl! It was so unlike the reasons one assumed men married. Martha's jealousy of T-Bone's wife returned, doubly intense, no longer mediated by the thought of her stuck home alone with the kids.

All these miles away from his wife, T-Bone spoke of her as if saying her name could somehow bring her near. Did Dennis have a story about Martha? About how he knew he loved her while defrosting her fridge? Did he still describe her as someone who understood what he meant? Probably he said it just to torture Lucinda. But even that was better than his forgetting her completely. Didn't everyone want someone thinking of them all the time, mentioning them at every chance, trying to bring them closer? Wasn't that what the religious sought in a god or goddess: someone to keep them always in mind without the messy human complications.

Suddenly Hegwitha cried, "Wait! Hey, look, there's Sonoma!"

"Is that her?" said T-Bone. "She looks like a fucking ghost."

As T-Bone slowed to a stop, Sonoma scowled at the truck. She was wearing her white cowboy hat and white fringed satin shirt. The angle at which she stuck out her thumb was wonderfully aggressive. Her blond curls shone like the glossy fur of some pampered pet. Like the Virgin in a votive painting, Sonoma appeared to hover inside an oval of luminous mist.

Years later, in what seemed like another life, Martha sometimes remembered how they'd found Sonoma. Mostly Martha recalled it when one of her children wandered off and gave her a moment of terror in some supermarket or park, and Martha would run around searching, panicking, trying not to seem panicked, and at last she would find her daughter or son, in the clothes she'd put on that morning, their sweet familiar bodies and faces that had never looked so lovely, and she knew she could never explain how exhilarating it was: the thrilling speed with which her worst fears popped like bubbles and vanished. Sometimes she would think of that silvery dawn when they'd found Sonoma: a whispered promise of that other joy, waiting in her future.

Hegwitha and Martha had jumped from the truck. Sonoma's jaw went slack—and then, despite herself, she'd grinned.

"Hey, dudes. How did you find me?" Her voice warbled, her face was white with raccoony rings of mascara encircling her brimming eyes. As they watched, a tremor rose up through her body until her lips and her fleshy cheeks began to wobble like aspic.

Martha and Hegwitha ran over and put their arms around her. Martha pressed her cheek against Sonoma's head and inhaled the dusty scent of her hair. T-Bone had climbed down from the truck and was watching from a distance. Sonoma leaned against Martha and burrowed her damp face into her neck.

Sonoma was talking and crying at once, gulping back spit and tears. Gesturing incoherently, pointing at the cactus just behind them, she seemed to be saying something about the giant saguaro with two huge arms that curled in a tilted loop, roughly parallel to the ground.

At last Sonoma quit sobbing. She said, "I got tired. I stopped to rest by this awesome cactus. I stood there, just like this, between its arms—and I heard the arms talking. They were chattering to each other in their crazy space-creature voices. But the weirdest thing was that somehow I knew, I knew they were talking to *me*. They were giving me a message, telling me to stay put and do nothing and stand here and wait for you guys to come get me. They were saying you would find me . . . Hey, listen. Come on. It's still happening. Hear that? Hear the cactus talking?"

No one asked Sonoma how she'd got there or where she had been or why she had run away from the camp or where she thought she was going. Motionless, barely breathing, the two women and the girl stood on the desert floor near the cactus, not far from the edge of the road. Like human arms, the cactus branches entwined them in its embrace.

"Hey. Voices," said Hegwitha.

In the distance crickets chirped—or was it the hum of telephone wires? A high-pitched twitter, an answering murmur, a question, call, and response.

"What is that?" said Martha. "What *are* those sounds?"

"Hush," said Sonoma. "Listen. Stay tuned. Are you listening? Hear it now?"

They huddled closer together. **(247)**

"I think so," Martha said.